Publisher's Note: This is a work of fiction. Any resemblance to actual events, or persons, living or dead, is entirely coincidental. Names, characters, places and incidents are either the product of the author's imagination or are used for the purpose of this fiction tale.

Cover Design by: Marie-France Leger

ISBN Paperback: 9798747275416

For more information, updates, and/or teasers, follow @mariefranceleger on Instagram.com.

GUARDIAN GATES
TRILOGY

THE GATES OF GABRIEL

THE GATES OF RAPHAEL
(COMING SOON)

THE GATES OF MICHAEL
(COMING SOON)

To my family and friends,
for always believing in me.
To the wishful and pure, the ones who endure, and
all those in between.

HE WILL RENDER TO EACH ONE ACCORDING TO HIS
WORKS: TO THOSE WHO BY PATIENCE IN WELL-
DOING SEEK FOR GLORY AND HONOR AND
IMMORTALITY, HE WILL GIVE ETERNAL LIFE; BUT
FOR THOSE WHO ARE SELF-SEEKING AND DO NOT
OBEY THE TRUTH, BUT OBEY UNRIGHTEOUSNESS,
THERE WILL BE WRATH AND FURY

ROMANS 2 : 6-8

THE GATES OF

GABRIEL

MARIE-FRANCE LEGER

EDITED BY: STEPHANIE LEMIEUX
& SOPHIA REYES

THE GREAT DRAGON WAS HURLED DOWN – THAT
ANCIENT SERPENT CALLED THE DEVIL, OR SATAN,
WHO LEADS THE WHOLE WORLD ASTRAY. HE WAS
HURLED TO THE EARTH, AND HIS ANGELS WITH
HIM.

REVELATION 12 : 9

Prologue

PORT HOPE, 1842

Beau stood at the edge of a rocky cliff, staring down at the hundreds of feet separating him from the dark rapids below. The water crashed against each stone peak like metal, ripping the waves apart briskly. Pellets of rain blinded his eyes, parachuting down like cannonballs.

A shooting pain of fire and ice brought Beau to his knees. Every nerve, every muscle constricted as an excruciating burn latched itself to his temples, banging against his skull.

The glowing white light of his halo blinked in beats before melting away to the rain and disappearing into the winds.

He scratched at his bare back, feeling only the jagged scars of his torn-out wings. Beau stood up in anguish, creeping further and further until only the base of his heel kept him grounded to the precipice.

"It won't kill you, Beau." A familiar voice startled him, causing him to fumble backwards.

Beau yelled in anger. "He took my wings! I have nothing left!"

Gabriel's grace lengthened the edge of the cliff by a few more feet, ensuring that Beau wouldn't jump.

"Come to me," Gabriel gestured. But Beau didn't move. He remained cemented to the ground in the heavy storm, staring at the white archangel in despair.

"I've fallen," Beau began to cry. "What have I done to deserve such a fate?"

Gabriel walked towards him and held out his hand. "Beau, you have served the Lord willingly and graciously. You have not fallen for a reason of malice or threat. He has greater plans for you, and you shall bear my name as the messenger. A *Nuntius*."

Beau took Gabriel's hand and stood up, soaking in the beaming radiance before him that he now could never be. He didn't understand why God would strip him of his wings and cast him away, like the pack of Lucifer's fallen.

"What if I refuse?"

"Then, you refuse," Gabriel spoke calmly.

No denial or compliance. Gabriel spoke again. "A chosen martyr will die by the name of Sophie Brixton. She was selected by the Lord to do His work but will suffer a necessary fate. She will have a daughter, Maya, and she is the *Puritas*. She will be the sole mortal descendant of God's chosen martyr, and she will end the war of the fallen."

Beau gasped in horror. "But the war is being contained. You – and Michael, and Raphael –"

"– will fight until the light conquers. The world is tearing itself apart, Beau. Lucifer is gaining an army in numbers. Find Maya Brixton and deliver this message to her as Beau *Gabriel*. Let my protection of grace guide you through your mission, I trust in you as He does."

As quick as lightning, Gabriel grabbed Beau's hand and seared it with holy fire, transferring Gabriel's archangel grace to Beau. Line segments of shimmering white beams coiled up his arm, snaking around his skin like taut vines. Each beam emitted a pain so intense, Beau didn't even realize how hard he'd bitten down on his lip. He tasted blood.

Then Gabriel vanished, leaving only the remnants of two radiant white feathers. Beau picked them up and squeezed tightly, looking towards the sky. The rain subsided and the clouds parted to an opening sun.

The gloss of Beau's grey eyes twinkled as he knelt on one knee and bent his head. "I will serve."

Chapter 1

KLEATON'S GATE, PRESENT DAY

... *It wasn't long before my feet began to*

sink, submerging into the mud like hot lava. I curled my fingers around a wilted branch, hanging over my head, taunting me. I sunk deeper, and deeper, clawing and crying to the sky... but no one heard me. Behind me, I could make out the distant sounds of the dark figure approaching, the crunch of sticks underneath their boots. Then the blade, a metallic silver, shining through the blanket of black nothingness. It burned, slowly slicing the paper thin skin on my neck. Only then did I remember to scream, but no sound came out – only a dark laugh.

The echoed hum of a hooting owl woke me from my nightmare. Pitch black darkness filled my bedroom, aside from the dimmed illumination of the moonlight. *Another one,* I thought, wiping the beads of sweat dripping down my forehead. I rose out of bed and flung my legs over the edge of my mattress. The alarm clock read: **2:24am.**

I rubbed my eyes and sighed, leaning sluggishly over my knees. The past few nights were sheer torture for my sleeping schedule. I tried everything from melatonin to sleep-time tea; *I guess I'm just a lost cause.* I always started off good, you know, be in bed for eleven which was reasonable.

Then, every night, variations of the same heinous nightmare woke me up and painted my mind with lasting fear for hours to come. Someone or *something* was following me, stalking me like a lion hunting its prey. Normally the dark figure never did anything, just... *watched.* But tonight, their blade had pierced my skin, scouting for ligaments and muscles underneath my torn flesh.

I traced a lone finger along my throat, remembering where the imaginary slit had been in my dream. I shuddered, thinking about that dark, sinister laugh that escaped my throat, replacing my screams. Why had I been laughing? *Who laughs at the face of death...*

Most nightmare nights, I found myself in a shaded wood, running for miles, running away. I knew the presence was there, calculating their next move, but they never caught me. I almost wanted them to, only minus the execution. At least that way, I could figure out what was secretly haunting me behind the caged walls of my oh-so-active mind.

But tonight was different. Tonight, the figure caught me, trapped me in a black hole of tar-like mud... *right where they wanted me.*

I shook away the remainder of my grim thoughts and checked the alarm clock: **2:27am.** "Ugh," I moaned.

I pulled open my bedside drawer and grabbed my mom's cross. I was religious, sort of. More often than none, I questioned having to worship a higher power, but my mom believed more than anyone... and she carried that belief to her grave. *How can God be almighty, righteous, and giving if He took you away from me mom...*

I stopped myself. I didn't have it in my heart to stop practicing my faith, especially now that she was gone. She wouldn't want me to. So, I prayed every night before bed and before the occasional exam I didn't study for. *Like that counts for anything.*

But maybe it did. Maybe every time I wore my mother's necklace, she'd feel closer to me. At least in my case, when her cross was around my neck, my thoughts felt at peace, made me miss *her.*

Tears filled my eyes and slowly dripped onto my lips. The salty taste of liquid hit my tongue before I quickly wiped away the sadness and pulled the cross down over my head. I held the small silver pendent tightly, clenching my jaw.

The moonlight gleamed brighter through my room, lightening the atmosphere around me. I swallowed and tucked my body underneath the covers, hoping to silence my thoughts. The luminosity hit my angled wall, focusing on a photo of my mom and I. I felt calm.

Shutting my eyes, I turned over and released one more tear, forming a penny-sized puddle on my pillowcase.

"I miss you, mom." I exhaled softly, drifting into a deep sleep.

A continuous ring chimed through the morning air. Sunlight penetrated my window as the blasted noise continued. My eyes felt sewn together, heavy, and unable to open. *At least I slept.*

Moments passed and the ringing stopped. *Thank God.* Then again, the chime began before I could blink. The alarm clock read: **10:04am.** *Shit! Shit, shit, shit.* I picked up the phone instantly and cleared my throat, hoping to disguise any trace of morning voice.

"H-hello?" I stuttered.

"Did you seriously forget about this morning?" Mags nagged.

I didn't forget, how could I? My best friend finally reported her abusive ex-boyfriend to the cops. *About damn time*, I thought. They broke up months ago but he'd still been stalking her up to now.

Needless to say, I was so ready to put him in place, permanently.

The events of last night weighed heavy on my brain. The encompassing darkness, the sinking mud, *the blade against my throat...* "No, no I'm sorry. I had another –"

"Nightmare? It's fine, I get it. I'll be at yours in ten, okay?" *At least she understood.*

She hung up and I let out a breath, forcing myself out of bed. I walked over to my closet and picked out a pair of faded blue jeans and a white t-shirt. The dirty wall mirror beside me approved of my mediocre appearance, so I did too. Grabbing an elastic, my purse, and some lip balm, I hurried out the door and into the bathroom. I stared into the mirror, my hazel eyes returning my gaze. My face had definitely seen better days, and apparently so had my bird's nest of hair. I messily combed through my brown roots and finished brushing my teeth, debating on whether washing my face was of high importance. *Nah.*

A muffled car beep sounded from outside and I knew Mags had just pulled in.

I rushed downstairs and spotted my dad dressed in casual work clothes, making coffee in the kitchen. "Oh, mornin' Maya. Want a cup?"

A fresh plate of toast was sitting on the marbled countertop, waiting for me to take one. "No thanks Dad, Mags just got here. I'll be back later." I snagged the bread and smiled playfully, holding it between my teeth as I tied my hair.

"Where you headed?" he asked, taking a sip from his mug.

"The police station, remember? I have to bring in the witness statements for Mags' restraining order against Braum."

A strained gurgling noise escaped his throat and I couldn't help but chuckle. "I forgot about that," he said. "Stick him where it hurts."

I nodded with a smile and opened the door, looking back at my dad before leaving.

"Be home by five kiddo, I'm making fajitas for dinner."

Oh... Great. "Love you!" I called out, shutting the door behind me.

"How you feeling, Mags?" I asked.

The fresh Spring dew frosted the top of her windshield and the sky was cloudy. Living in a small city left a bitter taste in my mouth, but there were moments when the air seemed magical. The town itself was about a half an hour drive out from where I lived, and I liked it that way. I dealt with the chatter when I was in high school, but graduation saved me. In just a few months, Mags and I would move to Mayfield and attend college together. *Away from this bullshit.*

She sighed. "I'm a little nervous, honestly. At least his friends are the ones giving in statements and not him. He'd definitely lie through his teeth and deny everything."

"How can he? You have all the proof."

And it's true, she did. She recorded every encounter they'd had on her Apple Watch, saved all the nasty screenshots, and took pictures of the damage he'd done to her. Not to mention all her friends, including me, saw him hit her at her birthday party. It pained me to watch him do that to her every day for so long. Mags was such a pretty girl, but she never believed it because of him. She had bright blonde hair and a model body that anyone would kill for. I still couldn't wrap my head around the fact that he made her think otherwise. *Ugh, he should have been locked up a long time ago.*

Silence. I was proud that she had finally made the decision to ax him after two years of deprived happiness, but it couldn't have been easy.

I grabbed hold of her hand and squeezed tightly. "Just think about it. You do this, and then he never bothers you again. Right?"

She let out a breath. "Yeah," and cleared her throat. "How about you, though? Um, you're going to have to see Tom –"

"I'm aware."

I forgot to mention that my ex-boyfriend was Braum's best friend. The only good thing that came out of that relationship was meeting Mags. If I hadn't dated Tommy, I never would've met her.

Don't get me wrong, the relationship wasn't horrible and nothing bad really happened. We just wanted two different things; I was ready, and he wasn't. Nonetheless, he wasn't someone I wanted to keep close tabs on, especially because he was defending Braum despite knowing everything he'd done.

We pulled up to the police station at around eleven. "Ready?" I asked.

She nodded her head and collected all the police report files in the backseat. We got out of the car and walked inside the station where Liza and Max were already waiting. Liza was more Mags' friend than mine, but we still got along pretty well, and Max was a flamboyant character; wasn't hard to get along with him. They were both handing in witness statements as well.

Liza embraced us instantly. "I'm so glad you're going through with this Mags."

"Baby, that waste of a man never even deserved you, not for a damn second!" Max added.

"Thanks for all being here," Mags said.

I pressed my lips together and forced a smile. The line was decently long, bustling with people, and I expected it to be at least half an hour until the cops came to talk to us.

A short man walked by me with an open-lidded coffee, and my mouth could practically taste its contents. *I should've taken my dad up on that freshly brewed cup this morning.*

I licked my lips. "I'm going to get some Starbucks while we wait. Do you guys want anything?" I asked. *Might as well make good use of my time.*

Max and Liza shook their heads, but Mags looked at me and smiled. "My usual, please."

I nodded and pushed the double glass doors open. The Starbucks was just around the corner and I doubted there would be many people since Kleaton's Gate only populated two percent of the human race. And I was right. There looked to be about three other people ahead of me and one dine-in who sat near the sugar stool.

The pungent smell of spiced lattes slapped my senses upon entry. I peered down and fumbled with my coin purse, scouting out any loose change I could use instead of my credit card. *Nickels and dimes are the worst crimes,* my dad always said.

Startlingly, my body slammed into a large frame, scattering all of my coins.

"Sorry, I'm sorry I wasn't looking." As I bent down to pick up my stuff, we made eye contact.

Holy saints...

The last of my change was in *his* hands. His messy hair was the shade of midnight, curling down over his ears. He towered over my petite frame like a skyscraper, zeroing down at me with what looked to be... grey eyes? *Grey?* Was that even possible? A slight grin formed on his mouth as he corrected his posture, handing me the money.

"My fault," he said.

The smile lines on his cheeks deepened and a small dimple surfaced on the right side of his face. He wore a white t-shirt that contrasted his tanned skin, exposing the apparent results of his workout sessions and black Levi's. A cornucopia of black ink trailed down his left arm, a design that I had never seen before.

I shifted in place, admiring his appearance through my thoughts. Though, I couldn't scratch the itch that picked my brain. When I had scoped out the shop before walking in, I hadn't seen this guy anywhere. I definitely wouldn't have forgotten a face like his, *or a body that's for sure.* Where'd he come from? Maybe he worked here? But he hadn't been behind the cash or making drinks when I last checked. I probably missed him.

"Thanks," I let out. We stared at each other for what felt like forever, in the most comfortable, uncomfortable way. He didn't seem threatening, but he made me feel almost uneasy.

He released a small laugh and tilted his head. *Oh no, was there something on my face?*

"What?" I asked.

He licked his lips and chuckled once again. "You're blocking the door."

Embarrassment was not an emotion I often felt, yet I experienced it twice in the matter of minutes. I hadn't realized I was standing right in front of the entrance like a complete idiot.

My cheeks reddened as I moved aside instantly. "Sorry, again," I laughed nervously. *At least my face was clear.*

"Don't apologize." And then he was gone.

I shook my head, entranced by the moment I knew I had shared with him. *You read way too many romance books*, I thought. Better to agree with what my brain was telling me than conjure up an imaginary scenario of what could be. It was just a random encounter with a random man, nothing more, nothing less.

I ordered the coffee and headed back to the station, attempting to erase the last five minutes of my life. *Just forget it.*

There were obviously less people but still a bit of a wait. Mags leaned her head on Liza's shoulder while Max was sitting across from them, flipping through files.

"Venti iced caramel macchiato for the princess," I joked, handing the cup to Mags.

She pepped up and smiled. "You're a lifesaver."

"Did they tell you how much longer?" I asked, sipping my drink.

Before she could respond, the station doors burst open and in walked Tommy, Ky, and... *Braum.*

I nearly choked on my coffee. Braum's blonde hair was a disheveled wreck, glued to his forehead with sweat. His rage-filled emerald eyes showed no signs of pity, only hatred. *What the hell was he doing here?*

I darted my attention to Mags who sat frozen in fright, unmoving. Braum instantly spotted our table and plowed through the line of people, holding his middle finger up towards Mags.

"You *bitch*!" he screamed, marching over. Without a thought, I moved in front of her alongside Max and Liza. Tommy and Ky grabbed hold of his shirt and yelled for him to stay back.

"You don't think I'll ruin you? *I'll fucking ruin you!*" he repeated, over and over.
Two male police officers stepped in and cuffed Braum, pulling him into a completely different room.

Thank God. I was as weak as a bag of sticks and Max and Liza weren't exactly pro-wrestlers. Truthfully, I would have been scared to find out what could've happened if they hadn't intervened. The line of people moved away from the scene, staring at all of us with blank expressions.

"Nothin' to see here people, you got issues of your own!" Ky addressed the crowd. Low chatter followed but they all went back to their business.

I held Mags until a female cop came up to us with a clipboard in hand. "Hey there, which one of you is Maggie Lake Harthrow?"

Mags lifted her arm and shook like a deer in headlights, moving slowly towards the officer.

"Can you come with me please? I have to ask you a few questions. Don't worry sweetie, you're safe." She smiled. She was kind.

Mags gathered all the witness papers and disappeared into an empty room with the cop. An awkward silence followed while the rest of us remained.

Ky's stalky frame approached me and gave me a slight punch to the shoulder. "How you doin' sport?"

I didn't mind Ky. His brown eyes were always forgiving, warm like chocolate. He was nothing but nice to me always, and probably the most mature person Braum had the privilege of having in his life. Why Ky was friends with him was beyond me, but I knew he had good intentions.

"Why the hell did you bring Braum?" I questioned. "How can you still vouch for that kid, Ky? You know what he's done to her."

A soft sigh. "I've known him all my life, Maya. He wasn't always like this."

I scowled in disgust. "That doesn't give him the right to do what he's done."

"I know, and I agree with you but –"

"Can I cut in?" Tommy interrupted, shooting Ky a gentle look. Ky nodded and squeezed my shoulder, then walked over to Max and Liza, engaging in small talk.

"Hey," he let out.

"Tommy."

He looked nervous, scratching behind his neck and fiddling with his fingers. I hadn't seen Tommy in months. He looked the same; a little scruffy and gained a pound or two but other than that, same brown hair and green eyes. I loved Tommy at one point or thought I did. He'd been a good boyfriend in the beginning, and I knew he was a good guy deep down. Just, he never knew what he wanted and led me on for months after apparently falling out of love. I doubt that he even loved me in the first place, but it's over now.

"Been a while."

His inability to make eye contact made me all the more uncomfortable. I could tell he was awkward and unaware of how this conversation would turn out. *Not like I cared.* No matter how hard I tried to focus, I was distracted. I felt a palpable presence of someone breathing down my neck or staring at me, but no one caught my eye.

"Yeah, yeah it has," I responded hastily. I kept looking around, but all that surrounded me were beige walls and distant chatter.

"Do you think we can go somewhere and talk?" he asked quietly.

Are you kidding me? My attention was now on him and I internally rolled my eyes. "Now's really not the time, Tommy."

I felt him hold back his words before speaking. I knew he was going to say something stupid like *you look good*, or *maybe we can hookup one last time*. Yeah, wasn't in the mood for another tragedy at a go-again.

"I know but –"

And that's when I saw him.

The guy from Starbucks sat in the corner of the station, his eyes fixed on me. *How long had he been sitting there?* I knew for a fact that he wasn't there a minute ago, I had done a thorough investigation of everyone in this place.

Before I could stop myself, my legs began to move in his direction, leading me to stand directly in front of him. His grey eyes glanced up at me, intensifying the longer I kept his gaze. With the little confidence I had, I managed to capture his attention. *Don't lose it.*

"Starbucks guy," I pointed.

"Starbucks girl."

I touched my chin and leaned on my heel, confused as all hell. "You don't look like a felon. How'd you wind up here?"

A slight upturn of his lips formed at the corner of his mouth. "I could ask you the same thing."

"I asked you first," I shot back. Again, that feeling resurfaced. The uneasy calmness when I first met him invaded my senses. Was he following me?

"I'm visiting a friend." He was mellow, and what seemed to be amused.

"You have a friend in jail?"

Another laugh. "I guess you could say that."

I hated that his smile was nice. I could feel the condescending arrogance radiating off of him like fire. He ran his fingers through his hair without taking his eyes off mine. The veins in his arms flexed as he stretched out and leaned back into the seat. Kleaton's Gate was small and I recognized almost everyone. Obviously, there were a few passersby that I would have no account of, but I familiarized myself with the mains. *Where did you come from?*

"You know, a jail is a dangerous place." I contended.

"Hm," he smirked. "Then why are *you* here?"

"I have my reasons."

A quick response. "As do I."

I wanted so badly to demand what those reasons were. What could a man like this be doing at a police station? Who was he visiting? *Why do I even care?*

Out of nowhere, a subtle smile painted his lips. My face heated.

"Do I amuse you?" I asked, pithily.

He took a moment, pausing before clearing his throat. "In a way."

Something about his tone screamed trouble. *Run.* But my feet remained glued in front of him, once again, like an idiot. His angled features were so captivating... *And those grey eyes.*

"That your boyfriend?" he interrupted my thoughts and nudged his head over to Tommy who was eyeing me like a hawk.

I furrowed my brows and shook my head. "Not anymore."

"So, you're single?"

My cheeks instantly flushed, and I swallowed, snapping back. "Wouldn't you like to know."

A crisp laugh rose from his throat. "So, you can ask the questions, but I can't?"

"*Beau Gabriel, proceed to the back bars for visiting.*" The intercom went off and he was on his feet, stepping right in front of me, leaving little to no space. He smelt of pine and mint, sending butterflies to my stomach.

Beau Gabriel.

"It's been a pleasure," he flashed a smug, saccharine smile and extended a hand out to me. For some reason, I was hesitant to take it, but I did. "I didn't get your name," he said.

I felt his warm skin against my palm, taking in the moment longer than I needed to and snapped out of my trance. Just then, I spotted a small golden cross tucked away underneath his shirt.

"Um, Maya." I released, rubbing my fingers against my sweaty palm.

He looked me up and down, smirking once before moving to my side and walking past me. "I'll see you around."

And once again, I felt his fleeting presence hook itself into me. The moment was brief, ephemeral, so why did I remain frozen in place like a stone statue? A million thoughts crossed my mind, all of them rationalizing sheer coincidences. But I couldn't shake it, not for the life of me.

This was no coincidence.

For whatever reason, I kept my eyes on the seat he had just sat on and realized one thing:

This wouldn't be the last time I'd see Beau Gabriel.

Chapter 2

NEW ORLEANS, 1987

*T*he chandelier vibrated above Beau's head, causing the lights to flicker in beats. Mardi Gras festivities were booming just outside his temporary loft, penetrating through the crusted brick walls. Ceiling residue peppered onto the blonde hookup who was nestled over Beau's body, kissing his neck.

She made her way down his back, carefully avoiding the connected v-lines engraved in his skin. When God took his wings, the scars were white like snow, powdery at the touch. But ever since Beau fell, he indulged himself in the impure vices that Earth had to offer; lust, temptation, and pride were just a few of his favourites. Now the cream coloured scars faded into an off black, darkening with an acute burn every time he committed a sin. Gabriel had assigned him to be the very first Nuntius; an angel able to walk the Earth for God's bidding. Although, Beau hadn't realized at first that he would be able to feel, and touch, and taste. And when he did, he did just *that*.

"Run off now, Brina. I'd like to be alone." Beau said, reaching for his trousers.

"But we've only just started," the blonde protested.

Beau now stood over her and gave her naked body a look down. He scoffed with disdain and motioned for the door, opening it briskly. When she didn't move, he pointed out the exit, to which she gathered her things and left in a hurry.

Beau poured himself a glass of aged whisky and walked towards the window, analyzing the coloured dancers and floating lights. "Hm," he smirked.

In the reflection of the window, he noticed a blinding white orb, growing behind him. He knew without turning around what it was, or rather, *who*.

"I was wondering when you'd show up." Beau chuckled, finishing off his drink.

Gabriel stood tall in white linen, accented with gold. "I've been watching you, Beau."

"I would hope."

"What reason is behind your wrong-doings? You are a messenger of the Lord, the first –"

"Nuntius, I know," Beau interrupted, curtly. He shoved past Gabriel, pouring himself another drink. "You should have one, brother. A toast for good fortune!"

Gabriel stood, displeased and concerned. "Beau, your scars are turning black. If they reach full darkness, you will become a part of the fallen. You will belong to Lucifer."

Beau stood in silence for a moment, trying to deny the truth that he had been pushing away for decades. He was turning dark. Lucifer had been pure once, like he was. A beautiful prince of Heaven, who chose power over eternal happiness. Now he led the army of the fallen in hell, torturing them for millennia and onward. The glass shattered in his hands, leaving hairline cuts in his palms that promptly healed.

Beau gripped the sides of his countertops, slamming down hard on the granite. "I haven't found her, Gabriel!" His bare chest heaved with anger, flexing the outline of his abdomen muscles. "What do you propose I do? Stay in hiding until the girl is born?"

"No, Beau," Gabriel breathed. "Sophie Brixton will be murdered in twenty-five years, on the eve of Maya's tenth birthday. She resides in Kleaton's Gate. Go there, and watch her. Protect her peace and yours until the time comes."

"The night before her daughter's birthday," Beau scoffed and took a swig of alcohol straight from the bottle. "Father has a twisted side."

Gabriel was now inches from him, searing Beau's hand with holy fire. Beau cried out, sinking slowly to the ground in agony. "Blasphemy does not look good on you, *brother.*" Gabriel spat.

He released him from the burn and hauled him brutely to his feet. "You enjoy this now, don't you? The craving for earthly vice and indecent satisfaction. Well with Lucifer, Beau, you will have none, worse than none! A black hole of fire and rage for eternity that will haunt you until you give full control. And then, once you do, he will laugh in your face and burn you twice more."

Beads of sweat dripped down Beau's forehead as he stared into the grey spheres of Gabriel's eyes. *He saw Sophie Brixton, gardening with her husband. She was a beautiful woman, with high cheekbones and straight brown hair. She looked happy and for the first time in a while, Beau felt solace. Sophie gripped at the silver cross pendant around her neck, smiling into the sky.* In a flash, he was sucked back into the present moment, puffing with breath.

Before he could get a word out, Gabriel declared, "Go to her, and keep her comfort. You will be her guardian from afar, while you still can. With divine providence, she will be in God's hands, and you will guide Maya."

Then, Gabriel was gone.

Chapter 3

KLEATON'S GATE, PRESENT DAY

"So," Mags hummed, pouring blueberry syrup on her pancakes. "What are you wearing tomorrow night?"

I flashed a faint smile and cut my waffle into triangular pieces, like my mom used to do. Today was the day that she died nine years ago, and my birthday just happened to be tomorrow. *Wonderful timing, I'm aware.* Because of this, I never did anything on my birthday besides order pizza with my dad and watch cult classics. It just felt wrong, you know, that she couldn't be there to celebrate with me. After all, she was the one who brought me into this world.

Mags dropped her fork and grabbed my hand, squeezing my fingers gently. "I know it's a hard day for you Maya, but your mom would want you to be happy. It's your birthday, the day you were born –"

"Yeah and the day after she died." I interrupted her. I knew how depressed I sounded, but I didn't care. I loved Mags but she had two brothers, a mom, and a dad. Her family was complete. I, on the other hand, had no siblings. My dad worked at a law firm all day and when he came home, he'd be buried in paperwork. Mags couldn't understand even if she tried. *Stop being so bitter, Maya.*

Despite everything though, Mags had been there for me ever since we had met two years ago. We hadn't been friends for that long, but she was family.

"Please just..." Mags took a pause, looking down. "Try to have a little fun tomorrow night. Even a little! Just a smidge. Tiny, mini, bite-size –"

"Okay, I get it." I laughed.

"Let me take you shopping after this. We'll get you a nice new dress for the club so you can impress a mysterious, handsome stranger." She winked, shoving the rest of the pancake in her mouth.

In that moment, *he* came to mind. Beau. It had been just over a week since I'd last seen him at the station; those grey eyes that I couldn't look away from. They were uniquely mesmerizing, almost *inhuman.* I felt like an idiot, thinking about a random guy I had coincidentally bumped into, twice,

The Gates of Gabriel | 33

in two different locations, one right after the other...
Nope, nope, not doing this.

I took a sip of iced tea and chuckled. "Pretty sure you're the one that's going to be on the prowl, miss newly single and free."

Mags clapped and grabbed her purse, leaving a twenty dollar bill on the table for both of us. "Well babe, that's expected!"

We walked out of Harv's diner and hopped into her Impreza. "I think they're having a sale at Bolly's Boutique, do you want to go there first?" Mags asked, backing out of the parking lot.

"Sure."

We shopped for almost two hours in one store. How that happened was beyond me. Mags was a different person when it came to shopping and devoted an exorbitant amount of time to styling herself and anyone who was willing to play dress up. Her fashion taste was Bratz mixed with Barbie doll. Mine, on the other hand, was vanilla and flat. It wasn't that I was a horrible dresser, I just preferred my comfy sweaters and mom jeans. But I decided to take Mags' advice and actually try to have fun for my nineteenth birthday. She was right; I knew my mom would've wanted me to. After trying on a bevy of outfits, I picked out a cobalt bodycon dress and some silver heels, then called it a day.

"Do you want me to drop you off at home?" Mags asked, turning down the car radio.

We were approaching the cemetery near the church, where my mom was buried. It was about fifteen minutes from my house so I knew I could just walk home. I wanted to visit her, talk to her, even if she wasn't physically present. Every year I would go there and bring her flowers with my dad. He never remarried after her, just nose-dived into ample amounts of work to get his mind off of it. I didn't blame him.

"Actually, can you just drop me off at the cemetery?" I asked, unbuckling my seatbelt.

"Yeah, of course."

After a few more minutes of driving, we turned into the small gravel entryway and she let me out on the side. "Call me if you need a ride, okay? There's a rain warning for tonight."

I nodded and closed the door, watching her drive off onto the country road.

The tall metal gates welcomed me, creaking as I stepped through. It was fairly cloudy without a trace of sunlight and a grey mist swept the ground. *Fitting for today*, I thought.

I walked past the rows and rows of marble tombstones, scanning over the names of lost loved ones with stories I knew nothing about. They all meant something, though, to someone. It was sad.

I rounded the corner and took in a heavy breath, wearily approaching the final tombstone to the left. The blue roses from last year were brittle and lifeless, crumbling apart at the touch. I swallowed back the sob prying its way out of my throat, strangling the familiar sadness I've encountered year after year. *It never gets easier.*

The barren soil pricked my legs as I knelt down and brushed my fingers over the engravement:

In Loving Memory of
Sophie Brixton
1962-2010
Fly High to the Heavens

A tear escaped my eye, then more, and more. It never got easier visiting my mom, knowing that six feet below me she was just a pile of bones. She was alive once; a breathing, human being. She held me, cared for me, raised me. Even though her touch was but a distant memory, I could still feel it on my skin, lingering every time I closed my eyes.

"Hi mom," I whimpered, wiping at my cheek. "I miss you, so much. Y'know, dad he's – he's going to make that vanilla buttercream cake that you used to make, the one with the butterscotch chips. He's going to butcher it so hard." I chuckled through sniffles, shaking my head. "I wish you were here."

"I got into MU for Cognitive Psych, so that's exciting. I'm going to head up there in a few months with Mags. You've never met her but you would've loved her. I bought a dress for my birthday tomorrow." The gentle pat of a raindrop hit my forehead, followed by heavier pellets. *Damnit.*

I rose up from the grass and wiped off my knees. "I better go mom, it's going to rain. I love you... I love you so much."

Just as I was about to turn around, I heard a rustling behind me. I whipped my head back to check, but no one was there. The wind began to howl and the leaves drifted against the tombstones, slapping them with light force. I swallowed hard, carefully making my way back to the direction of the exit, when the rain started to pick up harder.

In the distance, I could make out a shaded figure, moving in the shadows. I slowed my pace down, confused as to why someone would be visiting in the middle of a rainstorm. *Stop sketching out Maya, it's probably just the gravedigger.*

But the closer he came, the more I seemed to recognize him. It was a man, wearing a fitted black peacoat and black boots. His hair was dark and he was holding what looked to be flowers. Roses, blue roses.

My mom's favourite flower.

My heart stopped when his frame came into view, and the rain no longer hid his features. In that very moment, everything around me faded into a blurry horizon. I stopped in my tracks, faltering as he approached. *It can't be.*

His familiar grey eyes burned into mine when he stopped in front of me, flashing a sweet but mystifying smile.

"I knew I'd see you around," said Beau Gabriel.

Chapter 4

KLEATON'S GATE, 2010

*B*eau had watched Sophie every day since

Gabriel had visited him in New Orleans. He had acquainted himself with every bit of information there was to learn about her. She worked at the local hospital as a nurse and volunteered at the church on weekends. Everywhere she went, people seemed to know her. Though she seemed ordinary to Beau, everyone adored Sophie.

It bothered Beau, living in a small city with little to no excitement. He missed travelling to different countries, sampling different cuisines, sleeping with different women. To him, Kleaton's Gate seemed like the type of place where the elderly went to die and the young aged hastily.

The night that Sophie was to be murdered, Beau went out drinking at *Jinx*, a crummy pub in the rougher part of town. He slammed his hand on the bar and requested a couple rounds of drinks.

"Tequila, mister..." his eyes danced around the heavy bartender's name tag. "Can I call you, *Bones*?" he laughed.

The bartender rolled his eyes and scratched his beard, walking away to make the order. Beau looked around at the dark atmosphere. There were dilapidated dart boards and rusty steel tables lining the sides of the forest green walls. Pictures of classic rock stars covered the patch-up jobs the pub couldn't possibly afford. The crowd itself was mostly older men and women, with a few obviously underaged teens scattered around.

"$19.50," the bartender spat, sliding over the alcohol.

Beau quickly rolled his stool around and smiled. "I'll give you a twenty, just 'cause I'm feeling generous."

The bartender cursed under his breath and stomped to the back. Beau looked around and quickly grabbed the bottle of Patrón tequila next to the cash, hiding it under his peacoat.

He was making his way towards the door when the bartender noticed and started to yell. "Hey! Get back here you fucking rat!"

But Beau was gone, using his grace to make himself invisible. When the bartender came to check and saw nothing, he went back inside and slammed the door with a heavy grunt.

Beau walked a few blocks and took a seat by an empty trash can, right next to a park. He took a swig of the tequila and stared up at the sky. "I prefer this view anyways," he said, closing his eyes.

"Are you all right?" A kind woman asked Beau.

He woke in a hurry, looking down at the near empty bottle of Patrón. Then his eyes met hers.

Sophie Brixton.

She was beautiful up close, but not in a tacky way. Her brown eyes gleamed with golden flecks, even in the night. She had a silver cross pendant draped around her neck, just like in the vision he had seen when he looked into Gabriel's eyes. She was wearing a white maxi skirt and a navy blue sweater, carrying a small brown bag. Sophie was walking to the bus stop after she had just finished teaching an adult bible study.

Beau shook his head and sat up, rubbing his eyes.

"Here, let me help you," she smiled, extending a hand.

But Beau didn't take it. He swallowed hard and got up on his own, realizing this was the night she was to be murdered. She stepped back and grabbed something out of her purse: a necklace with a small golden cross.

"Here," she whispered. "Whatever troubles you will heal in time. Take it and remember that the light will always prevail."

Beau was hesitant at first, staring at her features while he still could. He seemed to remember all of the mistakes he had made while on Earth, just looking at her. Her face was pure and soft as she smiled at him, nudging once more for him to take the cross. So he did, and wrapped it gently in his palm.

He watched her walk away, into the darkness, a fleeting white aura following until... *Bang! Bang!*

Beau crouched behind the trash can and watched as a man dressed in full black ran into view. He was holding the little brown bag Sophie had once held, and a gun.

The world stopped spinning for Beau. A multitude of colours amassed together, blending into one from every angle he looked. Sirens rang in his ears as he stepped away from the scene, taking in every bit of motion. He peered down at his shaky hands, staring at the golden cross *she* had just given him. He inhaled once and bit down hard, clenching the pendant tightly.

When gravity could no longer stabilize Beau, he collapsed to his knees and watched the paramedics pull out a stretcher, retrieving the lifeless corpse disguised in a white sheet.

Sophie Brixton died on June 23rd, 2010 at 9:34pm.

Chapter 5

KLEATON'S GATE, PRESENT DAY

*R*ain pattered against my forehead as I
stared into Beau Gabriel's eyes. A million thoughts
crossed my mind but I couldn't focus on any of them.
I just stood there in bewilderment, sewn to the
ground beneath me.

"Hi," he smiled. "Do you mind?" he asked,
holding up the blue roses in his hand.

I watched him move past me and walk
towards my mom's tombstone. He bent down and
touched the soil, creating a small bed for the flowers.

When the wave of shocked had fizzled out, I wearily trudged towards him and tugged at his coat. "Are you following me? How do you know my mom?"

He got up and dusted off his knees, but didn't answer.

"Is the rain too loud for you? Can you not hear me?" I demanded, harshly. "Who are you?"

The assertiveness of my tone caught me off guard, but I couldn't fathom addressing him in any other way. I didn't know Beau Gabriel, at all. If he was truly following me, then I didn't care how I came across, even to him.

Rain pellets clouded my vision, sinking into my skin. "How are you here, *Beau?*" I was losing my patience.

He ran his fingers through his dark, wet hair and turned to me. Those grey eyes flashed into mine, matching the sky above. His stare was blank, unreadable, sending a cold shiver down my spine.

"I drove."

Sarcasm. The rain picked up harder, pouring down from the sky like bullets. A distant boom of thunder startled me which Beau snickered at.

"Scared of a little thunder?" he provoked, walking towards the cemetery gate.

I shielded my eyes with my hand and followed quickly behind him, determined to get some answers. "Beau –" I started.

"Maya." He said flatly, facing forward.

"You didn't answer any of my questions! Who the hell are you?"

Another acidly laugh. "Beau Gabriel, but you already knew that."

A tsunami of discomfiture hit me like a truck, just like every other encounter I've had with him. Puddles of dirty rainwater filled my path, unavoidable yet undetectable. I cursed under my breath as my new white sneakers plummeted into the mud, which seemed to fuel Beau's amusement even more.

I finally got a grip of his coat and pulled him backwards, just before the exit. I could taste the smeared-off mascara fibres trailing onto my lips as I narrowed my eyes.

"You brought my mom blue roses," I huffed, swallowing drops of rain. "That was her favourite flower."

He stared at me with narrow eyes, pursing his lips. He said nothing.

I felt weak, small, desperate. "You knew her, Beau. How did you know her?" It didn't make any sense. I visited her grave every year since she had passed away, and I never once saw Beau.

Thunder rumbled in the air as the rain poured down violently through the clouds.

He looked up towards the sky and squinted at me. "Let me give you a ride home," he finally said.

My eyes grew wide, frantic. "Are you *insane?*"

He shrugged his shoulders. "Maybe, but the rain is only going to get worse."

I crossed my arms, scoffing with frustration. "I'm walking home."

An orchestra of thunder roared forcefully in the sky. "Your funeral," he mocked, glancing at the tombstones behind me. *Hilarious.*

I knew for a fact he was right, but I wasn't about to get into a car with a complete stranger who I knew absolutely nothing about. He wasn't deaf, he heard all of my questions. Was he purposely trying to antagonize me? Did he even know my mom or was he just stalking me? *He's crazy, he has to be.*

And yet, for some inexplicable reason, I *wanted* to go with him. The thought of being alone with him frightened me, but excited me at the same time. I couldn't rationalize it even to myself, but for some reason, it made sense.

"Look, whatever you want to know, I'll tell you. Just don't walk home in this." He pointed upwards without taking his eyes off of mine.

No, don't give in. I planted my legs firmly in the ground, shivering. "Tell me now."

He bit down hard on his jaw, focusing on me. His eyes were searching for something within mine, I could tell. What they were searching for? That's as big of a mystery as Beau Gabriel was.

"Trust me," he released, breathing in deeply.

I stared at him in bewilderment, forcing down every snappy insult that tried to pry its away out of my throat. I shoved past him, clenching my chattering jaw before he caught my arm.

"Your mother was very important to me," he admitted, sheepishly.

I found desperation in his voice, helplessness; like a child who was begging for his favourite toy. He slowly let go of my arm as I stood back, studying his expression through the hazy grey atmosphere. He couldn't hold my gaze, staring down at the mud. His peacoat clung to him like second skin, and his dark hair swooped down over his forehead in zig-zags. When he finally met my eyes, I took a step closer. I don't know what possessed me to feel what I felt, but a part of me trusted him.

I swallowed hard and bit my lip. "We better go." I released, waiting for regret to suffocate my conscience.

He nodded briskly, pushing open the metal gate for me to walk through.

"Stand under there." Beau directed to a little woodshed just outside the cemetery. "I'll bring the car around." Then, he disappeared into the rain.

What am I doing? I barely know him. *Can I even trust him?* He gave me nothing. *Then why do I trust him?*

A few moments later, a black Porsche came into view, pulling up in front of me. I took in a breath and shook my head, silencing my brain. *Award for the biggest dumbass goes to me*, I thought. And I got in the car.

"You warm enough?" Beau asked, turning up the heater.

The car itself was probably under a year old; matte black seats, all leather interior. The radio system glowed red, blinking every time the base dropped. *What does he do for a living? Jesus.* He didn't have many things inside, though. There was a black ice air freshener hooked onto his mirror, a stack of mint gum in his disc compartment, a silver ring and a pair of dark brown aviators in his cup holder.

When we came to a stop, Beau quickly peeled off his black peacoat and threw it in the backseat. He was wearing a grey t-shirt that stuck to every curve of his torso perfectly. As he lifted his arm to turn the steering wheel, I caught a glimpse of his large tattoo, spiraling up his skin like black vines.

"What is that?" I asked abruptly.

He reached for a piece of gum and tore the plastic wrap between his teeth. "What?"

I blushed. "Your tattoo."

It caught my eye the first time I'd met him, but I didn't get a thorough look at it until now. It started at the base of his forearm, a shaded web of speckled black lines, then continued further up his arm, coiling up his skin like snakes all the way up to his shoulder. What puzzled me was the lack of detail; it appeared to be just a bevy of line segments. *What an odd tattoo.*

"It's a cover up," he replied, keeping his eyes on the road.

Cover up? Of what? There was absolutely no trace of scarring, not even in the slim cervices that weren't shaded by dark ink.

A glimmer of gold caught my eye, poking out from underneath the neckline of his shirt; a golden cross, the same one I saw him wearing at the station.

It shone against his tan skin, glowing seemingly brighter the longer I looked at it.

I forced my eyes shut and turned my attention forward. "What did you cover up?"

He looked at me quickly and smirked, raising goosebumps to the surface of my skin. "Nosy, are we?"

My cheeks flushed with embarrassment. "I didn't mean to pry."

The golden cross around his neck flashed in my peripheral vision again, sending a shiver down my spine. A magnetic pull of energy kept my eyes from wandering off, and before I could think, the words came out of my mouth.

"Are you religious or something?" I blurted. I was aware of the fact that people wore crosses as accessories, but for some reason, that didn't feel like the case with him.

"Sorry," I shook my head, afraid to even face Beau's reaction. "I know that's a personal question but I –"

He interrupted me and chuckled, taking in a breath before responding. "I guess you could say that."

I kept quiet for a few minutes, remembering the reason why I was in Beau's car in the first place. He knew my mom, he brought her flowers. There were so many unanswered questions, and yet here I was sitting comfortably in Beau's passenger seat, engaging in small talk.

I was too engulfed in my thoughts that I hadn't even realized we pulled into a Starbucks drive thru.

"Brings back memories, doesn't it?" Beau said, smirking at me. "The origins of our meeting point."

He rested his hand on the gear shift, and I found my eyes analyzing every vein that popped from beneath his tanned skin. They were apparent, visible, pulsing underneath his flesh the tighter he held his grip on the stick.

I dismissed the butterflies that fluttered in my stomach. "Why are we here?" I asked, wringing out my hair.

"A man needs his coffee," he said. "Can you grab my wallet in the glove box?"

I nodded and opened the compartment while he ordered, finding a black wallet. Though just before closing it, *something* caught my eye. Two beaming white feathers were tucked behind an instruction manual, glistening like snow. I couldn't help but stare at them, sparkling with opulence. A soft chime began to ring in my ears and everything became hazy, encompassing me in a soft blur of pearly hues. The chime intensified, transforming into a distant word. Only it wasn't just a word, it was my name; something was calling out for me. *Maya... Maya...*

Like a puppet on a string, I couldn't help my movements. I reached out to grab the feathers when *he* touched my arm, instantly sucking me back into reality.

"Find it?" he asked, sharply.

I nodded my head and gazed into his unnerving grey eyes. I quickly handed him his wallet, taking one last look at the feathers before closing the glove box. I swallowed hard as he handed me a coffee, and pulled out of the parking lot.

My hands were shaking, staring at the glove box. I wanted so badly to open it, to reach for those feathers and consume myself in whatever energy that'd coursed through my veins.

"Drink up." Beau interrupted my thoughts, clenching his jaw. "It'll get cold."

I cleared my throat and diverted my senses to the warmth of the cup, pushing away the fleeting feeling that those feathers had given me.

I curled my fingers around the coffee, narrowing my eyes. "I only drink –"

"Half n' half."

I darted my gaze to Beau who didn't seem shocked. I couldn't even make out a sentence. *How the hell did he know that?*

I tried to think of logical explanations to debunk all of these uncanny coincidences, but there were none anymore. He wasn't being honest with me – that much, I knew.

"So what's your address?" he asked, casually sipping on his coffee.

I pressed my lips together, placing my drink in the cup holder. "Pull over."

"What?"

"Pull over, Beau. Now." I demanded.

He swerved the car to the side of the country road and parked on the gravel. The rain continued to

pour onto his windshield as we sat in complete
silence.

The air remained still around us, with only
the low hum of the heater providing ruffled noises. I
knew if I thought too hard about what to say, I
wouldn't end up saying anything. There was no doubt
that he had an inscrutable effect on me. Though what
that effect entailed was inconsequential, especially
when it came to my mom.

I fiddled with my fingers before clearing my
throat. "You promised me answers. I want to know
the truth."

He turned to me and sighed, "You're right,
but I didn't say when."

A vein in my neck twitched. *Was he for real?*
I fumed. "Beau I'm going to –"

"Relax," he laughed, taking another sip of his
drink. "I'm messing with you."

My tense shoulders eased back. "How do you
know my mom?"

He shut the car off and turned to face me,
glancing once, then down at his lap. "I knew your
mom, a long time ago. She was a delight."

My mom died nine years ago, but Beau
didn't seem to look much older than I did. How was
that possible?

"How old are you?" I asked, praying he wasn't
over thirty-five.

A calm laugh. "Twenty-two."

Phew. "Then how –"

He paused for a moment and took in a
breath, fiddling with the golden cross around his

neck. For the first time since I'd met him, he seemed genuinely lost for words.

"Let's just say when I was a boy, I got caught stealing. Your mom helped me out, gave me a new outlook on things. Never took a damn thing again."

My cheeks reddened. I bit the bottom of my lip, holding back the tears that tried to escape my eyes. This always happened when I thought of her; why did I think that this time would be any different? What answer was I expecting? My mom had always been an inspiration to everyone she met. She was my hero when I was a kid, always made me feel safe and protected and loved. She believed in second chances, hell, even third chances.

So... that's the story, then. She helped Beau out of a rough patch, guided him, and he changed... He never forgot her.

"She was an amazing person, Maya. And I'm really, truly sorry for your loss." His hand left his lap and hovered closer to mine, finally settling atop the gear shift.

A wave of tension filled the air and for a second I thought he was going to grab hold of my hand. *Snap out of it.*

A warm surge rose through my entire body at the thought and I instantly turned away. "I think we should go."

I blandly told him my address and he started the car, driving in the direction of my house.

We didn't say a word to each other the entire ride back. I didn't know what to say, and I didn't have it in me to ask any more questions. I knew there were more untold truths, like how he happened to be in the cemetery at the same time as me, or who he was visiting at the jail. I wanted to know more about his past with my mom, about him, but I couldn't process it all, not just yet. Maybe it was better left unsaid, at least for now.

Beau stopped in front of my driveway and unlocked the doors. The rain mellowed out and I was almost completely dry from earlier.

"Home sweet home," he smiled.

"Thanks for the ride." I said, forcing myself to step out of the car.

I didn't have it in me to ask any more heavy questions about my mom, mainly because I wasn't comfortable enough around Beau to show such a side of vulnerability. Though I couldn't help but pose the question that rattled my brain.

I turned on my heel before shutting the door completely. "How did you know I liked my coffee half n' half?"

A sly chuckle. "It was written on your Starbucks cup when we first met."

"You're quite observant."

"You have no idea." He flashed a small smile, starting the ignition.

I pressed my lips together, shaking off the tension, uneasiness and *butterflies*. I wanted so badly to stay, without saying a word, just taking in the moment I had with Beau. *What is it about you?*

I finally convinced my legs to move and walked around the car, stepping back onto my lawn. "Until we meet again, I guess."

I watched him watch me. He observed me intently, something obviously on his mind, but I couldn't figure out what. He always had a similar stare when he looked at me. I tried to analyze him, but everything went blank when I looked into his eyes.

"Looking forward to it." He flashed a smile. Then Beau drove away.

Chapter 6

KLEATON'S GATE, JUNE 15TH

*B*eau had been watching Maya from afar ever since she was born. He liked to think he knew her better than she knew herself, or understood her for that matter. From the time that Maya had been in diapers, spat peas into her parents' face and walk her first steps – Beau had witnessed it all.

He had boundaries of course, like when she'd gotten older and started to date her first boyfriend, Tommy. Beau never liked Tommy. *Spineless rat*, he used to say. Though, he underestimated how beautiful she would grow up to be.

Maya had wavy dark brown hair and hazel eyes. She was petite, around 5'4 with a smaller frame. She had an allure everywhere she went, yet was completely unaware of her effect. Beau watched her read on the porch outside of her house for years, wondering what type of literature intrigued her. Maybe she had read about angels, like him. Either way, she radiated a purity so strong, Beau couldn't even resist.

And that was the problem.

Beau hated how he didn't hate her. He felt as if he had lived three lifetimes being on Earth, protecting someone he'd never even spoke to. After over a century of turmoil, chaos, destruction and heartbreak... Beau just wanted to go home, and Maya was the only ticket out.

He thought about approaching her and fulfilling the mission that Gabriel gave him. He contemplated it on numerous occasions but couldn't bring himself to doing so. He didn't know what he would say. How could he? Telling a mortal that she was the Puritas and her mother was the chosen martyr of God? It would've sounded ridiculous. So he gave up. His impatience got the best of him and he left town for a little while. He didn't go very far, but far enough that he wouldn't have to think about Maya Brixton.

Then one day, Beau was sitting in an old diner an hour away from Kleaton's Gate when the TV caught his attention. There had been a break-in at the antique shop in the Kleaton district.

At first Beau laughed. "Humans never learn," he said.

It was only when the image of the intruder came up that Beau gasped. A man dressed in white linen with curly brown hair and grey eyes was arrested and brought to the KG police.

He dropped his coffee and stared at the still image of the man on the television. "You've got to be kidding me," he snickered.

Beau grabbed his jacket and left a ten on the table, walking out of the diner to the sound of the TV broadcaster.

"*The intruder has not yet been identified. No personal belongings were found on him but officials say he put up quite the fight –*"

He sat on his Harley and looked up at the cloudless blue sky, fastening his glove strap. "Oh, baby Blight," he chuckled. "Baby fuckin' Blight."

It was just as much of a shock to Beau as it was to Maya when they ran into each other at Starbucks. He hadn't planned it, nor was he looking for her. He wanted to see Blight, one of the younger angels in Heaven, but not before he fed his caffeine addiction. Beau didn't have the slightest clue as to how Blight got to Earth, but he was determined to find out.

"Sorry, I'm sorry I wasn't looking," Maya had said.

She clumsily dropped her coins when she ran into Beau. This amused and flattered him at the same time, especially since this was their first real encounter. He didn't know how she would react, but he was pleased with the outcome. Her evident nervousness stroked Beau's ego, *slightly*, to be modest. He was no secret to women; they practically gnawed at his shadow.

But Maya was different. Even though he'd never spoken a word to her, he felt like he'd known her forever, watching her all those years.

He didn't want to leave her side, knowing that fate had steered the wheel on this encounter. Deep down, he knew that it was time to tell her what she was, but Beau was also aware of Blight's grace, and how his presence on Earth was most certainly not a coincidence.

After Beau left the coffee shop, he scouted the perimeter of the police building, looking for a way in without having to talk to any cops. He didn't enjoy the company of authority, in any way shape or form.

When he realized there were no back entrances, he settled for the common route and entered the building. That's when he saw her again: Maya.

Fuck, he cursed under his breath. He didn't want her to think he was following her, although Beau rarely cared about what other people thought. He casually leaned behind the entrance wall, hoping she wouldn't notice him. Beau knew he had to break the news to her at some point, but with another angel from Heaven on Earth, Beau postponed the urgency to a later date.

To his advantage, a blonde female cop walked by him and smirked.

"Hey there," Beau smiled.

He grabbed her wrist and pulled her gently to his side, staring into her eyes. He used his grace to see her thoughts. Everything she had seen, he saw, including Blight being locked up in the **Bar6** holding cell. He released her and compelled her to give a request for his visit next, to see the intruder on TV. And she did what she was told.

When Beau slid into a corner chair, he noticed Tommy Weem, Maya's pitiful ex. It looked like Tommy hadn't talked to Maya yet, since Braum McPhee decided to go rampage before he had the chance. But Beau could sense the obvious attraction Tommy had for Maya. He watched Tommy stare and gawk like a helpless mouse.

Jesus, if I were Maya I would've dumped you too, he whispered under his breath.

Beau hadn't realized that his gaze was on Maya, so when she approached him, it didn't come as a shock. She questioned his presence, which excited Beau. She was snappy and quick on her feet too, not like many of the women he had been with.

"Do I amuse you?" she had asked him.

A knot tied in his stomach. He wanted to tell her, more than anything. He wanted to comfort her about her mother and explain why it had to happen. He just couldn't. Instead, he looked at her; no makeup, brown hair tousled in a bun and old jeans. She did look funny, but not in a bad way. She didn't care about her appearance, but she didn't need to. She was beautiful. *Snap out of it, Beau. Focus.*

He pushed those thoughts aside and responded. "In a way."

He felt Tommy's slimy gaze on them the entire time, which irritated Beau. Beau made a little comment which flustered her. He enjoyed that. Then just in time, he got called to the back bars.

"I'll see you around," Beau said to Maya. And he meant it.

There were five holding cells before Blight, filled with scoundrel drug dealers and overnight DUI's. He felt Blight's grace steps before he turned to the cell, and when he did, Beau laughed.

"You got ten minutes." The male cop said, shutting the cell door behind him.

Blight was still wearing his white linen and his curly hair was in a disheveled mess over his head. His hands were cuffed to the table as were his bare feet.

"Man, do you ever look homeless." Beau snorted, pulling a metal chair directly in front of Blight. "The young baby Blight. To what do I owe the pleasure?"

Blight reached at Beau with anger, slamming hard on the table. "If you had only done what you were told, we wouldn't be in this situation, Beau!"

Beau glibly rubbed the spit off his face as Blight calmed down. He stretched his arms and leaned back on his chair.

"I wouldn't call this a mess, brother. I call it freedom." He laughed but Blight didn't. "Why'd you break into that shop anyway?"

"Early birthday present for the Puritas." He snickered. "I had to get your attention somehow."

"What present?" Beau demanded, confused. Blight said nothing.

Beau grew impatient and rolled his eyes. "Blight cut the bullshit. Why are you really here?"

Blight leered in disdain. "Isn't it obvious? Gabriel gave up on you. You failed us, all of us! You had one job Beau, one job. Make it known to the Puritas who she is, but no." Blight calmed down and shook his head. "You've been feeding all your carnal desires with booze and *women*." He spat.

Beau flinched, knowing exactly what *woman* Blight had been referring to. He pushed the memory back into his subconscious and cleared his throat.

He knew that he hadn't fulfilled his mission, but he was convinced that Gabriel would've never given up on him. Although a part of him wondered, maybe he had. Maybe God was going to banish him to hell like He did Lucifer. Maybe he would become a part of the fallen... and maybe he deserved it.

"Gabriel sent me as the *Viatorem*, the traveller to clean up your mess."

Ever since Beau had been on Earth, the talk of Maya being the Puritas was all he could hear. He never quite understood what was so important about her blood, and why God had chosen Sophie to be the martyr sacrifice.

He crossed his arms. "Hard to finish something when you don't know why you're doing it in the first place." Beau scoffed. "Why Maya?"

And despite everything, he had to believe in what Gabriel told him. He had to believe that there was a reason for all of this, but he never understood why.

"Gabriel didn't tell you?" Blight questioned. His face lit up and he laughed.

Beau was silent, his patience running on a thin line.

"Most of Lucifer's fallen are mortal beings that died and went to hell. But they were mortal once, they had a choice. They chose to do evil, to follow him. Because of this, God can't interfere even if they ask for pardon. But the Puritas, she has the power to lift the fallen."

Beau furrowed his brows in confusion. Maya was a mortal, and to complete such a task would require an immeasurable amount of divine grace – if that. He couldn't believe there was a way to combat the eternal punishment of hellfire.

"That's impossible." Beau shook his head. "How is that possible?"

Blight eased. "When Maya was born, God took Sophie as a vessel. Although brief, He sprinkled a portion of His grace onto Maya. He wanted to offer a plea of redemption, even though He, Himself cannot grant it." Blight trailed off, his eyes darting around the stone-boxed walls that encased the two. "Maya is the sole mortal who can enter Heaven, purgatory and hell. But the only way to do that, is if

she willingly drinks from the Holy Grail. She is the
key, but she must believe it. Though, I don't believe a
thought so grand just appears in ones' head. So, that's
where you come in."

*The Holy Grail, the chalice carved by
Thrones and archangels alike. Could it be true?
Could Maya unlock a new portion of power
unknown by the Heavens and beyond?*

"But..." Beau stammered. "Why Maya?"

Blight reclined in his chair, eager to escape
the restraints he'd been put in. "Take it up with
Gabriel," he sneered. "He chose *you*. An odd gamble
of resolution, though who am I to question an
archangel?"

Beau recoiled at the apparent annoyance
radiating off of Blight. All he wanted were answers,
and if Blight was sent down as the Viatorem from
above, wasn't it his job to give provide those answers
graciously?

Nonetheless, Beau learned enough of the
truth and what he was fighting for. Maya had an
unbounding power inside of her, coursing through
her veins. Though, there would be no way of her
knowing that unless Beau told her. Now, he had a
clear understanding of fate, and all the paths he had
taken that lead him to her. His conquest was to help
Maya find *herself.*

Beau couldn't push away his mission any
longer – he needed to act fast. He knew how slim the
gates of Heaven were, especially living on Earth this
long. He watched humans tear each other apart, each
and every day. He watched humans *fall.*

"Where is it?" Beau demanded. "The Grail, where is it?"

Blight's prideful simper covered his face. "Are you willing to serve? As a true angel of –"

"Where is the damn cup, Blight!" Beau slammed his hands on the table.

In the distance, footsteps approached and keys rattled.

"Port Hope," Blight whispered.

Beau narrowed his eyes, wrinkling his forehead. "Where I fell?"

The footsteps grew louder. Beau turned around and cursed under his breath. "Where in –"

But when Beau turned back to Blight, he had vanished, leaving only empty handcuffs behind.

Chapter 7

KLEATON'S GATE, PRESENT DAY

"*Happy birthday to you!*" I woke up to the sound of my dad's wretched singing. When my eyes cleared, I saw him standing at the door, holding a small purple gift box and some roses. *Oh no.*

I buried my face in my pillow and chuckled softly, covering my blushed cheeks. "You know I hate gifts."

My dad's face fell into a child-like pout, which made me laugh harder. I swatted his arm and took the gift box in my hands. "Thanks though, Dad."

It wasn't that I was opposed to getting them, rather I just never understood how to accept them properly. The concept of birthdays was always weird to me. Like, my parents were the ones who brought me into this world, shouldn't I be giving them a gift? To thank them for my life? It didn't help that my mom's death anniversary was the night before my birthday as well...

Don't think about it Maya... She would want you to be happy on your day.

My dad stood in front of me, watching with a big smile. "It's not much, but I have a big breakfast downstairs with your name on it."

I unravelled the pink ribbon and opened the box to find a small silver ring with a red gem in the middle. I never wore any jewelry besides my mom's cross, but the ring was absolutely beautiful. The ruby red stone shone from every angle and the silver itself wasn't tarnished in the slightest. On the inner part of the ring was an engravement that looked to be written in another language.

I slid it onto my middle finger and extended my hand. "It fits perfectly," I beamed. "Since when did you get such good taste?"

He laughed then kissed my forehead, giving me a tight hug. "I got it from that old antique shop down by the bay. The owner said it was some sort of protection ring. Said if the ruby glowed red," he tapped the gem in the middle of the ring. "That there was danger nearby."

He exhaled softly and swatted my arm, moving towards the door. "Now that you're getting older you know, moving away for school, I thought it may come in handy... even if it's just a hoax."

I furrowed my brows and brushed my thumb over the gem. "So, this isn't a hidden camera disguised as a ring?" I joked.

His eyes grew wide. "They make those?"

I giggled, shooing him out of my room. "I'll be down in a little bit, just got to get changed."

The ding-dong sound of the doorbell startled both of us. "Expecting anyone?" my dad asked.

Considering my lack of friends, I only assumed who it could be. "Probably Mags."

"I'll go let her in."

I walked over to my closet and pulled out a pair of grey sweats and a white tank top, rounding my hair up in a bun. The picture of my mom, dad and I sat on my dresser, reflecting the sun. I picked it up and held it close to my chest.

"I wish you were here..." I whispered, shutting my eyes. *But I know that you are.*

I finished up in the bathroom and walked downstairs to find Mags shovelling a plate of eggs and bacon into her mouth.

"Ah!" she shrieked, wiping the grease off of her lip. "Happy birthday Maya bear!" She kissed my cheek and wrapped her arms around me.

The kitchen table held an array of my favourite breakfast foods: strawberries in sugar, banana pancakes, bacon, eggs and sausages. *Impressive. Either he ordered all of this or spent seven hours in the kitchen.*

"Wow dad," I smiled, picking up a strawberry. "You've really outdone yourself."

"Truly, Talon, this is all..." Mags stuffed a floppy pancake into her mouth. "Positively scrumptious."

"Breathe," I inhaled, mockingly. "The pancake isn't going to run from you."

"You know I have a sweet tooth!"

"Glad you're enjoying the food Mags," my dad laughed. "At least someone is." He threw me a side eye, pouting.

I huffed, leaning over the bowl of strawberries and snagged two slices of bacon, chomping obnoxiously. "Mmm...." I exaggerated. "*Phenomenal.*"

My dad fastened his tie with pride and slurped his coffee. "I've got to run to the office for a few hours, but I'll be back for supper. What are you girls up to tonight?"

Mags jumped up and grabbed her duffel bag, pulling out the cobalt dress I bought and silver heels. *Oops.* I completely forgot that I had left them in her car.

"Maya and I are going to the new club that opened up at the casino." She said, cheerfully.

My eyes immediately darted to my dad. He was decently lenient. He let me do whatever I wanted as long as I called him and told him where I'd be, but it was my first time going to a club and I had no idea what to expect.

"Arc Royale?" my dad asked innocently, fixing his briefcase. No anger, no fights. *Phew.*

"Yes sir, that's the one." Mags pinched my cheek as I ate my meal. "Going to celebrate this girl's nineteenth in style."

I swatted her away, taking a big bite of eggs. "Want to come, Dad? I hear they make a mean shrimp cocktail."

"Tempting," he chuckled and kissed my head. "I'll see you before you go tonight. Happy birthday again, baby." And he was out the door.

I looked over to Mags who had the biggest smile on her face, tapping her white acrylic nails against the table. "Time to hit up the liquor store," she smirked.

It was a quarter to nine and my dad had ordered a mass amount of Chinese food for supper. Mags ended up eating only one eggroll because she didn't want to look 'bloated' in her dress, yet ate four slices of dessert. *That logic was beyond me.*

In a pleasant turn of events, my dad actually hadn't butchered my mom's buttercream cake recipe after all.

"It's actually quite delicious, Talon," Mags licked icing off her finger. "I may come down for seconds."

My dad burst out laughing. "You mean fifths?"

Mags waved a playful hand at him, a sheepish grin crossing her face. After washing the dishes, I dragged Mags up the stairs, pulling her into my room to get ready.

Mags threw herself into beautification, singing along to old Metro Station. We took turns doing each other's hair; Mags wore her blonde locks straight down, and I curled mine into a pony. She brushed some pink shimmer on her eyelids and finished with a nude gloss. I reached for my neutral eyeshadow palette but Mags shoved a stippling brush in my face. Before I could protest, she was already going to work on my eyes.

She clicked her tongue. "Uh, throw away the boringness just for tonight, Maya. We're going for sexy, seductive, sultry and smoky!"

I wanted to roll my eyes, but she had them pinned shut with her finger. She leaned in closer to my face, her lips brushing the curl of my nose. I smelt the tangy mixture of vodka and buttercream cake from her breath.

After moments of exaggerated whining, she pulled back and held a mirror to my face.

"Amazing, right? You look amazing."

For the first time in forever, I was actually shocked with my appearance. I always bagged Mags for spending all of her free time watching makeup tutorials, but she had skills. A shimmering gunmetal shadow fell over my lid, darkening in the outer corner. A vibrant blue color rested underneath my waterline, just in the center, bringing out the hazel in my eyes. She accented my eyes with a black lining, smoking it out upwards.

I held back my words, knowing that if I praised her, she would claim her position as my permanent makeup artist – and that, I didn't want. Instead, I settled with a simple thank you. That was enough.

She pinched my cheeks and gathered her dress, slipping on the red silk mini. "I'm single now, Maya. I have to glow!" She stood in front of my mirror, sucking in as hard as she could. "I look good, right?"

I laughed, taking another sip of the wine we had bought earlier. "You're sucking in air at this point, Mags."

She threw an elastic at me and huffed. "But am I *fuckable*?"

"Always." I winked.

"So..." she started. "Have you been talking to that new guy? What was his name again? Blake? Bard?"

"Bard?" I was taken aback. *What the hell kind of name...*

"Oh shut it, you know I'm not good with names."

I took a sip of wine, trying to hide my blushed features. "Beau." His name tasted like sweet sin on my tongue. *Don't think about him, Maya. It's your night.* "But no."

"Ah," she said, distracted by her own reflection in the mirror. "Well, did you even give him your number?"

My cheeks heated. "No, Mags. I was too busy interrogating him." My thoughts wandered off, replaying our conversation that plagued my mind all night.

She grew quiet. "Insane how he knew your mom."

I gnawed at my bottom lip, fiddling with my fingers. *Absolutely insane.*

"But that car ride... Must have been an intimate car ride?" She winked, taking the wine out of my hands and sipping loudly.

"Mags," I grunted. "No." But I couldn't contain my warmed cheeks, no matter how hard I tried.

She spun on her heel, crossing her arms. "See, Maya, this is your problem. You can't flirt for the life of you!"

I – Excuse me? "But why would I –"

"Ah, ha! He could be an undercover cop, or a spy? Maybe an... assassin? God, how hot would that be?"

I killed the tensity and shook my head, giggling. "You're an idiot."

She turned back around and gawked some more at her appearance. "Oh well, his loss. You're going to find someone tonight, I can feel it! Maybe you'll even lose *it* tonight, eh Maya bear? Imagine that! A nineteenth birthday bang-bash. Ugh, a dream."

I almost choked on my drink. Mags hadn't been a virgin for some time now. She lost it to Braum when they first started dating. I, on the other hand, was. I'd done a few things obviously, I had Tommy. But I never felt comfortable enough to do, well, *that.*

Mags never really teased me about it though; just always called me the 'purest little soul' she'd ever met.

Before I could say anything, she took a huge gulp of her vodka-cran and twirled like a ballerina. "What the hell Maya? Get out of your sweats and get dressed! We have to call an Uber soon."

I took in a breath and chose not to reply to her comment, pushing away all recent memories of my cemetery excursion with Beau. "Okay, okay," I said, taking one last sip of rosé.

I slipped on the cobalt bodycon and silver heels, shying away at my appearance in the mirror. I didn't look like myself at all. In fact, I practically embodied Mags. The dress hugged my figure, accentuating the right places. It scooped low enough to show cleavage, but still left room for imagination.

Mags came up behind me and rested her head in the crook of my neck. "You look so hot." A ding sounded from her phone. "Uber's here! Let's fucking party!"

I took one last look at myself before grabbing Mags' hand and shutting my bedroom door.

The entire ride there we sang along to early pop hits and took pictures, sneaking the occasional drink in the backseat from Mags' flask.

When the Uber finally pulled up to Arc Royale, I was completely starstruck. Three grotesque fountains lit up the entrance of the palace-sized casino. The building towered over the enormous parking lot like a glass kingdom, magically ornate. Flocks of people dressed in glitter and suits scattered the perimeter, bustling raucously.

"Thanks again!" Mags waved off the driver and linked arms with mine. "Now this is what I call a birthday celebration," she said in awe.

Sapphire velvet rope separated us from the inside of the matte black casino doors. Crowds of people passed us, carrying the scent of tequila in the air.

"So many lights," I gasped in disbelief.

Maybe I was being dramatic, but I had never been anywhere this extravagant in my entire life. I vaguely remember going to the circus when I was really young, but this was incomparable. I'd driven by Arc Royale a few times, but only during daylight. At night really exhibited the sheer opulence of this place.

The two large hedges on either side of the fountain welcomed us, glowing in pastel rainbow colors. When I looked up, I saw that the hedges were connected by one huge crystal arc, sparkling like stars. *Well, that explains the name.*

"Come on!" Mags said, approaching the two bouncers dressed in all black.

"I.D ladies." The one with dark hair said.

"For you, anything." Mags laughed, clearly tipsy. She held out her ID and walked through the velvet rope, clicking her heels.

I couldn't help but chuckle and presented my own ID. The man looked me up and down with striking blue eyes. "Hm," then passed it back to me. "Happy birthday," he smiled. "Enjoy your night."

For whatever reason, a wave of confidence hit me like a truck. I returned his gaze with a flirtatious stare, winking at him as I walked through the rope. I could feel his eyes trail me as I passed by, but I didn't look back.

The warm surge of alcohol seeped through my veins, intercepting all sense of rationality. I never would have done anything like that sober; Mags was always the flirt between the two of us. But I didn't care. *Tonight's my night, my birthday.* When I was dating Tommy, he never made me feel pretty or important. But you know what, tonight... tonight, I did. So of course, I had to take advantage of it.

This was *my* night. The one night I could indulge in pure bliss, drink without a sense of guilt. *My* night to dance until the sun rises, ignore all of the misfortunes of my past and forget all of the chaos and coincidences of... Beau Gabriel.

"What the hell was that, tiger?" Mags giggled, lacing our fingers together.

I beamed with a face full of fire. "Let's have some fun," I said, walking up the golden steps. *Tonight is my night.*

Chapter 8

ARC ROYALE, PRESENT NIGHT

Various different sounds rang through my ears from every single direction. Slot machines and blackjack tables surrounded us, along with crowds of people throwing down what looked to be their entire life savings. My dad taught me how to play poker, but I wouldn't dare dream of sitting at one of those high roller tables. If I were to gamble, it would be roulette. Place a bet on black or red and if it lands on your color, you win.

"Want to grab a drink before we go to the club?" I asked Mags.

She nodded and led me to one of the three bars lining the casino walls.

"What can I get for the two beautiful ladies?" the bartender smiled, rinsing out a glass. His light brown hair was gelled back, cascading down just above his shoulders. He had a pleasant face, approachable and affable. *Probably why he got the job.*

"Fuck, is everyone who works here hot?" she flirted, evidently intoxicated.

The bartender laughed, probably out of politeness. I couldn't imagine working for hours on end getting hit on by drunks every two minutes.

I pinched Mags and smiled. "Two tequila shots please."

"Make it four!" she yelled, giving me a genial shove.

He looked to me with patient eyes, waiting for my approval. I shrugged. *Ah, what the hell.* "Make it four."

"As you wish." He lined up our shot glasses and filled the clear liquor to each brim. I plugged my nose and took two big gulps, finishing off both shots. *I am definitely going to regret this in about thirty minutes.*

And I was right.

We hung out around the bar for a little while longer talking to the bartender. He was actually such a good sport for a sober man entertaining two drunk girls and of course, Mags made sure to get his number. *I didn't expect any less.*

As soon as I got up, the dizziness hit me like a tidal wave. We hadn't even gotten to the club yet and I was already ruined.

"Shit, I can't even stand." I slurred to Mags, grabbing hold of her arm. *Screw these heels!*

"Oh come on, the party has just begun! Woo!" She yelled, gripping hold of my arm.

All the lights blurred to a phantasmagoria of flashing colors. We stumbled around the room, trying to find the club. We definitely looked like idiots, but to be fair we'd never been there. Every corner looked the same. Hundreds of slot machines and people, just on and on and on.

"It has to be here some –" Mags bumped into someone, and fell to the floor.

"Damnit, I'm so sorry!" I heard a man say.

We both reached to help Mags up, and once she was stable, I looked to the mysterious stranger.

Whoa. Holy *hell.*

My inebriated brain couldn't process the man standing before me. He was absolutely stunning, almost like an expensive painting. Light brown scruff lined his chiseled jawline, trimmed perfectly. He looked to be about 6'3, 6'4, wearing a black button down rolled up at the elbows. A tattoo of two coiling snakes travelled around his forearm partnered by another hand tattoo with random black symbols. His ashy blonde hair was slicked back messily, though his grass-green eyes were alarmingly vacant, impossible to read.

"I'm sorry about that, beautiful. I wasn't looking." He held Mags steady, throwing me a few glances.

I stirred, pushing down conflicting emotions. I didn't exactly know how to feel, or why I questioned feeling anything at all. His presence hulked over me, raising goosebumps to my skin. It didn't feel like that sweet, uneasy calmness I'd felt when I met Beau... it was just plain *uneasy.*

I looked down, fidgeting with my fingers when I noticed the ruby in my ring radiate a faint red glow. *Huh. Probably just the hue of one of these lights.*

Swallowing hard, I pushed away the hanging discomfort that loomed over me and adjusted my wilting posture.

"Oh, no, no sir. That was my mistake," Mags bit her lip and ran a flirty finger over his jawline. "Actually, not a mistake at all."

I shrivelled my face in disgust. *I need a drink.*

"You girls feeling okay? Do you need water?" he asked.

As I attempted to tear my eyes away from him, I noticed he had a nametag. "You work here?" I questioned.

He kept an arm around Mags, but not in a creepy way. More like a trying to keep her stable way, which eased up my wandering mind for a moment.

"Oh, yeah. I work at the blackjack tables over there. Siles Killian," he extended a hand to me, flashing a set of pearly white teeth.

Before I could shake his hand, Mags stepped in front of me and threw her arms around his neck. "Maggie Lake Harthrow, do *not* forget that name Mr. Killian!"

She stumbled back into me and stuck a pointy finger in her mouth, barely balancing on her heels. "Mr. Killian, can you point me to the direction of the club?" she purred.

He chuckled and stepped to the side. "I'm actually just about done my shift. I can take you girls there if you want? Just give me two minutes."

"Oh! Yes, we'll wait right here." She grinned, taking a seat on one of the leather poker chairs.

I watched Siles jog off behind the slot machines and disappear into a staff room. My buzz was fading quicker than I anticipated, but I gave it no thought. The only thing that seemed to plague my mind was the mysterious Siles Killian. Even though he was gone, I somehow didn't feel the absence of his company.

I chewed on my bottom lip, pulling my hair out of its ponytail. "Mags, we don't even know this guy." I tried staying rational. *At least one of us was.*

She placed her finger over my lips and slumped down on the chair. "He's cute, we're keeping him."

A few minutes passed and Siles returned, coming up behind me with two mini water bottles and a set of keys.

"She okay?" he asked, handing me a bottle. The brush of his cold fingertips sent a chill down my spine.

"Thanks," I replied tensely. "Yeah, she just had way too much."

His snake-like stare narrowed, and though he wore a smile, his eyes told a different story. "Good thing you're here," he whispered. "You know, to take care of her."

I clenched my jaw, digging my nails into the cracks of my palm. Goosebumps covered my skin like icicles, piercing my flesh. The heavy tension weighed between us and I didn't dare move. I examined him, just as he examined me. *But what am I looking for...*

In an instant, Mags sprung to her feet and grabbed hold of Siles' hand. "Are we just going to stand around talking or are we going to dance?" She giggled, googly-eying Siles like he was candy.

We exchanged one last heavy glance, then he ripped his eyes away from mine. "I choose dancing," he smirked.

Siles led us through a winding web of tables and crowds. I couldn't fathom how much money was being tossed down the drain by people who thought Lamborghinis were affordable. A distant boom echoed through my ears as we approached the front of a massive glass door. Inside, a bevy of coloured strobe lights bounced off the walls and rotated on the ceiling like propellers.

A Latin song blasted through the air while bodies of women and men bumped and grinded to the energetic beats. Two caged pole dancers were side by side in the middle of the room, and a large L shaped bar glowed luminescent in the corner.

Toeing further into the club, a sense of euphoria eased my weary state of my mind. A group of drunk girls wearing neon necklaces pulled us into the belly of the crowd, dancing against each other without a care in the world. *I want that to be me.*

Mags turned my hips to face her, wrapping her arms around my neck while Siles disappeared into the crowd.

"Let's dance baby!" she screamed over the music, pushing her bottom into a random guy.

Have fun... Have fun! My voice insisted. *It's your night... Let go.*

"Screw it," I smiled. And I danced.

After what felt like hours of twirling, grinding and spinning, my feet felt numb, and I knew what kind of blistery crime scene awaited me once I took my heels off. I drank enough at the club to maintain my buzz for a couple of hours, but it began to wear off by the second. *These stupid shoes!* I pushed through the crowd and leaned against the wall, checking the time: **1:14am**.

Mags and Siles were still centered in the middle of the dance floor, making out like no tomorrow. I was happy for her, now that she was finally being single. But I still couldn't shake that weird feeling for the life of me. *You don't even know the guy Maya, cut him some slack.*

When Siles grabbed Mags by her thighs, lifting her up around his torso, I thought it was time to look away. *Ew.* I rubbed my eyes, peering down at my ring once again, the red glow still radiating. *Is this thing defective?*

I shook my head and waved my hands in the air, yelling to Mags. "Hey, I think we should head out, it's getting late!"

She gave me a thumbs up but continued to grind on Siles, laced around his body like entwined vines. My eyes travelled up his silhouette, meeting his gaze. His green eyes burned into mine, and he flashed me a coy smile as he wrapped his arms tighter around Mags' middle.

My heart bounced in my chest as he continued to feel every inch of her body, watching me with a feral expression. I wanted to say something, anything, but the words died in my throat. *You're drunk, he's drunk, it's in your head... Yeah, that's it.*

His hands gripped at Mags' dress and for a second, I could have sworn his green eyes blurred into a different color. A darker green maybe? I narrowed my stare, attempting to get a better look, but only then did I wish I hadn't.

Through the neon lights, the horde of bodies and the encompassing darkness, his shifty eyes were clear as day.

His eyes were crimson red.

Chapter 9

ARC ROYALE, PRESENT NIGHT

Go get some air... You've had too much to drink.

I had to rationalize it to myself, I had to. If not, who would? I know what I saw, I couldn't have mistaken it for any other color. They were red.

When I turned to look at him again, his eyes were that familiar grass-green... only there was nothing familiar about them.

I managed to capture Mags' attention and pointed to the entrance of the club, crossing my hands over my legs. Whenever we were out, Mags and

I used that as a signal to use the restroom. And once again, she threw her hand up and waved at me to go, but didn't follow.

The cool levelled air was refreshing upon exiting the club. My ears rang faintly and the booming music faded into the distance the further I walked. I took in a breath, feeling surprisingly calm now that I was out of that crammed cube and away from... *him.*

I pulled out my phone to check the Uber cost. *I was just about done with this night.* But my phone wouldn't turn on. I pressed hard on the power button, but nothing. Completely dead. Black screen. *I'm so screwed. Of course I forgot a charger too.* I had one too many scary instances taking taxis, so that was out of the question, and my dad was surely asleep by now. *Think Maya, think.*

I decided to walk around the area and ask people if they had a charger I could borrow. Of course, every single person shook their head. I knew damn well they were lying, but I still carried on. *Snobs.*

I rummaged through my purse, checking all the little zipper compartments to see if I could find a spare phone cord. Maybe that way I could –

"Watch it!" I said, bumping into a hard frame. The contents of my purse poured out onto the red velvet carpet. *Are you serious?* As I bent down to pick them up, a familiar tone sent my nerves spiralling.

"Maya?"

I stopped dead in my tracks, gripping my lip-gloss tightly. *There's no way.* My eyes began at his shoes, slowly moving upwards until I met his shaded grey eyes. I swallowed hard, unable to comprehend the fact that he was standing right in front of me. "*Beau?*"

A crisp laugh rose from his throat. "We have got to stop meeting like this." He bent down and picked up the mini water bottle Siles had given me. "Interesting size," he smirked, insinuating a dirty joke.

I swatted it out of his grasp, shoving the rest of my things into my purse. "What the hell are you doing here?"

He ran his hands up and down his all black attire. "I work here. What are *you* doing in that dress?" He took a step back and eyed me like a doll on display. "Not that I'm complaining."

I rolled my eyes, forcing an attitude. "It's my birthday. Well, was."

The corner of his mouth lifted to a smile as he rubbed the stubble on his jawline, not taking his eyes off me. "Well, you certainly look the part. Happy birthday."

I scoffed and avoided eye contact. Of course, Beau worked at the one place I was having my birthday at. Of course, the one night it was acceptable to make mistakes, I couldn't, because of Beau Gabriel. I didn't want to let my guard down around him, I couldn't. What would he do if I did? Would he stomp on my heart like it meant nothing? *Why are you thinking about this?*

"Why so glum?" Beau asked, sucking me out of my own head.

"I'm not glum." I lied.

Of course I was. My feet hurt, Mags was fawning over some strange man, and worst of all, the one person who never left my mind stood right in front of me, eyeing me with intrigue.

I almost wanted to forget him completely, at least for the night. With all the strange coincidences that seemed to have brought us together, I thought maybe tonight, I could just remember me. I could remember what I was like before I'd met Beau.

I looked down at my phone and sighed, pushing away all of my trivial thoughts. "I need a charger, do you have one?" I asked, bluntly.

There was no way of telling how long I'd been gone for since my phone had died, but I knew I had to get back to Mags. There was something off about Siles that I couldn't put my finger on, and I left her alone with him. If my gut was right on this one, then I needed to save her quick.

"In my car, yeah. Do you need a ride?"

Thoughts of sitting next to Beau in the passenger seat resurfaced in my brain. The warmth in his car, an intoxicating smell of pine and mint engulfing my sinuses. *No, not again.* I crossed my arms. "No," I finally responded.

"Well," he chuckled, "I bid you good luck getting home." He took a step forward, positioning himself directly in front of me. Lifting two fingers, he dusted a loose strand of hair from my face, a slight grin forming at the corner of his mouth. "Better."

I stood still, cemented to the ground beneath me. I dug my nails into my palm, sweaty from his touch. A million thoughts raced in my head, but I couldn't focus on any of them.

He walked past me, nodding once. His grey eyes burned into mine with satisfaction. "Get home safe."

Before I could stop myself, I reached out to grab his arm. He turned to me with a coy expression, lifting his eyebrows.

I hated the fact that he was standing in front of me, waiting for me to ask him for the ride he had already offered. I hated that he made my heart flutter, even though I hardly knew anything about him. He was a complete and utter anomaly, but yet when I was around Beau, I felt safe. I couldn't lie to myself any longer, I *wanted* to be around him – and the universe seemed to be giving me exactly that.

I inhaled a deep breath and kept my posture erect. "It's a free ride," I released, acting unfazed. "So yeah, you can drive me home."

"I thought you'd never ask." He snickered, bowing playfully.

"But we have to get Mags first. She's still in the club."

He pursed his lips and glanced at his watch. "I'm cut in five minutes. Go get her and meet me here, sound good?"

I nodded and watched him run off to a poker table, slapping the shoulder of one of his coworkers. I caught myself analyzing the contours of his silhouette, admiring the black on black attire he wore that

✜

hugged his muscular frame like second skin. A sharp pain stunted my senses, and I realized I had been biting my lip. *Ew, no. Ew.*

By the time I had reached the club, most people were leaving. I shoved past the crowd and made my way to the dance floor that was covered in confetti streamers and glitter. The lights were already dimmed to a jaune hue and the DJ was packing up his equipment. No sign of Mags.

I grew fidgety, scouting the perimeter, running back and forth from the inside and outside of the club. No Mags.

"Mags?" I yelled out to the remaining people shuffling away to the door. "Mags!"

Oh, no, no, no. My phone was dead, I couldn't even contact her. *This is bad, this is really freaking bad.* If only she wasn't drunk and my phone was fully charged. But... I left her. I left her with a complete stranger, in a foreign environment filled with people. *Oh you idiot!*

I ran up to the DJ and slapped my shaky palm on the wooden booth. "Have you seen a girl with blonde hair and a red dress?"

He scratched at his bald head in annoyance. "Try fifty blonde girls in red dresses."

Oh my God, I can't believe this is happening! "She, uh she was dancing with a guy! He works here! Blonde, tall, all black outfit – Siles. His name is Siles!"

"Sorry." He shrugged.

Damnit! I wanted to scream, darting my eyes around the near empty room. Beau trotted through the glass door with his black peacoat, holding car keys and a backpack.

"Did you see Mags?" I demanded, running past him. "She's blonde, wore red, she –"

He grabbed hold of my arm and pulled me in front of him. "Hey, whoa, hey. What's wrong?"

The warmth of Beau's touch slowly levelled me back to reality. He pulled up the strap of my dress and rubbed his thumb gently against my collarbone. I could have melted at the gesture if it weren't for my best friend being lost and inebriated in the possession of a stranger.

And the anxiety is back. "I looked everywhere, I can't find her, I can't find Mags. She's just gone." I talked through panic breaths, rubbing my temples. "I wasn't even gone that long Beau, I –"

"It's okay, sh." He gripped tightly of my hand, intertwining our fingers. Tiny tingles erupted underneath my skin. "She's probably somewhere in the casino. We'll find her."

But we didn't find her. Beau and I scouted the entire place for over half an hour and she was nowhere to be found.

"This is insane. She wouldn't just leave." I let out a sigh of exasperation, scraping my scalp.

Beau stood silent for a few moments, then nudged for me to follow him. We walked past rows of slot machines until we reached a door that read:

MAINTENANCE.

He pulled out a set of jangly keys from his back pocket and looked both ways before entering.

The tiny, congested room was filled with TV's and cameras.

"Shut the door." He said, typing away on a computer.

I did as I was told and looked at the monitors. "Are you even allowed in here?" I asked, nervously.

"Perks of being liked," he winked.

I rolled my eyes and sat behind him, gnawing at my lip. All I could think about was Mags. *She couldn't have gone far. How did I not see her leave? She would've had to walk past me, no?*

"What time did you leave the club?" he asked, adjusting the security footage times.

I rubbed my temples, retracing my timeline. I remember pulling out my phone when I got tired of dancing, when I watched Siles practically screw my best friend on the center floor. I grimaced, shoving the memory as far down as possible. "Uh, around 1:15 I think."

He scrolled through the camera recordings and set the time from 1:15 onward. The video footage showed several minutes of people dancing... and then I saw Mags.

"There, stop!" I exclaimed.

Mags was leaving the club, hand in hand with Siles. As they were walking out, Siles seemed to have looked directly at the camera and... smiled? *What the hell? My eyes have got to stop playing tricks on me.*

So, that's it then. She was with Siles. She left me, to sleep with some random guy she didn't know.

Impossible. She never would have done that, she never has. *That isn't Mags.*

Beau leaned back on his chair, pointing to the screen. "Who is that guy?"

I bit down hard on my bottom teeth, attempting to control the betrayal of being abandoned by my best friend, without warning, on my *birthday.* "I should be asking you that. You work with him." I scoffed.

It didn't make any sense. If she wanted to leave with him, why didn't she tell me when I was there? She left only minutes after I did. She must have talked about it with him at some point... *and just forgot to mention it.*

Beau turned his head to me, narrowing his eyes. "Maya," he said, concerned. "Did he tell you he works here?"

"Yeah?" I responded bitterly, leaning up from my seat. "Why?"

He bit the inside of his cheeks and looked at the monitor once again, shaking his head. "I don't just work at the tables, I work in management. Look, I know everyone who works here."

A hollow pit formed in my stomach and I knew I wasn't going to like what he had to say. "And?"

He let out a deep breath and stared into my eyes, his jaw twitching. "Maya, whoever that is... he doesn't work here."

Chapter 10

HELL

"*Faster,*" Marina moaned. "Baby, faster!"

The screams of condemned souls rang loudly through the heated air. Hell fire painted the walls of the onyx cave, mighty and ardent.

Siles huffed into her red hair. "How do you like that?"

Their deafening whines went on for a few more minutes until Marina got irritated and shoved him off of her.

"Boring." She spat.

Marina was a succubus: a female demon who appeared in dreams to seduce, usually men. If said person was riddled with mortal sin, the succubus would be able to control them with just one kiss. Siles was the same, an incubus who too, possessed this ability.

Marina stood up, wrapping a red silk robe over her naked body.

"Nothing pleases you, Marina." Siles scoffed, placing the black sheets over his sweaty torso.

"*You* don't please me," she hissed.

The granite doors flew open, causing Marina and Siles to jump. When they saw who had entered, they quickly gathered themselves and stood up side by side, regaining composure.

With the flick of his wrist, the hell fire receded into the cave walls, leaving a trail of crimson mist. "Having fun, are we?" Lucifer joked. He crossed his arms, leaning against the granite door. "Please, don't stop your salacity on my account."

Lucifer had been one of the most beautiful creatures in existence. He had brilliant blonde hair and piercing grey eyes, much like his archangel brothers. But when he fell, the golden aura he possessed turned to black and red. He lived in a world of blood and midnight, with only fire illuminating his paths... and that's how he liked it. The sound of terrorized, trapped souls was music to his ears. He had complete control over everyone and everything in hell, which is what he had always wanted.

Power. Control.

He wanted to rule, but never below his brothers. He wanted to rule the sky, but God stood in his way. *Pride* overtook his being, until it consumed him.

Then one day, his crystallized grey eyes turned red with rage while the veins underneath his skin morphed into soot-colored snakes, stamping his body like thorned weeds. Nothing was ever enough for Lucifer, even though he seemed to have it all.

He dressed in all black with an engraved white pendent hanging from his chain. The ivory hue radiating from his neck seemed to be the only thing that lit up the darkness that followed Lucifer.

Before he fell from Heaven, God rewarded Lucifer the power of the moon, hoping that Lucifer could prove his potential for containing power. Instead, Lucifer captured the grace filled inside God's creation and stored the grace-fueled moonlight in an amulet around his neck. When God saw that Lucifer had no desire for purity, he cast him down to hell alongside the band of angels who worshipped sin – the fallen. In a heaping rage, Lucifer scratched God with the archangel's sword, the sword that since then, has been locked and guarded by the archangel Michael. He combined both graces in his necklace, saving it for the day he would finally take his revenge on Heaven: the war of the fallen.

"Master," Siles and Marina bowed simultaneously.

Lucifer rolled up his sleeves and curled his slender fingers around Marina's neck, brushing a kiss on her cheek. With one hand, he hoisted her up in the air and pinned her thin frame against the cave wall violently.

"Pet," he spat directly in her eyes. With two fingers, he pushed opened her robe and danced around her skin, exploiting her in front of Siles. Then he released her harshly, like a lifeless sheep.

Siles swallowed hard as Lucifer approached him, watching him with beady red eyes. He stopped in front of Siles and put his knuckles to his chin, analyzing him with purpose.

"Are you afraid?" Lucifer asked, tracing his pointed nail across Siles' throat. A patch of flesh parted underneath his jawline, secreting thick blood. Lucifer pulled away and licked the gore from his finger.

Siles dug his nails into his palm, his teeth chattering incessantly. "N - no," he blurted out. "Master." He bowed cowardly.

Lucifer broke out into a roaring laugh, clapping his hands together giddily. "Ha-ha! What fun." He signaled for Marina. "Come, come before me my sweet."

Tapping both of their faces, he paced around them, circling like a shark. He held up a flaming finger and opened his mouth. "Something... *happened*," he emphasized.

"What –"

"Ah, ah." Lucifer interrupted Siles. "I need you two to fix this, how should I say... minor discrepancy."

Lucifer pulled out a small black bead from his pocket, an *orbionyx*, and threw it into the air. A growing orb began to form, blurring into the vast land of Earth and its creatures. He swirled his fingers

for a few seconds until a glossy visual of Beau and
Maya appeared.

"My Father is trying to make a fool of me."
Lucifer's red eyes burned at the sight, watching Maya,
the *Puritas*, in the cemetery the day before her
birthday.

"Who are they, Master?" Marina asked,
peering over his shoulder.

Lucifer rubbed his jaw, eyeing Beau with a
twinkling expression. "Hm, what a familiar face."

The orbionyx burst, dropping gloppy grey
globs to the stone floor. Lucifer turned on his heel
and looked to the two demons, placidly. "Kill them in
whichever way you please." He moved past them,
then quickly turned around with wide eyes, holding
up a graceful hand. "But have some fun first."

Marina and Siles exchanged stares of
confusion, frozen in place. "But... why?" Siles
questioned.

Silence.

A vein in Lucifer's forehead twitched,
darkening with each pulsating beat. His blonde hair
fell out of its gelled place, covering his crimson eyes.
He halted before the door, turning around slowly to
face the demon.

Siles blanched, paralyzed from his stare.
Within seconds, Lucifer had him by his throat,
squeezing until Siles' eyes turned beet red. "Since
when do *I* need a reason?" He hissed.

Marina shivered, taking slow, tentative steps
backwards to the granite door.

Without turning around, Lucifer snapped his fingers and the door slammed shut. Marina fell to the ground in a thump as burning red chains sprouted from the wall, imprisoning her ankles.

Lucifer dragged Siles by the neck and pinned him to the cave, igniting scorching blue embers from the wall. The red chains coiled around both Marina and Siles, the scent of burning flesh filled the air as they screamed in pain.

Lucifer laughed, watching their twitching bodies convulse. "Do we have an understanding?" he snarled, using his spit to gel back his hair.

They cried agreements in agony, begging to be released. And when he released them, their skin bubbled with grisly, black boils.

Lucifer stepped over their spazzing bodies, kicking them over with the point of his shoe. With squinted stares, they could see Lucifer's tall figure standing over them, black wings stretched out with a smile.

He let out another icy laugh, crouching down close enough that they could smell his spiced breath.

"Never forget," he growled, "I own you."

Chapter 11

KLEATON'S GATE, PRESENT NIGHT

My hands shook violently in my lap but I couldn't feel them. The entirety of my body went numb, like I was paralyzed from head to toe. Sweat poured down the nape of my neck as I buried my face in my palms. Flashes of anxiety began to skyrocket while a heaving pain formed in my chest, stomping on my heart. *Mags is doomed.*

Tears welled in my eyes and before I knew it, a sob escaped my throat. "She's dead! She... She has to be dead... I let her leave with a serial killer, Beau!" I wailed.

My brain couldn't even consider the possibility of her being alive... there was just no way.

Siles, whoever *he* was, kidnapped her. Maybe they went to get some air and he drugged her. What if he stabbed her? *Oh my God she is dead. This is my fault. I killed my best friend.*

My legs bobbed frantically, I couldn't sit still. Pacing around the small maintenance room, I tried to catch a breath; any breath that would ease my mind... but I knew that breath didn't exist.

All I could think about was her. Where was she? Where did he take her? Some secret underground holding cell with all of his other victims?

I remember the feeling I had around him. That intoxicating, off-putting impression he gave. His snake-like stare that fixated on my every move, watching me like a hawk. I played it casual though, because I was stupid and drunk and did I mention, *stupid!*

"Sit down." Beau insisted.

I darted my eyes towards him, my chest heaving up and down. He patted the seat next to him and extended a hand out to me. "Come on," he motioned.

I looked to him with a daggered stare, digging my nails into my palm. *One breath in, one breath out.* I shut my eyes and found solace in the darkness behind my eyelids. *Stay here forever.* But I couldn't – not with Mags in danger. I inhaled another long breath and took the seat next to Beau. *Relax, Maya.*

"Panicking isn't going to do much for you or her." He said.

But I couldn't relax. I scowled at him and moved away, unable to control the mixture of fury and solicitude. "Do not tell me what to do right now. Unlike you I actually care if she dies." I snapped, my seething anger reaching its boiling point.

I knew he was right, but I couldn't temper the vexation burning inside of me. Taking it out on Beau definitely wasn't the right decision, but I'd clearly already made a list of bad ones... what was one more?

He cupped my knees in his hands and turned the rolling chair to face him, drawing me in between his legs. His face lowered to mine, close enough that I could feel his breath linger against my lips. His grey eyes turned dark like coal, hypnotizing me.

"Don't make an enemy of me, Maya." His voice was low and demanding.

I swallowed hard, eyeing his lips. He was so close to me, *too* close... and I wanted him to be. I held his gaze for a moment until he let go of my legs and leaned back.

"Look, let's start off by going to her house. Maybe she took him home? And if she's home, you can get your beauty rest." He snorted and made his way to the door, holding it open for me.

And the moment's over. I rolled my eyes and walked through, glancing one last time at the empty room before Beau shut off the lights. *I hope he's right.*

"That's hers, right there." I pointed as we pulled into Mags' neighbourhood. The porch lights were completely shut off, leaving only the solar motion beams in the garden providing illumination.

"I don't think she's here, Beau." I shook my head, unbuckling my seatbelt.

He turned off the engine and stepped out of the car. I made my way around and matched his pace.

"Only worry when you have a reason to worry." He said sternly.

I was never really good at controlling my temper, and I'm sure Beau had figured that out by now. I didn't know what he got out of irritating me, but he did a great job of it. "Oh? And my best friend being abducted isn't –"

"Hey," he put his finger over his lips. "Keep your voice down. Neighbours." He pointed around the area, furrowing his brows.

I could feel him smiling which pissed me off even more. When I looked over at him, I was right. *The nerve.*

We made our way up the walkway to her house. I knew Mags' parents were sleeping, and both her brothers were off to college. I checked the time: **4:47am**.

Beau had already rang the doorbell three times before I could process my thoughts. I shot him a look and he shrugged his shoulders.

"No time to waste," he whispered.

No response, nothing.

"I hate this." I bit my fingernail anxiously, waiting for an answer that could possibly make my night, or break it into a million pieces.

Beau banged the door a few more times with his fist, then rang the doorbell once more.

"Beau!" I snapped, agitated.

Just then, a faint light in the corridor came closer to us. The door slowly unlocked to Mags' mom dressed in a blue pyjama set with her blonde hair in a bun.

"Maya? What on earth –"

"Grace, is um, Mags home?" I asked eagerly. Every knot in my stomach tied and constricted, hoping the answer would be a yes.

She rubbed her eyes and turned off her phone flashlight. "Maya, it's almost five in the morning."

I felt bad knowing she had to get up in two hours for her job, but I felt worse knowing I lost her daughter. "I know, but we went to the casino for my birthday and she left. I don't –" Guilt. "I don't know where she went. She left with someone and I can't get a hold of her."

Grace was like a second mom to me. When Mags and I first met, we became inseparable. I practically lived at her house, spending countless nights in a row there when my dad was working late. Grace knew about my mother's passing, and offered her home as a safe haven if I ever needed an escape... *I always needed an escape.*

I knew I could tell her anything, and in this case, I had to. I didn't care if Mags would get mad at me the next day, or not talk to me for a year. As long as she was safe.

Grace's mouth dropped. "What? You can't get a hold of her?"

I shook my head. "No. My phone died at the casino and I've been calling ever since it's been charging."

She frantically turned on her cell and put in the passcode, dialling Mags' number.

After a few rings, a familiar voice sounded through the phone... Mags. *Wait... what the hell?* I looked at Beau who remained unfazed.

"Mags, hun, where are you?" Grace asked.

I could hear quiet mumbles on the other line but couldn't make out what was being said.

"Okay, okay. Maya's here with a uh –" she stopped and eyed Beau up and down. "A man." She cleared her throat. "Glad you're safe. See you tomorrow. Love you."

She hung up the phone and turned to me with a smile. "She's fine, sweetheart. She's staying at Liza's right now and she said she'd text you tomorrow."

I opened my mouth to speak, searching for the right words to say. I knew in my gut she wasn't at Liza's... she couldn't be. But Grace wouldn't believe me, why would she? She'd just talked to Mags who told her everything was fine.

I looked at Beau once again and bit the inside of my cheeks. "Thanks Grace, sorry to disturb you at such a late hour. I was just worried." I responded, forcing a smile.

She isn't at Liza's, she's lying to you! Demand where she is, pick her up, your daughter's in danger! Was what I wanted to say. But the fact that she answered the phone meant that she was fine... at least I hoped. *Stop this Maya, she answered the phone. She's okay.* Maybe it was just a misunderstanding since we were drunk and we thought he worked there. But he went into a staff room? He wore the same uniform as Beau? *Something isn't right.*

"Go home, get some rest. You're a good friend, Maya." Grace yawned, closing the door. "Goodnight, both of you."

Beau wiggled his fingers into a witty wave as we turned away. "Told you not to worry." He bragged, opening the car door for me.

I shut it and buckled in, trying to kill the uneasiness that infiltrated my thoughts, but it wouldn't die.

"I know we heard her, but I don't know. Something still seems off." I stressed, shaking my head.

I rubbed my fingers together, mindlessly tracing over the ring my dad gave me as Beau drove to the direction of my house.

The ring.

The ring that glowed red when Siles was around. Did it really work? Was it trying to tell me something but I ignored the signs?

I plucked it off my finger and stared at the ruby, shaking it to see if it would shine. Were there batteries somewhere? Nothing. The ruby was beautiful, but it was just a stone.

"Beau, this ring..."

He glanced at it quickly then returned his eyes to the road. "Very pretty."

I leaned forward from my seat, shaking my head. "No, listen. My dad gave me this protection ring for my birthday." I held it up. "He said if the ruby glowed red around someone, that meant they were dangerous."

He shot me a look of confusion but let me talk.

"I know, I sound insane. But I remember the ring glowing around Siles. Is that crazy?"

He cleared his throat and tightened his grip around the wheel. "I think you're just sleep deprived."

I leaned back into my seat, sluggishly. *Ugh, maybe he's right.* Maybe I was sleep deprived. Maybe it was all in my head and I conjured up this weird hallucination while the tequila controlled my rationality... Or maybe I didn't. *You need sleep, Maya.*

I squeezed the ring in my palm once before sliding it back onto my finger. *Mags is fine...*

Beau pulled into my driveway and unplugged the charging cord of my phone. His fingers tapped the screen until he found my contacts list, adding his number in.

"Just in case you need me again, I'm not leaving it up to fate," he released, handing it back to me.

Butterflies filled my stomach, fluttering around in a medley of contentment. I blushed and turned away, concealing a smile. The thought of having Beau's number in my phone put my mind at ease. I wouldn't have to rely on sheer coincidence if I wanted to talk to him anymore... and I wanted to talk to him.

On the horizon, I watched the clouds turn to a faint pink. "Sun's coming up." I mumbled, avoiding eye contact.

I always hated this part. Leaving. I didn't know why I felt such a pull towards Beau, or why he left pleasant knots in my stomach. Leaving his side, as much as I hated to admit it, pained me.

"That it is." He smiled.

I turned to him, twiddling my thumbs. There were so many things I wanted to ask Beau, so many coincidences I needed answers to, but did he even have them? *How could he?* So I thought to ask the one thing I knew he had control over. "How did you know I was at the cemetery that day?"

"I didn't."

I narrowed my eyes playfully. "If I remember correctly, you were so confident that you'd see me again."

He took a pause, then met my gaze. "I guess I was just lucky."

A warm heat rose to my face, one that I couldn't hide. I sat in the seat a little longer, taking in the faint aroma of his cologne. My eyes searched his car innocently, hoping to find something else to spark up a conversation. *I really don't want to go.*

My gaze landed on the silver ring in his cupholder. I picked it up and analyzed its simplicity.

There were no scratches, no tarnishes; it looked untouched. Only the inside was engraved with the letter R. *R? For what? Why does he never wear it?*

"It's a nice ring." I remarked. *Get out of the car, you look desperate.*

And what a mistake that was. The air between us grew heavy, and Beau's shoulders tensed up. He remained silent, though I could tell he was biting back words. *Great job Maya, you struck a nerve. Can this night get any worse?*

I swallowed down my embarrassment and quickly put it back in its place. *Stupid, stupid, stupid.*

My body practically shoved me out of the car, my hand hovering over the door handle ready to click it open. But before I did, my mouth decided it wasn't done humiliating me.

"Thank you for tonight." I spluttered, red-faced. "You didn't need to help me, but you did. So, thank you."

He let out a soft chuckle. "What are friends for," he replied.

I forced a smile and stepped out of his Porsche, watching him pull out of my driveway and drive off into the dusky morning.

I stood at my front door for a few moments, staring at the parking spot where he was only a few seconds ago. I replayed all the events of tonight in my head, wondering why his last remark stung more than it should have.

"Friends." I whispered under my breath. *Just friends.*

Chapter 12

KLEATON'S GATE, JUNE 24TH

Braum was out drinking at a local pub the night of Maya's birthday. Of course, Maya and Braum had very different ways of celebrating their night. After Mags put a restraining order against Braum, his father beat him senseless every night for a week. His father was a drunk and worked at a gas station, spending most of his earnings on booze and cigarettes. Braum's mother had passed away due to cancer when he was a boy and his sister had emancipated herself years ago. He had to obey court-ordered volunteer work at a soup kitchen on top of working at a convenience store, hoping to save enough money to move away.

He crashed at Tommy's place a few nights a week, and another few at Ky's. They couldn't let him stay though; their parents weren't too keen on the fact Braum now had a criminal record.

Braum decided that he had enough of his personal pity party and wanted to let loose. "C'mon boys, let's just go!"

Tommy and Ky were playing video games in Tommy's basement, ignoring Braum's senseless invitation. It wasn't that they didn't want to go; they just saw what he was becoming and wanted to protect him from it.

"Ky you got me covered?" Tommy asked, playing Call of Duty. "Braum, man, I'm not feeling Pinkie's tonight."

Pinkie's Up was the only strip club in Kleaton's Gate. It wasn't posh, but it wasn't dingy either. Some professionals would go there, but reserve a back room so no one would see them. The young and dumb who turned the legal age would also have little celebrations there as well. Then of course, the regulars who practically lived on their doorstep.

"It's half-priced drinks tonight, Tommy. When'd you get so boring?" Braum scoffed, taking a huge gulp of beer.

"I'm with Tommy on this one, dude. Just chill here, we got enough beer for nine weeks." Ky added. "Tommy... acquiring target!"

The following moments were silent while the boys concentrated on the game. *Concentration, concentration...*

A collective scream followed by a high five. "Yes! *Target acquired!*" Tommy cheered, crushing his beer can.

Braum bit the insides of his cheeks and marched in front of the TV, unplugging the console with force. He ran his fingers through his tangled blonde hair and watched the boys, agitated.

"The hell?" Ky swore, throwing his arms up in protest.

"Dude?" Tommy questioned.

Braum didn't say anything. He dragged his legs over to the mini fridge and pulled out two beers, sliding them over to his friends.

"I'm not drinking by myself while you guys play video games. There's tits and booze calling my fuckin' name." Braum took another huge swig of his brew. "Now, will you quit being boys and grow some fuckin' chest hair, will ya?"

Tommy and Ky both looked at each other in bewilderment, confused and concerned. Neither one of them moved; neither one of them touched the alcohol. The silence weighed heavy in the air while Braum stood, jittery and annoyed.

It was Tommy who decided to break the tension, standing up to grab the beer bottle from Braum's hand. "Buddy, you need to sit down."

Braum moved away quickly, flailing his arms. "Don't touch my fuckin' beer!"

The boys stared at him.

"Now I'm goin' to Pinkie's, and if you guys don't want to come so be it. I'm out of here." Braum waved his hand in the air and snagged another beer bottle on the way out, slamming the door.

Pinkie's was about a half hour walk from Tommy's place, but Braum knew a shortcut. He got there in under twenty. The pink neon entrance flashed through the darkness, inviting him in.

Braum took one last sip of his brew before throwing it to the side, and pushing open the doors. "Home sweet home." He grimaced.

Low, sensual music boomed over two enormous speakers. Crowds of men sat in groups at metal tables, placing dollar bills into the thong straps of the strippers.

Braum passed a dark haired woman who sported a bright blue bikini bottom and orange pasties. He whistled and winked, making his way to the luminescent bar.

He pulled out a twenty dollar bill and slammed it down aggressively. "Two rum and cokes, double the rum."

The bartender was a young blonde in her early twenties, wearing a small white tank and a padded pink bra. She made the drink quickly and handed it to him with a smile. "Here you go."

"Mm," Braum spoke hoarsely, gawking at her cleavage. "You got that bra in red, too?"

The bartender rolled her eyes and grabbed the twenty, shoving it in her bra cup.

"Whore," Braum snarled, walking towards a vacant leather couch.

He ogled salaciously at the strippers on stage, tossing whatever loose change he found in his pockets onto the ground beneath them.

And he drank – more, and more, until his pockets were dry.

The night passed in a blur. A few women took interest in Braum, sizing him up and complimenting him. He'd engage for a few moments, but the women quickly realized he had no money to give. Their initial lap dances quickly turned to angry bartering.

"Bitches! All women are bitches!" he raged, taking a huge swig of his drink.

No one paid attention to Braum, even though he desperately craved it. If a woman hadn't given him her time for more than fifteen minutes, he would throw ice cubes at the wall like a spastic infant. He wanted to feel something, anything. Braum was aware that his life fell apart as a young boy, but thought to turn it all around as he got older. When he finally accepted the position he was in, it ate away at him. The excessive drinking was just one of his many coping mechanisms.

"Easy there, tiger." A red-haired woman approached Braum, the first one in a couple of hours.

The mystery girl was tall and slim, all legs. Her wavy red hair swooped down just over her chest, soft like silk. She wore a tight green dress and fishnets, accompanied by yellow stilettos.

"Mind if I sit?" the redhead asked, plopping down right on his lap. She smiled at him, brushing away strands of his sweaty blonde hair.

Braum grew fidgety, nervous. He'd never met a girl who exuded this much confidence... a *woman*, rather. He didn't know where to place his hands, so they settled on the curve of her spine. "Do you uh –" he choked.

She laughed, throwing her arms around his neck. She traced a finger over his jaw, then his chin, then his lips.

Braum wanted to say something, anything, but all the words died in his throat. After a few moments, he managed to ask, "Do you work here?"

She shook her head and glanced around the room, grimacing at all the strippers grinding on titillated customers. "I'm too good for a place like this. Or maybe," she grabbed the drink from Braum's free hand, "too *bad*." She smirked, licking the rim of the glass.

Braum shifted in his seat, subtly trying to hide the growing erection in his pants. He wanted this woman, every inch of her, right now. Just barely touching her, she'd already satiated his every fantasy. Sleeping with girls was one of his many hobbies, but that's all girls were to him, *hobbies*. He hadn't really been interested in anyone since Mags, but this woman... this woman changed the game. He wanted to know her. He needed more.

The mystery woman climbed to the other side of Braum, stretching over him seductively. She got to her feet and extended a hand out. "How about you take me home and I can show you just how *bad* I can be?"

Braum nodded slowly, his lips dry, waiting to kiss hers. Everything about her was enticing, captivating, *desirable.*

He wore an intoxicated expression as she led him outside, but not from the alcohol. "Can I get a name at least?" he flirted.

The woman smirked and curled her fingers around Braum's, looking ahead. "Marina."

Chapter 13

KLEATON'S GATE, PRESENT DAY

*M*ags and I hadn't talked for a few days after Beau and I visited her mom's house. She told me she would text me but to my surprise, she hadn't. I called her numerous times just to hear her direct me to voicemail.

"*Hey this is Mags, say you love me and I might just call you back. Mwah.*"

"Are you serious?" I muttered, tossing my phone onto the bed.

I found comfort underneath my blankets, burying my face, and problems into my pillow. It was hard for me to believe that everything was fine, especially after the near abduction that could have been, at Arc Royale. At least Mags was okay... *Keep telling yourself that, Maya. Maybe one day you'll believe it.*

I closed my eyes, shutting out the world. "What is my life." I murmured against the silk casing.

I must have dozed off because when I looked out my window, the mid-day clouds turned into a fading sunset. I rubbed my eyes and checked the time: **7:32pm.**

"Maya?" my dad asked, knocking on my door.

"Come in," I said, forcing myself to consciousness.

My dad stared at me, confused. "Since when do you nap?"

I shrugged my shoulders, placing my pillow back on top of the others. I noticed a wet line of drool on the silk. *Okay, yuck.*

I quickly shook my head and turned my attention back to my dad. "Since today I guess."

He chuckled and opened my door a little wider. "Mags is downstairs. She said you girls had dinner plans?"

I practically flew off of my bed in shock. My eyes grew wide with bewilderment, wondering if I'd heard my dad correctly. "Mags? Mags is downstairs? Right now?" I asked, utterly perplexed.

My dad nodded slowly, puzzled. "What's wrong? Did you not have plans tonight?"

I knew that if I said no, my dad would bombard me with more questions. I hadn't explained to him what was going on the past few days and the fact we hadn't spoken. It's not that I didn't want some moral support, but I myself, had no idea why she wasn't talking to me. Though if Mags really was downstairs, I could finally get some answers.

I scrambled for my purse. "No, yes. I mean, yes we have plans. The nap made me woozy," I said, hurrying past him. "See, this is why I don't nap."

I didn't wait for his response as I bolted down the stairs. Only, I wish that I hadn't bolted. I wished that I stayed in the comfort of my blankets, huddled underneath its protection. Because who was standing in my kitchen, staring at me with piercing blue eyes, was far from who I expected.

"*Mags?*" I shivered, slowing down as I reached the bottom step.

A heavy weight balled in my stomach, anchoring me down in place. A girl who looked like Mags, yet not at all, turned to me with a poisonous smile that halted my movements. I held my breath, looking at someone who I thought... I *thought* I knew. Her eyes were icy, beady and bloodshot. Everything in me told me to run away, to send her out and never invite her back in my home. But... why?

She faced me, slicing her stare into mine like pointed blades. "I've missed you," she smirked.

The tension in Mags' car could have shattered a window. I shifted in my seat a handful of times, attempting to relax, but I couldn't. Panic loomed over me, feeding my fear.

"So..." she broke the silence, clicking her tongue. "How've you been?"

She kept her eyes on the road while I quickly stole a glance. Her makeup was done differently. She had dark eyeliner smudged underneath her waterline and scarlet lipstick. Mags loved playing with makeup but never the dark shades; she said it contrasted against her skin and blonde hair. A nude lip and mascara was her staple. This, however, was the complete opposite. Her blonde hair had two dark brown streaks cascading down both sides of her face, bristly and dry.

"You uh –" I stuttered. "You changed your hair."

"Mhm," she smiled. "You like it? I thought it was edgy. Blonde Mags was getting a little too *boring*."

I swallowed hard, fighting the urge to jump out of the moving vehicle. If I were to die, it would be a kindness compared to the harrowing feeling I felt around her. She was not the same girl that she was a few days ago, she wasn't Mags. The thought of her ever going dark never crossed my mind; she wouldn't have even considered it for a billion dollars. One time she wore a brown wig for her Halloween costume and took it off in the middle of the night because she said it gave her food poisoning. *Food. Poisoning.* And now... now I'm supposed to believe she changed her appearance to this, willingly? *Absolutely not.*

"It's different." I responded quietly.

We hadn't exchange many words the entire ride into town. I didn't know what to talk about, or how to ask questions. The air remained heavy, intoxicating. Everything that I thought to say slipped my head and fell into a dark abyss. Each glance I stole, the grim feeling resurfaced. It tugged and prodded at my psyche, repeating over and over again. *Something is wrong. Get out of the car.*

After a torturous half hour, Mags pulled into one of the fanciest restaurants in Kleaton's Gate, one that I could never afford unless I was splitting with three or more people.

I wiggled my brows in confusion. "What are we doing at Fondos?"

She shut off the ignition and turned to me. Her blue eyes narrowed, darkening. "Eating, what else?" she laughed, grabbing her purse then slamming the car door shut.

I followed after her as she marched up to the glass entrance. "Mags, I can't afford to eat here."

Mags and I only ate at fast food joints or local diners. We weren't a fan of the elite community, especially at Kleaton's Gate. Fondos was beside Swan Lake's golf course which held the top tier millionaires and their bratty partners. Needless to say, I was baffled that Mags even considered bringing us here.

She turned around quickly and held up her hand, tapping together her black acrylic nails. "Your mom saved thousands of dollars for you in a trust fund before she died. Now she's dead, and you can use it."

My jaw dropped.

Her words cut me like a knife, hacking at my heart. I fought every urge inside of me to slap her across the face, shocked that she would ever mention my mom in such a distasteful light. She watched me with a smile, as if she was waiting for a reaction.

My teeth chattered as I held back tears. I wanted to hurl myself in front of a car, or jump off a cliff... whichever was most painful. Mags would never say anything about my mom unless it was in good faith, never. We would rarely even talk about her because she knew how sensitive a topic it was for me.

"How dare –" It took everything in me to stop myself.

I knew that I had to control my anger to get answers. At this point, that was all I wanted. Something happened that night with Siles, and I needed to know what. I bit my tongue and trailed behind her. *What happened to you...*

I always judged the upper class lifestyle, but there was no denying its opulence. The ambiance of the restaurant was absolutely breath-taking. A waterfall with a koi pond was directly behind the host stand and glass chandeliers hung from the baroque ceilings. A white linen banner hung to my left reading:

Welcome to Fondos! We specialize in the world's finest Italian cuisine!
Yeah, if you can afford it.

The man behind the host stand was very handsome, wearing an all white ensemble with gold hemming. I glanced around the room to find that everyone working was quite good-looking as well. I expected that much.

"Table for two." Mags said, flatly.

I was sure she would have hit on him. She flirted with everyone if they were attractive enough for her, and this guy seemed to be very much her type. Tall, muscular, charming smile... but she didn't even bat an eyelash.

He led the way to a table near the balcony, overlooking the lake. "Here you are ladies, can I start you off with some water?" he asked.

Before I could speak, Mags took the reigns. "Gin and tonic, light ice."

The host looked taken aback by her attitude but kept his composure all the same, looking to Mags then to me. "I'll tell your server right away. Yourself?"

I forced a smile, hiding my discomfort. "Water's fine," I said, taking a seat. He left.

"Since when do you drink gin?" I questioned, glancing over the menu in horror. The only thing I could afford were garlic sticks for twenty-three dollars. *What a scam.*

"I like to try new things, you know that." She said, folding her arms over the table.

Hm. "Do I?"

A moment of silence passed when our server returned with our drinks. She was a very pretty, curvy brunette. "Hi ladies, my name is Sam and I'll be your server for tonight. Have you decided what you'll be having?"

Mags pointed her finger at the menu. "I'll have the steak and potatoes."

"And how would you like your steak done ma'am?" Sam asked, writing on her notepad.

Mags closed the menu and handed it to her. "Rare."

I swallowed down my words. Mags never ordered steak because she said red meat interfered with her diet plan and she was extra peculiar about raw meat. All my life I watched Mags avoid steak at family barbecues, practically convulsing at the sight of a pork-chop.

"For you?" the waitress asked, turning to me.

I bit down hard on my bottom teeth. "Nothing, I'm uh, I'm good." I replied, folding the menu and handing it back to the waitress.

"Are you sure?" Sam asked. "We have a great –"

"She said she's good, now go." Mags sneered.

The waitress quickly scurried away and disappeared into the kitchen.

I've had enough. "You didn't need to be rude."

Mags ignored my comment. "So sorry I've been MIA for the past few days. Siles and I have been having the best time." She brushed her hair back to expose two plum hickies on her neck.

Disgusting. I pushed the mental picture out of my brain, knowing that this was my chance to ask about Siles.

I took a swig of water, eying her carefully. I knew that I needed to play it cool, but it was so damn hard, especially after her insensitive comment about my mom.

Nonetheless, I mustered up the courage and posed the question. "So what happened the other night? You went ghost and didn't talk to me for days."

She perked up, as if she was waiting for me to ask that. "Oh, well Siles and I were in such a hurry to get privacy so we could have alone time, if you know what I mean." She winked, sipping her gin and tonic. "Yeah, we've just been having so much fun together so I kind of spaced. Totally my bad, but we're together now, aren't we?"

There had to be more than that. Everything about her changed; the way she walked, the way she talked to people as if they were below her and she was the queen.

"Honestly, I think I'm in love. He's so great. He's so sexy and amazing in bed." She added.

"You met him a few days ago, Mags. Do you even really know him?"

Flashbacks of Beau and I figuring out that Siles didn't even work at the casino came into mind.

She raised her voice, gripping the tablecloth. "Of course I fucking know him. Are you insane?"

Her pupils were dilated and her expression feral, like a lion who hadn't eaten for weeks. I knew it was time to tell her about my discovery with Beau; I couldn't keep pretending any longer. Siles wasn't being honest and I wasn't about to let him take advantage of her, even if she'd end up hating me for it. I took in a breath, smoothing out the white cloth she practically yanked off the table.

"Mags, the other night when you left, I ran into Beau at the casino who *actually* works there. And, um –" I stuttered, trying to calculate my words properly. "We found out that Siles doesn't actually work at Arc Royale. He lied to us, he lied to *you.*"

Her face flushed, reddening with anger as she pushed back her drink. She stared at me in silence, her blue eyes intensifying. "*Beau,*" she emphasized. "You know Maya, I've never actually met *Beau.* Does he even exist? Or are you just making things up because you're lonely?" She laughed. "No, no. I can't be so harsh. I bet you know him so well, don't you, Maya? Have you even fucked the guy? Does he even *want* you, Maya?" she snapped, her voice strained and sharp.

I buried my nails into my palm, finding comfort in the acute pain that followed. *Does he even want you, Maya...* Her words replayed in my brain, taunting me with spite. Everything that came out of her mouth was an intentional shot to hurt me, to get under my skin. She knew about all the encounters I had with Beau – the police station, the cemetery, all utter coincidences. She knew how he made me feel; she was my best friend, of course she knew that I cared. *She's trying to hurt me.*

The ability to control my emotions was a mere balancing act at this point. I watched her in utter disbelief, my thoughts fraying into a vexatious frenzy. *Leave, run, please. Stay, hit her, slap her!* I didn't even have time to defend myself before Sam returned with the food.

"Steak and potatoes for you," she said, placing the dish in front of Mags. "Anything else I can get you girls tonight?"

"What is this?" Mags demanded in disgust. "This isn't rare enough."

Sam turned bright red. "Miss, I –"

"I am not paying for this." Mags said pushing the plate in front of her. "Cheque, now."

"I can get you the manager, I'm sorry I thought –"

"My father co-owns Swan Lake's golf course. I don't need to talk to your *manager* to get you fired," Mags spat.

Sam wasn't the only one who turned red. A surging heat rose to my cheeks as I looked around, observing the sheer disgust in everyone's expressions. Our waitress was shaking, visibly about to cry, while Mags egged her on, lying through her teeth. Mags' dad was an accountant and most definitely not the co-owner of a golf course.

"Don't worry about the check ma'am," she whimpered. "The drink is on the house."

Mags flung her bulky black bag around her shoulder and stood up. "As it should be."

The waitress ran off in a hurry.

My stomach turned with utter humiliation. I paled as the room began to spin and my head weighed heavy. *Get away from her, get away from her.* The last thing I wanted was to be around Mags for another second. I didn't care about the questions or the answers anymore. I was determined to be as far away from the 'new' Mags as possible.

"I'm going to the bathroom." I seethed, clenching my teeth together.

The light fixtures were glossy, sparkling like diamonds above me. Only they were blurred, like the sea of bodies around me, melting together into a kaleidoscope of shadowy figures.

"Meet me at the car?"

I ignored Mags and darted for the ladies room, locking the door. I stood in front of the mirror and stared at my reflection, panting. Beads of sweat trickled down the base of my neck as the anxiety hit with full force. I ran to the stall and kicked it shut, hurling up my breakfast from the morning. Everything spun. *Stop, make it stop!*

A sharp pain banged against my skull as I scrambled for my phone, dialing the only person I wanted to see.

Three rings. "Hello?"

His voice was distant, but I knew it was him. "Beau," I groaned, wiping my mouth.

"Maya? Are you okay?" he asked.

"Pick me up, please. I'm at Fondos by Swan Lake."

A moment of silence. "I'll be there in ten." The call cut off.

I sat on the cold floor with my head between my legs, trying to process my band of thoughts. I didn't know Mags anymore, whoever she was, whoever Siles made her. *What did he do to her?* How did she become so vile? So unrecognizable? This wasn't her; there was not a piece of her new persona that resembled the old Mags. *New Mags is a cold-hearted bitch.*

I forced myself steady, pushing up off the ground and found the emergency exit that lead to the parking lot. I didn't want Mags to see that I was leaving with Beau, considering that she ripped me to shreds about him at dinner. *She doesn't even know him. But... do I? Does she have a point?*

Mags was sitting in her car texting, unaware that I was approaching. She smiled at her phone, holding it up for a picture. I rolled my eyes, walking up to her window and tapped on the glass.

"Hey, I'm not feeling well so I called my dad to pick me up." I half-lied. *I'd rather eat my own hand than spend another minute with you.*

"What? No, boo. I can drive you back home." She replied, re-applying scarlet lipstick. She didn't even look at me.

I wanted to grab her throat. *Control yourself.* "I don't want to get you sick. It's fine, my dad's almost here."

I backed away from the car, turning around slowly when she called my name. "Maya, wait!" She reached around to the back seat and pulled out a small purple box.

"Before you go, I made you a cupcake. To say I'm sorry for not texting you because I was having amazing sex." She smirked, holding out the box to me.

I stared at her, hesitant to take it. Everything about her smile made me want to run for the hills. I didn't know who she was anymore. I didn't want to know. Whatever happened during those few days wasn't my concern anymore. I didn't want anything to do with my best friend. *What the hell is happening? Do you hear yourself?*

But... do you see her?

With tentative movements, I grabbed the box and fully stepped away from the car. She flashed an elusive smile and rolled up the window, then drove off into the night. It was only then that I noticed the faint hue radiating from my finger. A knot in my stomach constricted, forcing out a gasp. All of the hair on my body was standing when I realized...

My ring was glowing red.

Chapter 14

KLEATON'S GATE, PRESENT NIGHT

*B*eau was deep in thought on his drive home from work. He hadn't seen or heard from Maya since the incident with Mags a few days ago. He fought off the feeling of missing her, even though that emotion was undeniably present. *She doesn't matter to me. She's necessary to win the war, to contain the evil... She doesn't matter to me.* But Beau knew he was lying to himself. Whether it was God's plan or fate, it frustrated him that he couldn't get her out of his head.

He gripped one hand on the steering wheel and scratched his scalp. "*Fuck,*" he muttered.

Beau felt something growing inside of him; an unfamiliar sentiment he had never felt for a *mortal.* He'd been with many women from different countries, but never stuck around long enough to find out if something could develop. But with Maya, he was obliged to stay for years and years. Because of that, he couldn't distinguish whether or not his feelings were out of genuine protection or if something more was beginning to sprout.

Beau pulled into his parking spot at Glass Hill Condos and turned off the engine. He sat in the car for a while in silence, occasionally glancing at the passenger seat where Maya once sat. Amidst all the panic that night, he had fun in a weird way and it made him smile, but he could never show her that. *Maya's the mission... that's it, that's all.*

He took in a breath, peeking at the silver ring in his cupholder, pushing away all the memories that it contained. He fiddled with it in his fingers, staring bleakly at the engravement: R.

After a few moments he tossed it in his glove box, grabbed his keys and got out of the car. *No distractions.*

Beau had finished an early shift at the casino and was home by nine in the evening. He sometimes questioned why he even worked in the first place; it would be so easy to compel his landlord into thinking he paid the rent every month. Although, Beau rather enjoyed sucking the greed out of foolish mortals, and brushing up on his gambling skills at the same time.

He threw his keys on the entrance table and shut the door behind him. Letting out a sore gasp,

Beau's features twisted in pain as he scratched at his scars.

Every night for weeks, heavenly fire burned through his back as a result of him prolonging the mission. It was a consequence, forged by the archangels if he strayed from his purpose... and that's all Beau seemed to do.

He walked past his kitchen, fighting the urge to drink away the pain like he'd done several nights in a row. He knew he had to tell Maya who she really was soon, otherwise –

"Beau." A booming voice startled him.

Beau was standing by the glass window when Gabriel appeared. "Funny, I was just thinking about you."

Gabriel stood in the middle of the room, dressed in all white linen. "You haven't told the Puritas."

Beau walked over to the couch and plopped down. "Why is it never a simple hello with you? How are you doing today? You have a lovely place."

In the blink of an eye, Gabriel had him pinned against the wall. "We don't have time for this, Beau!" Gabriel held him by his shirt for a few moments before releasing him and stepping back. "Michael's army is growing weaker and Lucifer's fallen are moving up. He has convinced them that if they overthrow Heaven, God will bow down and the eternal burn of hellfire will cage the angels."

Beau found it ridiculous that the fallen would even entertain Lucifer's whims, but then again, he was no secret to Lucifer's manipulations.

"There are several fallen that still want redemption. Their souls are trapped in hell, but they can help us. We need Maya, she has God's grace; she can lift their souls." Gabriel spoke desperately, eying him with suspicion. "Have you looked at your scars lately, Beau?"

Beau avoided looking at his back. He knew that he'd been disobeying God's orders by not telling Maya, and the longer he stalled, the darker his scars would become. And once they reached full darkness, he would belong to Lucifer.

Beau gritted his teeth. "No."

He knew it was time to tell her, hell, he should've done it a long time ago. But if he was being honest with himself, he didn't know how. He almost wished that he told her back then, back when she was still dating Tommy Weem or sneaking beers to bonfires. At least he didn't know her yet... not in the way he knew her now.

Running around with Maya these past few days made Beau realize something – she was completely and utterly normal, innocent. How could a normal girl accept such a title? The Puritas? A saviour of the afterlife? He didn't want to place that burden on her back, he couldn't.

"What if she doesn't believe me, Gabriel? What if she does nothing?"

Gabriel approached Beau slowly. "Believe it or not Beau..." he paused. "She does trust you."

They exchanged a momentary stare in silence. Beau thought back to their encounter at the cemetery, yet another inexplicable coincidence. The rain practically drowned them, though Beau had a car to cover him and Maya did not. So he offered to drive her home, but she didn't make it easy. When he used his grace to manipulate Maya's trust, it didn't work. Only when he showed a side of vulnerability did she soften. She trusted him on his own, without his power, but by her own will.

Somewhere deep down, Beau knew that Maya cared for him too. He didn't want to admit it to himself, because if he had, what then? They could never be together. Did he even want that? An angel and a divine mortal, thrown together by twisted fate? He saw her mother die – he lived on Earth for over a century, watching wars, galivanting the globe, satiating the darkness that grew within him...

But Maya's warmth was a glimmer of hope.

Every time he looked into her hazel eyes, wide and gentle, his sins melted away, even just for a moment.

"Gabriel," he bit his tongue, but the words fought to come out. "I... I feel something for her."

Gabriel didn't seem surprised, taking hold of his hand. "I thought you might, Beau."

Beau stood quiet in his thoughts. He didn't want to lose Maya, but he was at risk of losing everything else. The war, his brothers, his home, all of it. He was afraid. He didn't know how she would react, but did it matter anymore? Time was treading on a very thin line, a line that he could cut or save. Beau became clouded with affection that he was forgetting the mission, his position as the Nuntius. He couldn't battle his fear any longer. He needed to do what was right. And when he finished the mission, he could go home. *Yeah... Home.*

Gabriel handed a small white cloth to Beau. "Maya must say these words before drinking from the Holy Grail."

Beau unravelled the message, written in Latin. It translated to: *From the chalice I drink holds the power of the trinity. By His name, I accept its grace.*

Whoosh. Beau looked up to find that Gabriel was already gone.

Shutting his eyes, he took in a long breath, grasping tightly of the cloth before putting it in his pocket. *Time for that drink.*

He walked over to his kitchen and pulled out a bottle of whisky, pouring himself a glass.

Taking a huge swig, he finished the liquor in one gulp. "She's my mission, that's it. That's all she is." He uttered, wiping his face. "That's all fuckin' is."

A twinkle glinted in his peripheral vision. Beau held in a breath and glanced over at the wall mirror across his table, dreading what was to come. He felt his scars becoming worse, the pain almost unbearable, but he was too afraid to look.

He shut his eyes and glanced at the mirror once again, then back to his alcohol. "Fuck it." He took one more sip and walked to his reflection.

Steely grey eyes pierced back at him, dark and weary. His midnight hair swooped down over his forehead messily, curling over his ears. He stood for a moment, staring, attempting to control his nerves, then removed his black shirt. Beau glared at his abdomen, squeezing his fists tightly. He didn't want to turn around. Though his appearance taunted him, demanding him to look. *I have to do this.*

With dithering hesitation, he slowly turned, gasping in fright. A cornucopia of black veins coiled in every direction from his scars, sprawled like snakes underneath his skin. Beau gripped and pulled at his flesh, heaving with agony.

"No, no, no!" Beau wailed ferally, scratching at his back. "God, no!"

I can't, I can't be like them... I can't fall, I won't fall! He didn't want to be in Lucifer's possession, anything but that, anything but the fallen. In Heaven, he was just an ordinary angel. Gabriel chose him to carry out this mission. God and the archangels trusted him; they crowned him the first Nuntius... but he failed.

"Fuck!" he screamed, punching the mirror with brute force. The glass shattered into a hundred pieces, leaving micro cuts on his skin that quicky healed.

He collapsed to the ground in defeat. No one was perfect and no one could be perfect, Beau knew that. If he made one more mistake, the gates of hell would welcome him with open arms for eternity. *An eternity of suffering.* He sat in silence over the broken shards with his head in between his legs. *I'm fucking doomed.*

The soft vibration of his phone startled him. He met his gaze in the mirror, staring at his sharp, bloodshot eyes, then pulled out his cell. The call display read: **MAYA BRIXTON.**

Maya? With aching muscles, he pushed himself up off the floor and cleared his throat, pulling himself together as best as he knew how. "Hello?"

"Beau..." Maya sounded anxious. He knew something was wrong immediately. "Pick me up, please."

Without explanation, Beau replied, "I'll be there in ten."

He hung up the phone and threw on his shirt, scrambling for the door. The panic in Maya's voice repeated in his head the entire drive. He tried to think about the mission, Gabriel, home... But all he could think about was her. Many of their encounters were coincidental, but not this one. She reached out to him on purpose. She needed him, and that was enough.

He pushed on the pedal harder, digging his nails into the leather of the wheel. "I'm here Maya," he breathed. "*Always.*"

Chapter 15

KLEATON'S GATE, JUNE 25TH

"*I*'m sorry, my room's kind of a mess."

Braum said to Marina, sitting on his bed.

His buzz had slightly worn off, which excited him. As much as he hated to admit it, alcohol always lowered his performance in the bedroom department.

"Oh don't apologize," Marina replied, tracing her fingers over his desk. "I enjoy a little chaos."

She kicked off her heels and pushed Braum onto the mattress, taking off his shirt. He slid off her dress and left the fishnet tights on, yanking at the cross-patterned string. Braum moaned as she went down on him, bobbing her head.

Marina knew what she was doing. It would only take one kiss, and Braum would be a slave to her. The more he wanted her, the less he would want anything else.

Braum pulled her up over his legs and leaned in close to her face, but Marina pulled away. She was taunting him, and she quite enjoyed it.

"Ah, ah, ah." She chuckled, straddling him.

"*Please*," Braum pleaded, digging his fingers into her back.

Marina traced his neck with her lips, her fingers sliding over every inch of his body.

Over time she grew agitated, finally facing him with venomous eyes. "You're going to be *mine*," she laughed, cupping his face. "Poor Braum... You do not know what I have in store for you."

And she kissed him.

PRESENT DAY

Tommy hadn't heard from Braum since the night he left for the bar. They never went more than two days without communicating with each other, so he began to worry.

"What if he overdosed on something, man?" Tommy suggested.

Ky shrugged his shoulders. "Should we call Mike?"

Tommy shook his head. "You'd get a better answer from a brick than his own dad."

Tommy paced around his basement, thinking of logical solutions to get in touch with Braum. He never wanted to go to his place unannounced; last time he had, two half-naked girls chased him away with sharp stilettos... *Yeah, never again.*

Though, Tommy was running out of options. "Fuck it, let's just drive to his house. Mike's probably workin' right now so he won't give us a hard time."

Ky agreed and they were out the door in minutes. When they reached Braum's house, they noticed his 2006 Corolla in the driveway.

"Well, he's home," Ky muttered.

Braum had given both Tommy and Ky spare keys to his place just in case something bad happened between him and his dad. They knew how short fused Mike was when it came to Braum; anything could happen at any given time. He treated him like his own personal punching bag, as if Braum was the reason for his addiction issues. It seemed as though Braum had a bruise for every inconvenience that set off Mike, and Braum had *many* bruises.

Tommy hesitantly unlocked the door and called out, "Braum!"

"Buddy, you here?" Ky added. "We saw your car in the driveway."

No response.

Tommy walked to the kitchen, noticing a bowl of soggy cereal on top of the table. Overhead lights flickered on and off, emitting a buzzing sound. *Huh?*

The air was heavy, and something didn't sit right with Tommy, but he had no idea what it could be. He glanced to Ky with uneasiness and made his way to the staircase.

Tommy took one tentative step before placing an arm out in front of Ky. A pungent odor engulfed his senses, putrid and rotten. He sniffed the air. "What's that smell?" He sniffed again. "Ky, do you smell that?"

Ky scrunched his eyebrows and stuck out his nose, taking a whiff. "Kind of, what is that?"

Together, they crept up the stairs carefully. As they got closer, the smell grew more intense, almost intolerable.

"Fuck," Tommy spat, covering his nose. "It smells like death in here."

Ky took the lead and climbed to the top of the stairs. All three doors were closed except Braum's. Light spilled out from a small gap in the doorway.

"Braum?" Ky called out again, covering his face with one arm. "Braum, buddy, you've got to crack a window."

Tommy opened his door and peeked in, but Braum was nowhere to be found. The room was still messy and nothing seemed to have changed. They paced around until Tommy's eye caught a small piece of paper sitting on his bed.

In messy red ink, the note read:

acquiring target

Tommy raised his eyebrows in confusion. *Acquiring target? Like, in Call of Duty?* He wondered if Braum was still angry about the other night when he hadn't gone to Pinkie's.

"What is this shit? Is he messing with us?" Ky asked, irritated. "Fuck man, that smell!"

Braum loved playing pranks on them ever since they were little kids, but this seemed... different. A gut feeling told Tommy that something was very wrong, no matter how much he wanted to believe otherwise.

They took one last look around the room before backing into the hallway. "Let's just go, he's probably at the bar again." Tommy said.

As he strode by the bathroom, a shadow moved quickly in his peripheral vision, underneath Mike's closed door.

A pit formed in his stomach. "Ky – Ky, did you see that? Did you fuckin' see that?" he panicked.

Ky's chocolate eyes darted around the corridor. "No? What?"

Goosebumps surfaced all over his body, picking at his flesh like hornets. "I saw... I saw something in the corner of my eye, in Mike's room." Tommy's voice cracked.

They moved past the staircase cautiously, tiptoeing to the front of Mike's door. In dead silence, only the floorboards creaked beneath them. Tommy buried his nose in his shirt, plugging it with disgust.

"On three?" Tommy whispered.

Ky nodded wearily.

"One... two... *three*!" they yelled in unison, kicking the door open.

The silence was deafening. A crow sat on the open windowsill, its merlot eyes fixated on them. Tommy remembered the days when he used to go hunting with his dad; the smell of a rotting animal abandoned by other hunters. When his dad would skin the carcass, their lifeless eyes stared back at him while their blood dripped and dripped.

Tommy couldn't stomach the gruesome scene that painted the room. Years of hunting could have never prepared him for this moment. His heart leapt into his throat and his guts clenched, paralyzing his breaths.

He stood by Ky, frozen in fear.

Neither said a word.

Not a sound came out.

"T – Tom..." Ky stuttered in shock.

The mutilated corpse of Braum's father hung from the ceiling fan, spewing blood from every hole like a fountain. Just above his navel, two words were carved in red:

target acquired

Chapter 16

KLEATON'S GATE, PRESENT NIGHT

"Thanks for picking me up." The familiarity of Beau's car eased my panicked thoughts.

His dark hair clung to his forehead, shaggy and wet. Sweat glistened atop his tan skin like gloss. *Shit, did I interrupt his workout?*

He kept his eyes on the road and cleared his throat. "What happened?"

Well that is the question, isn't it. I kept quiet for a few moments, picking at the edge of Mags' cupcake box. My phone was vibrating like crazy, but I was too anxious to check it. Every time I hit decline, it kept ringing and ringing.

"Could be important," Beau said.

I briskly flipped it over and saw thirteen missed calls from Tommy. *Really not the time.* I shook my head and turned my cell off completely. I didn't want to deal with him, not after what just happened.

I slid the phone into my back pocket. "Just my ex, Tommy."

"The guy at the station?"

I nodded, adjusting the heat warmer in my seat. The night was humid but being around Mags left chills all over my body. I couldn't stop shaking. My thoughts buzzed around like bees, trying to comprehend what happened at the restaurant. Who was she? I wanted to scream, but at who? Her, or Siles? Was this part of a prank? No, she insulted my mom. She stabbed my heart numerous times, and twisted the knife. How could she? *Now she's dead, and you can use it...* Her words repeated in my brain, jabbing at my skull. *Forget her, Maya. She chose Siles over you.*

"Do you want to talk about it?" Beau sucked me back to reality.

Did I want to talk to Beau about it? What if Mags was right? Maybe I hadn't known Beau as well as I thought... Or wanted to believe. What if I can't trust him? But I could trust him. I've trusted him before, and he never hurt me. Beau was closed off, mysterious and if I was being honest, a tad shady. But... I trusted him. He picked me up, and without an explanation he was here, when I needed him most. That counts for something. *Let him in.*

"I just –" I stuttered, searching for the right words to even describe what happened. "Mags and I hadn't spoken since the casino. Then out of nowhere, she randomly showed up at my house with apparent dinner plans that I was obviously unaware of. Then we came here, to this place that I – *we*, couldn't even afford."

Beau chuckled softly. "Who doesn't love overpriced cob salad?"

"Exactly!" I continued to talk. I thought maybe saying it out loud would help me rationalize the situation. And in a weird way, it helped.

He listened to the whole story, from start to finish without interruption. I told him about the way she looked at me, the scene she made, and the insensitive comment she said about my mom, which Beau flinched at. I also mentioned the price of the garlic sticks, which he laughed at.

"She was so mean Beau, to everyone, to me. It was like she was a completely different person, I didn't even recognize her."

My stomach grumbled and ached. Food was the last thing on my mind at the restaurant, around Mags' cold demeanour. But all this talking made me realize that I hadn't eaten anything at all and puked up all of my breakfast. *I was hungry.*

"I need food." I opened Mags' cupcake box and took the dessert in my hands.

It was red velvet with buttercream frosting, covered in heart shaped sprinkles. She knew I hated

the cheesecake icing. *At least she remembered that.*
The sweet smell of sugary goodness filled my stomach.
I took a mouthful and leaned my head back, moaning
with satisfaction. After a few more bites, I finished
the entire thing.

"Jesus. Ever look into competitive eating?"
Beau joked.

Only his laugh was distant. It started with a
soft chime, then the ringing grew louder, penetrating
my ears with metal clangs. My vision blurred, the stop
lights twisting together like a tornado. A hollow pain
bubbled in my stomach as the cupcake began to crawl
its way up my throat, begging to come out. Everything
spun, and spun, and twitched and shook. Nausea hit
me as I squirmed in my seat, trembling.

"Maya?" Beau. "*Maya!*"

Close your eyes. Close your eyes. I reached
out to Beau but couldn't feel a thing. *Close your eyes.*
The motion, it stopped. Darkness encircled me,
fading fast, *fast, faster...*

Then, nothing.

I woke up in a bed with a heavy wool blanket
draped over my body. The yellow hue of a small lamp
was the only source of light aiding my vision. *Uh...
where am I?* The room was small and blackout
curtains hung on the steel rod next to me. My head
pounded against my skull, my eyes still configuring to
the dimness of my surroundings. Behind the closed
door, I could make out a faint nose in the distance.

I shut my eyes again, trying to ease the pain. My head fell back onto the grey pillow, and only then did a familiar scent ignite my senses. *Pine and mint.*

I scrunched my eyebrows and held my head, attempting to sit up. My eyes darted around the room, almost fully adjusted to the lack of light. There was practically nothing in here. A black cabinet in the corner, a laundry bin and a lamp atop a white bedside table.

A knock on the door startled me and Beau's tall physique slowly crept in, holding a glass of water. He was wearing grey sweatpants and a black t-shirt, exposing every curvature of his arms. His dark hair swooped down over his forehead and his grey eyes twinkled, clear as day. Only then did it really settle in... I was in Beau's bed.

"Hey," he smiled. He sat down on the edge of the mattress, handing me the glass. "How are you feeling?"

I shifted in the sheets and took the water, chugging it back. The cold liquid cooled my throat with icy bliss. *Water never tasted so good.*

My mouth was so dry and my head rattled. "Been better." *Isn't that the truth.*

Beau sat across from me, watching with concern. I felt like a stray puppy that had just been rescued.

"Beau," I said reaching out to him. "It was just an anxiety attack. I must have passed out, I'm okay. It's happened before."

But Beau didn't budge. His features only grew more unsettled.

"What is it?" I asked, placing the glass of water on the bedside table.

Beau stood up and paced for a few seconds, lifting his hands over his head. I couldn't help my wandering eyes from drifting to the v-lines trailing directly to his...

"Maya, you don't know what happened, do you?" he interrupted my thoughts. *Thank God.*

I kicked the sheets off my legs and stretched. "I do, I had an anxiety attack."

He sat in front of me and swallowed hard, his grey eyes piercing directly into mine. The air was still, heavy. Beau remained quiet and serious, which worried me. He always had a comeback or an obnoxious line to ease any situation, but not this time. He was dead silent.

"Earth to Beau?" I teased, pushing his arm.

He cleared his throat and got up, leaving the room. *What the hell?* What was going on? *Why am I even in Beau's bed right now?* I thought he was just going to drop me off at my house. He could have let my dad deal with the anxiety attack; he'd seen way too many episodes, especially after my mom passed away. It never really got any easier.

Beau returned with two familiar white feathers in his hand, the same ones I saw in his car glove box a while back. He sat back down in front of me and placed them to the side.

I couldn't help my laughter. "What are you going to do? Tickle me to death?" I always made jokes when I was uncomfortable, and the uneasiness was reaching the point of awkwardness. I couldn't help myself.

His expression was dark. "I honestly don't know how to tell you this," Beau muttered.

Putting aside the tension, Beau's indirectness began to irk me. "Beau what is it? You've been dancing around –"

"Maya, you were poisoned." His voice held no trace of humor.

I stared at him for a few moments, trying to process what I just heard. *Poisoned? Poisoned!* I chuckled once, then again and again. "You're joking. I mean, really."

A vacant pain began to form in my gut, pushing against my insides. The uneasiness heightened, but not to a point of laughter... to a point of *fear*. I got up from the bed and moved back towards the wall.

"Maya –" Beau reached out.

I shoved him off, feeling the surging warmth erupting underneath my flesh. "No, no, was this – Was this your way of getting me into bed?" My thoughts raced a mile a minute. "I didn't ingest anything, I didn't –"

And just like that, a tidal wave of emotions struck. Mags' cupcake. I ate... I ate Mags' cupcake.

No, no. *No!* She wouldn't do that. *She couldn't do that. Mags... she wouldn't try to kill me. She wouldn't poison me.*

"Mags – Mags didn't do this. I had an anxiety attack, Beau, that's it." I mumbled. "It was me, I had – I have anxiety, I have..."

I sunk to my knees in the corner of Beau's room, covered in sweat. As much as I didn't want to believe it, as much as I *couldn't* believe it... why did I believe it? How could I question my best friend in the whole world?

Tears drowned my sight, dripping slowly down my cheek the more I contemplated the possibility. Through my glossy vision, I glanced up at Beau who kept his eyes fixated on mine, his expression inscrutable. His lips were pressed together and he didn't budge.

Why are you staring at me like that! What are you looking at! My head throbbed with pain, anger and confusion. "Say something!" I yelled to Beau, desperate, desperate for anything.

Beau languidly pulled out a small transparent bag from his pocket and moved towards me, crouching down to my level. A small grey particle the size of a raisin was sealed inside.

"This is a death cap mushroom." He held up the baggy with two fingers. "It's one of the deadliest mushrooms in the world."

He fully sat down, crossing his legs. "Look, I considered a lot of other possibilities too, Maya. Trust me, it's not like I wanted to believe Mags would try and hurt you. But when I finally got you to rest, I checked the cupcake box and saw this."

Tears flowed down my face like a river, my mind tangled in hysteria. "How do you even know what that is? You could have drugged me!" *She wouldn't do this to me!*

"Maya!" Beau cupped my face in his hands, breathing heavily. "I never fed you, I never handled that *fucking* box!" His chest heaved up and down, eventually relaxing.

"These mushrooms grow primarily in Europe and I..." he paused, pressing his lips together. "I lived there for a little while. The person I bunked with told me about them." He twirled the bag in his hands and scrunched his eyebrows.

Grim flashbacks resurfaced in my brain: Mags and her aimless outbursts, her seething anger, the smile on her face when she handed me that cupcake box... I wanted to hurl. I squirmed at the thought of eating the whole thing without realizing it was killing me by the second.

"Why... Why would she do this?" I sobbed. I felt defeated. I felt hopeless, confused, shattered. I felt... like I didn't even know how to feel. "How am I okay? How am I not dead?"

Beau stared at me, somber and sincere. He had a blank expression, but his eyes told a different story. I knew he had a million things on his mind, but Beau was never the talking type. His grey eyes glossed beneath his long, dark eyelashes.

I don't know how long we had been sitting on the floor in silence, but Beau finally stood up and walked towards the bed. He scooped up the two white feathers and stood against the door, leaning back on the handle.

"Maya..." he twirled the feathers between his fingers.

My attention was on Beau, until... until it wasn't. Something was distracting me. A faint hum, quiet but clear. My name was being called, over and over. *Maya... Maya...* Hushed whispers encircled me. *Where is that coming from?*

"I need you to listen to me." Beau spoke sternly. "Fuck," he scratched his head, looking to the ceiling. "I don't even know how to say this without sounding insane. I didn't think it would be this hard."

Dried tears cemented my cheeks like concrete. I slowly got up, standing with wobbly knees. "What are you talking about?"

What more could there be? My best friend poisoned me with a mushroom!

He walked over to me and grabbed my hands. "Maya, you are an extremely important person."

Agitation combatted my sadness. A conglomeration of wrathful emotions infiltrated my ability to control my senses. "That doesn't explain why my best friend would try and kill me!" I flung his hands away.

He backed up and clenched his fists. "But it does! It does. She's not herself because she's being controlled by an incubus. Siles - Maya," he huffed. "He's an incubus from hell."

My legs moved before my brain processed anything he'd said. *Run.* I rushed past Beau and made a B-line straight for the door, but he was faster. He moved in front of me, blocking the entrance.

"*Let me out!*" I yelled, batting his chest with my fist. His muscular frame deflected every hit without flinching. "You're fucking crazy, let me out Beau!" I wept.

I couldn't control my hands, I couldn't control anything. My movements were no longer mine; they belonged to my fight or flight. I swatted and slapped his chest repeatedly, and he let me. *He's crazy! He's crazy!* I was losing my mind. Beau had been so normal up until this point. He never showed signs of being one screw off from losing his shit. He was always composed, and enigmatic. What the hell happened to him? *Is he on drugs?*

"No, I'm not on fucking drugs Maya." Beau said flatly, grabbing my wrists.

Wait? I didn't say that out loud... did he just? Did he just –

"Yes, I read your thoughts." He replied, releasing me. "I need you to listen to me, and I mean really listen to me, okay? Don't make this harder than it has to be."

I sunk to my knees in defeat. My thoughts bounced and smashed against my skull, making it impossible for me to think straight. Tears waterfalled down my cheeks but I was no longer sobbing. Crying took no effort.

I sat there and looked to Beau with weak eyes, completely numb. "I'll listen."

You know when the world around you stops spinning and for one millisecond you feel like you're floating? As if nothing matters and the worries fade? In between the pauses of Beau's implausible fiction tale, I felt that. I listened to him, I did. He told me about the archangel Gabriel, and how I was the Puritas destined to end the war of the fallen. He told me how he had watched me and my mother from the day she was born and to the day I was born, to the day she died... yes, he told me it all. He told me that Mags was being controlled by Siles who's a demon from hell. Lucifer is trying to kill me, apparently. And Beau, Beau... he's an angel, he is an angel from Heaven. I have to drink from a chalice that will supposedly permit me to walk through all three stages of the afterlife. It's all planned out. Pre-destined. Like I said, an implausible fiction tale...

"That's why your ring glowed around Siles, Maya. Do you remember when you saw me at the police station when we first met?"

I nodded gently, staring blankly at the wall behind Beau.

"I was visiting an angel named Blight. He was arrested that day for breaking into an antique shop. He told me that he came to Earth to give you a birthday present... at the time," he shook his head. "I didn't know it was your ring."

My mouth was dry. "An angel, from Heaven..." I whispered. "Was arrested on Earth. Because he broke into a store." I spoke slowly.

Beau now stood up and extended a hand out to me. I blandly grabbed it and faced him. I couldn't help my docile state, I was a shell of myself. My body was disconnected from my thoughts and every nerve was stunned. I didn't understand what was happening, how could I? My mind was blank and empty, and my head, heavy. *I'm going to be sick.*

Beau was psychotic. He was a literal psychopath. The one guy who finally made my life interesting, who made me want to wake up in the morning since my mother died... was a lunatic.

"I know you don't believe me. I know it's going to take a while to process, but here," he handed me one feather, the feather of an *archangel.* "If you hold this in your hands and pray to Gabriel, it will all make sense."

He opened the door and let me pass. I turned to look at him as my legs dragged me out of the room. I stepped slowly through the dim lit apartment, glancing once to a corner that housed shattered glass.

"I texted your dad to come pick you up. I just assumed that you wouldn't want to be near me for another second, so..." he said, handing me my phone.

I took it with shaky hands, staring at Beau. *Turn around. Walk out. Leave.*

A vein in his forehead twitched as he gritted his teeth, unlocking the front door.

I stepped through and took one last look at his mesmerizing grey eyes that I no longer recognized.

"I'm here Maya, *always.*" He breathed.

This was the last time I'd see Beau Gabriel.

Chapter 17

KLEATON'S GATE, PRESENT NIGHT

"*She* didn't fucking pick up!" Tommy panicked.

Tommy and Ky drove frantically around town trying to find Braum. After seeing the bloodbath of Mike's remains, he couldn't stomach explaining it to the police. At least not yet. He wanted to give Braum the benefit of the doubt, hoping it was a suicide.

"Try again, damnit!" Ky slammed the steering wheel.

Tommy threw his phone to the side. "I called thirteen fucking times Ky, Maya shut her phone off!"

Ky huffed. "Try Mags."

Again, Tommy attempted to call Mags a handful of times. "Directly to voicemail." Tommy mumbled.

"Man, Tom," Ky scratched at his forehead, holding back tears. "What the fuck is happening, man what the fuck? What do we do?"

"Do we go to the police? We have to report it, we can't just –"

Within seconds, Tommy's phone began to ring. He picked it up briskly and gasped at the caller ID: **BRAUM MCPHEE**.

"Ky... it's Braum." Tommy stuttered.

"Pick it up, fuck, pick it up!"

Tommy cleared his throat nervously. "H – hello? Braum?"

Heavy breathing.

"Buddy, is that you?" Tommy asked again.

Silence for a few moments.

"Meet me at my place, ten minutes. There's someone I'd like you to meet." The line went dead.

"Well?" Ky questioned. "What did he say?"

Tommy swallowed hard. He heard Braum, or what sounded like Braum. But at the same time, not at all. He knew something was wrong, he could feel the icy chill in his bones. The way Braum spoke was hoarse, different, *cold*. He needed to find out what was going on. He needed to know his friend was okay.

"Braum's at his place... We have to go back." Tommy stuttered.

Tommy had walked through Braum's front door a thousand times, but tonight was different. He didn't even want to step foot on his driveway, let alone enter the house again. The swaying corpse of Braum's dad imprinted on his brain, latching to his thoughts.

They stepped out of the car and wearily toed their way to the entrance. With sweaty palms, Tommy turned the door handle and walked in.

Smoke filled the room, slapping their faces upon entry. Tommy coughed repeatedly until Braum appeared with a small hand-fan.

"Stupid smoke." Braum spat, inhaling a cigarette.

Braum had dark bags under his eyes and his blonde hair was gelled back messily. He wore a white tank top and blue jeans. The chain his father gave him as a boy was no longer around his neck.

Movement startled them in the kitchen. When the smoke cleared, Tommy could make out a red-headed woman in sheer tights and a tight red dress.

"Boys!" Braum embraced them. "Come in, come in, close the fuckin' door!" Braum irately kicked it shut.

They hesitantly followed him into the kitchen where the girl in red became clearer. She was very pretty with an undeniable allure. She looked older than Braum but still very youthful. Her high cheekbones and red lipstick drew the most attention.

"Boys, I'd like you to meet Marina." He planted a slobbery wet kiss across her collarbone. "My girlfriend."

Tommy and Ky exchanged looks of confusion. They hadn't seen Braum for a few days and he already had a girlfriend... nothing made sense. They'd seen Braum reject girls left, right and center. He would have sex, then leave. It was a given at that point, but suddenly, Braum had a girlfriend?

"I've heard so much about you. Both of you." Marina kissed their cheeks, then retreated back to Braum's side.

But I haven't heard anything about you, Tommy thought. Shakily, he nodded and smiled but was left speechless at Braum's demeanor. Braum didn't seem fazed at all that his father had been hanging in his room. Did he even know?

"Braum..." Ky started. "Where have you been? It's been days. We came by earlier but –" He paled, thinking about Mike's blood splatter all over the walls. He couldn't continue.

Braum threw a pot in the sink and scoffed. "When'd you get so clingy, eh?"

Tommy put a foot forward and eyed Marina. He had no idea where Braum picked her up from. She didn't look like the typical woman in Kleaton's Gate, nor Braum's choice of lady.

Tommy then looked to the ceiling and realized the kitchen was directly underneath Mike's bedroom. He choked back the vomit that was crawling up his esophagus. The initial shock wore off and Tommy's emotions took control.

"Your dad is dead, Braum! He's dead, hanging in a fucking room upstairs!" Tommy blurted out.

Silence.

Ky began to shake incessantly, stuttering on his words. "Did you – did you do it? Did you kill Mike, Braum? Did you kill your dad?"

Marina and Braum exchanged a look of irreverence that made Tommy queasy. Their expressions were blank yet amused.

Braum smiled slyly, then chuckled. He walked up to Tommy's face and slapped him playfully on the cheeks. "You drunk, Tom? Eh, how many beers in, huh? Five?"

Tommy bit his tongue. Braum's touch was icy and calloused. He wasn't acting like himself, he didn't look like himself... *This isn't Braum.* To Tommy, Braum looked like a puppet being controlled by a ventriloquist, helpless and hollow.

Marina smirked. "They're cute, Braum. Funny."

The thorny tension heightened between the four of them. Ky slammed his fist on the table in aggravation. "Cut this bullshit out! I don't know what the fuck is going on, but we saw your dad hanging from the goddamn ceiling, Braum!" He took a breath as tears formed at his waterline. "Did you do it? Did you... did you fucking do it!"

In one motion, Braum aggressively grabbed Ky by the shirt and pinned him against the wall.

"Watch your tongue, Gerber. Or I'll cut it out of your fucking mouth."

Marina jumped in, breaking them up. "No need for violence." She looked to Ky. "Why don't you boys show us what you saw?"

Tommy wanted to be as far away from the scene as possible. The smell of Mike's rotting corpse clung to his memory, clear as day.

"I'm not going back up there." Ky shook.

Braum marched to the stairs in a huff, Marina in hand. "Go on, go on! I want to see what you're whining about. Go!"

Tommy felt caged, as if he had no other option but to see the body once again. He sluggishly climbed the steps, his feet weighing him down in fear. When he reached the top of the stairs, he ordered Braum and Marina to go first.

"Open the door. I'm not touching it." Tommy commanded.

And they did just that.

Only Mike's room was completely intact. The windowsill had been shut, the blood splatter on the floor was clean. There was no body hanging from the fan; everything was palpably spotless.

Ky's jaw dropped as Tommy shoved past Braum and Marina, entering the room in utter disbelief.

"But - no," Tommy stuttered, faltering. "He was right here. There - the blood, it was everywhere." Tommy buried his face in his hands and sank to the ground.

"No, this isn't fucking right." Ky pointed a finger to Braum. "You buried his body, you did something! We aren't crazy, we aren't –"

Marina and Braum smiled pleasantly, watching the boys in hysterics.

"Now what were you saying about a body?" Marina smirked.

Chapter 18

HELL

*T*he distant sounds of screaming souls entertained the demons. Marina and Siles waited for Lucifer beside his throne in the hall of hell fire. Scorching blue flames lined the black velvet seat as well as the stone perimeter.

"Do you think he'll be proud of us?" Siles asked Marina.

She admired the red acrylic manicure that she obtained on Earth. "I hope so. Having sex with Braum is like fucking a bunny. So weak, small, incapable, spineless..." she trailed off.

Siles grabbed her neck and twisted it to face him. "I don't enjoy the thought of you sleeping with that feeble insect."

Marina laughed and licked her lips. "And how are *you* treating Mags?"

He let her go on a whim, smoothing out his dark dress shirt classily. "Leave it to your imagination."

She chuckled.

The granite doors burst open and Lucifer walked in wearing a saccharine smile. "My two favourite pets!" he opened his arms wide. "What progress have we made?"

Siles and Marina jumped up and took their place in front of Lucifer's throne.

"They're under our control, Master." Siles bowed. "Mags used the poison mushroom that you gave me. Might I say, you chose a rather specific means of death."

Lucifer lifted his chin. "I have my reasons." He then clapped, directing his attention to Marina. "And you, my dear?"

Marina flipped her red locks behind her neck. "Well, I suppose that my kiss is as sweet as it is deadly. I controlled Braum to kill his father."

Siles threw a sharp look at Marina, confused as to why she didn't tell him her plans. Siles and Marina spent most of their time together in hell, working their way up to be a part of Lucifer's army. But to Siles, the mission was only eliminating Maya. He hadn't realized that loose ends were a threat.

Lucifer laughed out loud, narrowing his eyes. "And was the life you took, worth eternal punishment?"

Marina smirked. "He was a bad man, if that's what you're asking, Master."

Siles swallowed hard and kept silent, digging his nails into the crease of his palm.

The granite doors opened by Lucifer's power. "Well then, I shall personally introduce myself to our new guest." He pinched Marina's cheek as he passed. "Good job, my sweet."

The blue flames died down and a still, unnerving silence followed Lucifer's parting.

Siles turned to Marina in bewilderment. "When were you going to tell me that you took a mans' life?"

Marina scoffed and patted Siles' chest. "When were you going to tell me that you've gone soft?"

Chapter 19

KLEATON'S GATE, TWO WEEKS LATER

Beau's thoughts weighed heavy on his drive home from work, fraying out of control. He hadn't spoken to Maya in weeks, and he couldn't find it in him to sit from the sidelines while demons roamed the Earth – their sole purpose: Maya.

"You cannot interfere," Gabriel had said in a prior visit. "She must come to terms with her title, *alone.*"

Beau scoffed. "You really expect me to stay away? When Siles and Marina are out there waiting to –"

"She is protected."

"Not well enough!" Beau's bare chest heaved, his pupils dilating with anger.

Gabriel approached him, standing tall and indomitable. Beau swallowed hard, backing away. For the first time since his creation, Beau didn't see Gabriel as his brother... he saw him as the mighty *archangel.*

"You have broken every rule pertaining to her," Gabriel grabbed his wrist, searing it with holy fire. "Do not break this one, *Beau.*"

And Beau listened.

Sort of.

On his drive home, he took the exit off to Maya's neighbourhood and turned onto her street. *I'm technically not doing anything wrong if I just scout the perimeter*, he thought.

He parked on the side of the road, a few houses down from hers and stepped out of the car. The night was chilled and eerie, the cold wind danced with the trees. He spotted Maya's porch lights as he hid in the distant wood, flickering on and off like clockwork. Beau thought about normalcy, and how in another life, where he wasn't an angel and Maya was not divine, that maybe he could have fixed those lights for her. Maybe he was a carpenter, and Maya was a successful author. And maybe, their twisted fates would have aligned in a passionate unity, away from angels and demons and death. *In another life.*

A yellow hue of light illuminated the beige walls of Maya's bedroom window. Beau couldn't see anything other than two hanging frames on her wall and a chalkboard calendar. But then, he saw *her*.

She was brushing her damp hair, wearing a white tank top with a design Beau could not make out from his distance. Though even with the space between them, Beau was enveloped in her warmth. Her cheekbones were high, her eyes sad. He couldn't even imagine what she was going through, all of the thoughts in her head... the thoughts he had given her.

A faraway rustling ruffled the bushes. Beau crouched down behind a tree and spectated, expecting it to be a racoon or a squirrel, some puny creature that meant no harm.

But Beau was wrong.

Red eyes glowed from beneath the fern, aiming directly at Maya's house. A figure emerged, crawling out with hidden calculation. Her pale skin absorbed the moonlight, irradiating her devilish features. Her hair was the shade of blood, tangled in loose curls. She smirked, moving out of the bush and creeping closer to Maya's lawn.

Without hesitation, Beau's grace carried him briskly through the wood, planting him directly in front of Marina. He coiled his fingers around her neck, and she let him with content.

"I was wondering when we'd finally meet." She smiled.

He hoisted her body up higher, tightening his grip around her throat. "What are you doing here?" Beau asked, sharply.

"Oh you can't be that stupid, *Beau*."

"Your darkness will never rule." A white hue radiated from beneath Beau's grasp, the scent of burning flesh filled the air.

Marina withered in pain, her face turning purple. She gurgled, digging her pointed nails into his wrist. Blood trickled down his forearm, burning his skin with fire.

She fell out of his grasp and scurried back, rubbing the thin skin on her neck. "I follow orders."

"Of a menace."

"Of a *king*." Marina countered, coughing out blood.

Beau narrowed his eyes, bewildered at the fact anyone could view Lucifer as a king, a ruler of anything other than the damned. Murderers, adulterers, the greedy and the envious... the fallen.

Beau almost pitied them, their souls and what broken promises he bestowed upon the fallen. He wondered what Lucifer did to wrap Marina around his finger, that she would enslave her entire existence to serve him.

"You can be redeemed, Marina." Beau let out, eyeing her carefully. "Maya has the power to free your soul. You don't need to do this."

Marina's low, sinister laugh carried with the winds. She stabilized herself upwards, spitting on the ground.

"And what makes you think I want redemption?" She stepped closer to Beau. "I am perfectly content in hell."

As fast as lightning, she grabbed Beau's arm, burning hell fire into his tattoo. The black lines glowed crimson, flashing red from beneath his skin.

Beau whined in pain, sinking his knees to the ground. He felt his grace paralyzing by the second, freezing him in place.

"What..." Beau said through strained breaths. "What did *he* promise you..."

Marina released Beau and kicked him over, digging her pointed heels into his side. "Power."

She marched through the wood, crossing the road. Beau couldn't move, he could only watch. He trembled, his eyes glossy. Marina would kill her in cold blood. She was so close. Everything would be over; the mission, Heaven, the war, his time with her... *She can't fight. She doesn't have God's grace in her, not yet. She'll die, she'll die, she'll* –

A beam of light rippled in the air, sending Marina flying back onto the pavement. Her body shook violently, her skin smoking with grey embers. Beau's eyes grew wide, staring at Maya's house in disbelief. A glint of golden shimmer sliced the air, impossible to detect unless one possessed divine vision. *A holy barrier... Impenetrable from the outside.*

His eyes flickered to the road, and Marina's body was gone. *Fuck*, Beau mouthed, digging his nails into the soil for support. The hell fire was almost out of his veins, dripping off his skin like liquid. It burned, but Beau didn't care. Something else caught his attention.

At the top of Maya's roof, a shadow stood, dressed in white linen. Even through the silence of the night, his presence spoke volumes. He peered down at Beau from a distance, his grey eyes intense and sharp. With a single nod, he stretched out his

glowing white wings and turned away, flying into the
moonlight and disappearing in the clouds.
   Gabriel.

Chapter 20

KLEATON'S GATE, ONE MONTH LATER

I was back in the forest, a shaded wood of darkness and despair. I'd been here for so many nights in a row that I felt the weight of my presence from my previous visit; the familiar feeling of my body sinking into that tar-like mud, drowning my corpse. I looked to my left and spotted the dark figure approaching, trudging at me with lightning speed. The figure pushed me to the soil and kicked my abdomen, securing me in a place of defeat. My eyes squinted to the ink-stained moon, adjusting to the figure standing above me. And with the tiniest glint

of light, I saw movement behind the figure –
something stretching out wide. I saw... I saw wings –
Black wings.

   I awoke in a blanket of sweat, clinging to
every part of my body like glue. I couldn't silence my
panting, my esophagus begging for air. Beads of
perspiration stained my forehead, dampening the
loose locks of hair around my face. I huffed for more
oxygen, wrapping my arms around my middle...
knowing damn well it was a dream. Yet, I still felt it –
I still *saw* it. The muscular build of the figure, its dark
wings stretched out wide. Its... *familiarity*, though not
at all.
   Another nightmare.
   I lost track of every vicious dream I've had
since I left Beau's apartment. When I first started
having them again, I was a wreck... and I had every
reason to be. Though after a while, I almost
welcomed the grim fears and patronizing thoughts.
   I hadn't talked to Mags, Tommy, anyone for
that matter in a little under a month. My brain waves
were out of whack; one second I was fine, dealing
with the fact that everything in my life turned upside
down and the next, I was in a ball of heaping sadness,
wailing on the ground. Tommy rang my phone every
day for the first two weeks, but everything stopped
after a while and I didn't care to ask why. Mags...
Mags tried to poison me. *No, she wouldn't do that.*
Beau was making it up. She's your best friend! But,
someone did. And frankly, I wouldn't have put it past

the new Mags. She went completely ghost after Fondos, but that I expected and that... I was too afraid to explore.

Then there was Beau.

I hadn't spoken to Beau since I left his apartment... since he told me *everything*. Every night for the past month I've had nightmares. Some were the same as before, but others became more graphic... more *familiar*. Black wings, dark and deadly, rippled through my psyche. Those dreams screamed danger. After I met Beau, the nightmares came to a halt. But now, for some reason unbeknownst to my knowledge, they were back in full force. As if the nightmares weren't bad enough, some invisible figment of my imagination woke me up, repeating my name over and over like clockwork. *I owe my deteriorating mental health to Beau being a psychopath.*

I tried my very best to push out everything Beau said to me that night. It was almost impossible to believe that I, Maya Brixton, a nineteen-year-old girl from Kleaton's Gate was the key to stopping a war between Heaven and hell? Beau Gabriel, an angel from Heaven, was cast down to Earth to protect my mom before she died? None of it – none of it made sense. It *couldn't* make sense.

I looked at the alarm clock: **10:03pm**. Nothing thrilled me more than staying in bed. I had hardly moved from under my sheets for the last little while. I didn't feel the need to. Everything around me was distorted; reality and fiction intertwined to a new wave of fucked up.

I couldn't bring myself to communicate with any other human being. What if they turned out to be a zombie? Or a wizard? Hell, if angels existed, wouldn't every other mythical creature in fairyland exist too? *God, I wish I could talk to my best friend about this.* But I couldn't. Because not only did she did she try and poison me... *allegedly*, according to Beau, she was being controlled by a demon. *Ha! Ha-ha.*

Mags fell off the face of the universe, *not like I cared anyway.* But I did, and I couldn't help that I did. *What if Beau was really telling the truth and she was under the influence of Siles? What if Mags was still Mags, just buried underneath this... Snap out of it! Do you hear yourself?*

My head and heart took a major beating trying to rationalize the incomprehensible. But there was nothing to figure out; none of it was real. Beau was delusional and I had to accept that I fell for a complete and utter psychopath. *Some things really are too good to be true.*

My door creaked opened slowly and my dad walked in with a plate of chocolate chip cookies. "You hungry?" he asked softly.

I hadn't talked to my dad all that much either since coming back from Beau's. It made it easier that he was always at work but I rarely ate meals with him. I would just order in late at night to avoid communication. I was aware of how bad it sounded, but I didn't feel like explaining the last month of crazy to him. I lost my best friend and I lost... well, it doesn't matter anymore.

I forced a smile, sitting up from underneath my covers. *He was trying.* "Just leave it there." I pointed to my bedside table.

My dad stood in silence at the door, staring at the family photo of him, my mom and I. "You know," he pressed his lips together. "Your mom was always good at this. Anytime you got into trouble at school, I'd always send her to talk to your teachers because she was just... so incredible with people."

Here we go. I knew I was about to get a lecture about being antisocial and distant. As much as I didn't want to hear it, I gave my dad a chance. *Those cookies smell really good.*

He paced cautiously around my room for a few moments then finally took a seat at the edge of my bed.

"I know I'm not your mom, Maya. I know I'm always at the office and I'm not around all the time. But," he paused. "I want you to know that you can let me in. I may not have the best advice and we can't, you know, paint our nails and gossip about boys."

I laughed. That, was genuine.

He smiled. "But – I still love you. I love you, and I'm here for you. If you allow me to be." He squeezed my hand tightly.

I felt even worse than before, guilty even. I realized that I was isolating the people who cared about me, but nothing felt right anymore. Nonetheless, someone who loved me was sitting right here, waiting for an explanation. He was right, my mom was always the one who comforted me. She was my anchor, my rock. My dad fell off the train when she passed away, we both did. But he was trying now, and I saw that.

I held back the urge to cry. "I love you, dad. I'll be okay." *Did I believe that?* "I've gone through worse." *Maybe not.*

Thump. Thump. I turned to my dad. "Did you hear that?"

Thump. He scrunched his eyebrows, searching the room. "I think it's coming from outside."

My dad reached over my bed and pulled the curtains open. I leaned over and scanned the road; a red car was parked in front of our house.

Thump. Through the darkness, I could make out the periphery of a familiar profile.

My dad looked at me in bewilderment. "Is that Tommy?"

I swallowed hard, remembering that I hadn't responded to any of his texts or calls for weeks. He motioned for me to come outside several times, continuing to throw pebbles at my window.

"Ah, Christ Maya, just go out there before the kid breaks the glass." My dad scoffed.

I threw on a black hoodie and some sweat shorts, snagging a cookie before following my dad downstairs.

"I'll be listening." My dad joked.

I shook my head, taking a bite. "Did you really heat up store-bought cookies?" I laughed, shutting the front door.

Tommy was standing in my lawn wearing a decrepit white t-shirt covered in stains and grey sweatpants. His brown hair was a mess on his head and he looked to have lost an unhealthy amount of weight.

I approached him slowly, eying him carefully. "Tom –"

He grabbed my hand and rushed me into his car, breathing heavily. Quickly locking the door, he checked his backseat and all his mirrors at least three times.

What the hell was going on? "Tommy, hey," I placed my hand over his forearm. "Hey, relax. What's wrong?"

Tommy's eyes were bloodshot and beady; he looked like he hadn't slept in centuries. "Where –" he stuttered. "Where have you been, Maya? I tried calling you for days... weeks, I tried." He was shaking.

Chills crawled up my spine, creeping their way to the nape of my neck. A horrible gut feeling latched itself to my insides, painting my body with fear.

I slowly moved my hand towards the door handle. "Tommy, you're freaking me out." *My dad is right there, he can hear me scream.*

Tommy's teeth chattered. "Braum... Braum is fucked, Maya. He's fucked! Marina's fucked, everything is so fucked!" he slammed his hand on the steering wheel repeatedly. "I'm not crazy, I saw the body. I saw – I saw it, with my eyes, Maya." He sobbed. His visage was inscrutable.

Anxiety hit me like a truck. I didn't know whether Tommy had taken drugs or if he was drunk. I didn't smell any alcohol on him, and Tommy never experimented with drugs when we were together but maybe things had changed. Everything he was saying wasn't making sense yet here he sat, engulfed in a full-fledged panic attack.

My palms sweat as I carefully reached out to him, placing my hands over his. "Tommy, breathe. Tell me what's going on, breathe."

He swallowed hard and wiped snot from his nose. He turned to face me with weak eyes. His back was hunched as he shook ceaselessly.

"Braum went out about a month ago, on your birthday actually. He went to Pinkie's and Ky and I didn't want to go so he just left." He took a pause and rubbed his eyes, evidently holding back tears. "I don't know what happened there, Maya, but he came back a different fuckin' person."

I sat in silence, allowing him to regain composure.

"Me and Ky, we - we didn't talk to him for days. And you know Braum, Maya, he bunks with us any chance he gets."

I nodded. Even when I was dating Tommy, Braum hated being at home because of his dad. I didn't know too much about the situation; Tommy thought it was best to keep me out of it. All he said was that his dad was abusive and Braum wanted out.

"We went to his house and his car was there, everything looked fine and - and then," Tommy began to shake again. His eyes welled up with tears and he buried his face in his hands.

I rubbed his back, holding in the uneasiness that loomed over me. "And then what, Tommy?"

He sobbed uncontrollably. "We saw Mike, Maya. He was dead, hanging from the ceiling fan. His body, oh God, Maya it was a fuckin' bloodbath."

My stomach sank. I felt the cookie that I just ate rise up to my mouth, prying its way to come out. "He..." I choked on my words. "His dad killed himself?"

Tommy turned to me instantly, a trail of snot dripping from his nose. "No! Braum killed Mike! He fuckin' killed Mike, him – him and his fucking girlfriend, Marina!" he spat. "Something's wrong with him, Maya, he's not him."

For a second, I watched Tommy's feral expression without emotion. Though, time began to slow down and I lost my train of thought. I had no words. Braum was a bad guy and his abuse was no secret to me, but I'd never take it as far to pin him as a murderer.

"The worst part, when Ky and I went back to his house, the body was gone. Braum didn't know what the fuck we were talking about but he did, he *knew!* Him and Marina, they laughed at us. Ky – he hasn't come out of his house in weeks! I haven't slept, I haven't eaten, I haven't – he's a liar, Maya. He's a liar. He's not him, he's a different person. Ever since that night, ever since her –" he stuttered.

The air around us was hot and heavy. Tommy sat in silence, breathing in spurts. He sat up and turned to me slowly; dried tears stamped his cheeks. "Ever since he met Marina. Maya, this girl, she's... there's something wrong with her."

Questions flooded my brain, stampeding from every direction. Yet, I knew this feeling all too well. I could see the defeat in Tommy's eyes, the confusion and the pain. He was telling the truth, or he believed it anyway.

"I'm not crazy," he whispered, sombre.

And I believed him. For whatever reason, I believed him. I didn't know the whole story, only what Tommy just told me. But I had felt the frustration once before... the uneasiness, the confusion. I had seen the deviant behaviour and the unidentifiable; the way your best friend could turn into a complete monster, could hurt everyone around them, and could hurt you.

I had seen it before, because I'd seen it in...

Mags.

Chapter 21

KLEATON'S GATE, ONE MONTH EARLIER

Beau unlocked his front door and shut it quietly behind him. He retrieved Mags' cupcake box from his car and held it in his hands, calculating his thoughts. Maya was asleep in his room, completely unconscious. It left Beau puzzled; he had never seen anyone spaz out like that before.

He placed the remnants of Mags' cupcake on his kitchen counter and dug through the remains carefully. *Something isn't right.*

In the corner of his eye, he caught a glimpse of a small grey particle underneath the crumbs. Beau picked it up and analyzed it closely. His eyes opened wide when he realized what it was.

"Death cap mushroom." A low voice whispered.

Beau turned around quickly, irritated. "Gabriel! Get the hell out of here, she'll see you!"

Gabriel plucked the poison particle out of Beau's hands in one swift motion. "If this doesn't kill her first."

Oh no, no, Beau panicked. He ran to his room and cradled Maya's head. She was convulsing, shaking rapidly. Her temperature felt like fire and foam began to pour out of her mouth. Beau placed one hand on the nape of her neck and one on her chest, pressing hard. A white light beamed from underneath his palms as he mouthed a prayer, healing her.

Within seconds, Maya's pale complexion regained its natural pigmentation. He huffed with breath, sitting still for a few moments, watching her. *You're okay, Maya. You're going to be okay.*

He quietly tiptoed out of the room and shut the door, trying to keep his composure. "She..." Beau shook his head. "Mags poisoned her?" he looked to Gabriel. "Gabriel, her best friend tried to poison her."

Gabriel was silent.

Beau remembered the moment he learned of the death cap mushroom, how poisonous it was, how *deadly*. "Death cap mushroom... how did she even get it? I've only ever seen it in Europe." *What the fuck is happening?*

Gabriel cupped his hands together and released a glowing *orbiopal*, floating between him and Beau. "We have company, Beau."

Beau watched a flashback of Siles and Marina, walking hand in hand at the casino. Their red eyes glowed as Marina pointed to Mags and Maya at the bar. Marina hid behind an empty corner and grabbed Keegan, one of Beau's co-workers. She slit his throat and undressed him in a storage room, handing Siles his uniform.

The crystal orb disappeared into the dim light of Beau's apartment.

"That explains why Keegan hasn't shown up in weeks." Beau kept one hand cemented on the counter. "Who are they?"

"Siles and Marina, two of Lucifer's fallen. He's an incubus. He's attached himself to Mags, to control her to kill Maya." Gabriel responded.

Beau clenched his teeth. Lucifer was behind all of this. *That explains the death cap mushroom.* This was the last thing that he could have wished for. He hadn't told Maya who she was yet and his scars were almost black. *Immaculate timing.*

"And what of Marina? Who is she?" Beau questioned, sternly.

"Succubus. But they've been impossible to find. Lucifer must have cloaked them on Earth."

Beau couldn't control the seething anger coursing through his veins. He shoved past Gabriel and made his way for the door. "I'll fuckin' find them."

"Beau –" Gabriel used his grace to seal the entrance.

Beau turned around in anger. "How hard is it to kill a sex demon?" Beau spat. "Put venom in their condoms."

Beau teemed with rage. He knew time was running out and the last thing he needed was a hound hunt for Lucifer's pets. He knew he had been stalling on his mission for Maya, but that was over now. There was a bounty on Maya's head, and in light of Lucifer's recent stunt, Beau knew he would stop at nothing until she was dead. Lucifer discovered the threat, the Puritas. She has the power to lift the fallen, undetectable and untouchable by poisoned grace. He couldn't let him kill her, because of the mission, because of home, Heaven, and because... *Because I can't lose her.*

A faint stirring sounded in Beau's room. Maya was awake.

"Fulfill the mission, Beau. Let it be known." Gabriel was gone.

Beau turned around and filled a glass of water, slowly walking over to his bedroom door. He knew it was time, he couldn't let this drag on another day; not with Lucifer's demons running around, their sole purpose to kill Maya. He inhaled one last breath and turned the handle. *No turning back now.*

PRESENT DAY

Beau glanced over to the four empty bottles of whisky on his countertop. He hadn't spoken to Maya since he told her everything a month ago, and he never visited her home again after his altercation with Marina. It worried Beau, knowing that Marina and Siles were still out there just waiting to pounce, but Gabriel assured him that she'd be protected, and he kept that promise. Nonetheless, Beau still thought about her every single day. He wondered how she was doing, how she was coping... *If* she was coping. He knew he couldn't intervene in the process of her accepting her divine form, but it ate away at him. *I'm never going to see her again*, he thought.

Beau walked over to the cabinet and pulled out a near empty bottle of whisky. He twisted the cap and turned the bottle upside down, shaking out the few drops of remaining alcohol.

He cursed. "Looks like I'm going to the liquor store." He placed the now empty bottle alongside the other ones, pointing to them. "To get you guys a new friend."

He wiped his mouth and threw on a black t-shirt, gelling his hair messily before grabbing his keys.

Beau had spent countless nights inebriated since he had last spoken to Maya. His days consisted of drinking, conning rich gamblers at work, then drinking more. The only upside to the situation was the fact his scars stopped burning. *If you count that as an upside*, he thought. His entire purpose and every single path led to *her. Nothing matters anymore. I just want to go home.*

He carelessly flung open the door and inhaled a familiar scent of lavender, stopping in disbelief. Standing before him was the last person he expected to see, but the only person that inundated his thoughts for weeks.

He stood in shock, staring into her familiar hazel eyes. She was wearing a black hoodie and worn out shorts. He took in everything about her, starting at the top of her messy bun, making his way down to meet her gaze. Her expression was inscrutable, yet solemn.

Beau swallowed hard. He scrunched his eyebrows softly, feeling the pounding of his heartbeat rattle against his chest. He hadn't said her name in so long, it felt foreign on his tongue. But when he did, it tasted of sweet sugar and warm cinnamon. It tasted like *home.*

"Maya?"

Chapter 22

KLEATON'S GATE, ONE WEEK EARLIER

Mags found herself in a cold, dark room.

A single lightbulb hung from the ceiling, blinking in erratic beats. An acute pain stabbed at her temples, her limbs aching and strained. When she came to, she realized that her hands and feet were bound to a metal chair. Mags shifted and twisted but was unable to set herself free.

"Help!" she cried out. "Help! Somebody help!"

But only silence responded.

Mags whimpered desperately. "Please, anyone..."

Mags had no recollection of what had happened in the last few weeks. The last thing she remembered was going to Siles' place after Maya's birthday party, then, nothing.

Maya. *Oh my God, Maya! Where is she? Is she okay? Where the fuck am I!*

Although Mags couldn't remember a thing, a vacant space filled her thoughts. It was as if there was a hole, a pool of memories concealed from her, waiting to be unlocked... but she lost the key.

Low grunts sounded somewhere in the darkness, followed by a series of clangs.

"Hello? Hello, who's there? Who's there!" Mags yelled, trembling. *Is that an animal? I'm tied to this freakin' chair! I'm going to die!*

Groans of pain continued more rampantly, then slowly faded, hiding in the black darkness. Next came a hoarse whisper of a male clearing his throat, groggy and strained. "Where - where am I?"

Mags froze, goosebumps surfacing to the top of her skin. *This... This can't be.* She was able to recognize that raspy tone anywhere, but a part of her hoped it wasn't him. "*Braum?*"

A still silence filled the air, then another painful groan. "Yeah... yes. Who is - who are you? Where am I?"

Mags couldn't stop the tears from waterfalling down her face. *It is Braum. We were kidnapped. We're going to die!* "Braum - Braum, it's

Mags. I don't –" she sobbed. "I don't know where we are. I don't know what the fuck happened!"

"*Mags?*" Braum groaned, his voice clearer. "Mags oh my God, Mags! Are you okay? Where are you?"

A tsunami of tears cascaded from her eyes, dripping down like pattering rain onto her skin. "I don't know, I'm tied to a chair!" She bawled.

Mags could hear the panic in Braum's voice as he too, shifted around, struggling to untie himself. An exasperated grunt followed, then more banging.

"Help!" Braum cried out.

"Help us!" Mags whimpered.

After a few minutes of continuous wails, two ceiling lights clicked on, illuminating the atmosphere. The room was small and bare, black graffiti stamped the walls and a metal door was stationed in the corner. Braum and Mags sat across from each other in tattered, bloody clothes.

"*Oh my God...*" Mags muttered in shock.

Braum had deep cuts all over his neck and arms, some fresh and some old. He wore a white tank top covered in stains and grey ripped jeans. His eyes were badly bruised and his bone structure, sunken.

Mags' hair hadn't been brushed in days. Her black long sleeve had been ripped at the chest, exposing the top of her cleavage. Her legs were covered in scrapes and she was barefoot.

"Mags, Mags!" Braum wept, tugging his chair forward.

But the chair was cemented to the ground.

They cried in unison, exerting all of their strength to escape their restraints, but it was no use. They were stuck.

"Braum what – what happened, where are we?" Mags whined. "Do you remember anything?"

The metal door creaked then unbolted, and in walked Siles and Marina, holding hands.

Marina was wearing shiny leather pants and a black bodysuit. Her red hair was slicked into a tight ponytail with loose strands framing her face. Siles had on dark jeans and a white button down, rolled up at the sleeves.

Marina instantly darted for Mags and slapped her hard across the face. "I couldn't listen to your ceaseless yapping for another second."

Blood sprayed from Mags mouth, staining the concrete below her. She spat and slowly turned her head back, facing Siles with weak eyes. He bit down hard on his jaw and quickly faced Marina who was already on her way to Braum.

"*Marina?*" Braum coughed out. "What – You... You're the girl from –"

"Shut up." Marina grabbed his neck in her hands, choking hard. She straddled him and licked her lips.

"You are riddled with impurity. You are so weak... it's just too easy." She laughed, squeezing his cheeks.

Siles cleared his throat. "Marina, enough. You said this business is necessary."

She viciously turned to Siles and scowled, digging her heel into Braum's foot before pacing back.

Marina clapped. "Business, right." She eyed both Braum and Mags, turning back and forth on her heel. "Why do you think you're here?"

Silence.

Marina raised her voice. "I asked you a question!" She stomped.

Braum gasped in horror. "Marina..." Braum spoke through staggered breaths. "Baby, look... I was wasted, I'm sorry if I hurt you during our –"

Siles immediately interjected, stepping in front of Marina. "She's not *yours*, worm." He spat.

Mags' heart pumped rapidly, beating out of control. She had no idea what was happening, why she felt anger, envy and... jealousy. *Who the hell is this?* She had never seen Marina before and Siles was protecting her. *But why do I care? I don't even know this guy?*

A wave of adrenaline hit Mags, submerging her fear. She was trembling, supressing all of her terrified thoughts, but remained strong. *I'm not going to die like this.* "Who the fuck are you?" she demanded, tugging the ropes on her wrist.

Marina laughed and walked up to Mags, pulling Siles to her side. She eyed Mags as she kissed his neck, making her way to his collarbone.

"The fuck?" Braum questioned from behind. "What the hell is happening?"

Mags felt like she was going to be sick. Her stomach growled with hunger; she couldn't remember the last time she ate. Every single thought and memory in her head blurred together, as if her brain didn't want her to remember. But yet... she felt everything. She felt things for Siles, that was undeniable, even though she had no recollection of their time together. A connection of some kind had formed and Mags was sure of it, but she couldn't pinpoint when. *What is fucking happening!*

"If you're not already aware kitten," Marina smirked at Braum. "I'm not interested in you."

Braum opened his mouth to protest but Marina blew a breath into the air, muttering a different language. "*Quies...*" she released.

And on command, Braum's mouth was sealed shut. He struggled to speak, but his lips were sewn together by an invisible force.

His eyes grew wide, feral, as he yanked at the ropes tying him to the chair; tears welled in his bloodshot eyes, desolate and hopeless.

"What... What did you do?" Mags cried. "Braum!"

"Relax, Maggie. He can hear you." Siles responded.

Maggie. No one had called Mags that for years, not even her own family. She stared at Siles and for a split second, Mags thought she saw a glimmer of empathy in his eyes. *I know you... I know more than I think I know... We – We shared something, a bond, a moment? This, this confirms it. Something we had was real, somewhere... I need to find it. I have to find it.*

He glanced at her quickly before turning his attention to Marina.

"Peace of mind, finally. Feeble little rat." Marina spat. "Siles, shut her up." She pointed to Mags.

Siles clenched his teeth, digging his nails into his palm. "She isn't speaking, Marina." He contested.

Mags swallowed hard, observing his discomfort. Was Siles protecting her from whatever mojo Marina had performed on Braum? Why would he do that? *What are you doing...*

Marina spun around and eyed Siles with aggravated suspicion. "I... don't... care." She emphasized each word slowly. "Do it."

He was silent, standing still for a moment. He took in a breath, glancing to Mags with pitiful eyes. "*Quies...*" he released to the air.

A sharp pain slit her senses. It felt as if someone had taken a sewing needle and stabbed her lips, over and over until it was sealed completely, unable to open. She squirmed in her seat, shutting her eyes in agony. Uncontrollable panic electrocuted her body, constricting her senses. *Who... Who are you! What are you? What is happening to me!*

"For now, I can't hurt that infirm Puritas of yours." Marina began, puckering her lips.

A vein in Siles' forehead twitched, his expression filled with bewilderment. He kept silent.

"But I grow very angry, oh! Can't you tell?" Marina continued. "So what is the next best option, hm?"

Us. Mags knew.

Marina clicked her heels, circling Mags and Braum like a shark. "Let's call this an intermission, because the act got *boring*. Siles and I have you pests under our control and I, a brilliant mind, was dying to see your state without our influence."

Marina and Siles flashed their red eyes as black veins coiled underneath their skin. Mags sat motionless in horror. Tears flowed down her cheeks as she and Braum both wrestled with their restraints, failing once more. *What are you! What the fuck are you! This isn't real, this isn't real, this isn't...*

"Before we put you under our control again, I thought it best that you had a good look at yourselves." Marina giggled.

She clicked her heels and made her way for the door, stepping out for a few moments before returning with a double-sided mirror. She propped it in between Braum and Mags, stepping back. Mags' blue eyes were sunken, her hair painted with dark stripes, brittle and choppy. This was a version of her she'd seen in nightmares, a version of her that never existed up until now. She sat in anguish, weak and defeated.

"Say bye-bye now." Marina laughed, kicking over the mirror. It shattered into a hundred pieces against the cold cement.

Mags took one last look at Siles through glossy eyes. His red pupils flashed into hers, slowly fading to an emerald green; a green that she remembered. Her thoughts unhinged, buzzing in her brain. The room began to spin, faster and faster.

Heated sweat poured from her neck, dripping down her spine.

>*Can you hear me...*
>A male voice, distant but familiar.
>*I'm sorry Maggie...*
>Darkness.

Chapter 23

HELL

"*W*hy didn't you tell me about Beau?" Siles questioned, pacing in the garden of greed.

"I can handle my own, Siles." Marina walked away, picking poison petals to place in her hair.

"We are a team! You've been keeping secrets from me, Marina. And what was that? At the cellar?"

Marina crumbled the flower in her hand, disintegrating it to ash. "*Fun.*"

Siles clenched his fist, his green eyes turned red with rage. "Since when do we play with innocent lives, Marina?"

"I grow tired of this conversation."

"I," Siles grabbed her wrist, turning her to face him, "have not."

"Why do you care about them? What good have they provided you?" Her voice was sharp. "We have all of this, all of hell! My love," she grabbed hold of his face. "We have it *all*."

He swatted her hands away, liquid burning his eyes. "You may think that, but that is far from the truth."

Siles stomped to the portal of Earth, glancing one last time at the demon he cared for, the demon he trained with... the demon he no longer knew.

Chapter 24

KLEATON'S GATE, PRESENT NIGHT

*A*fter Siles returned from hell, he and
Mags took a midnight stroll down by the coastal lake.
When Siles was first tasked to kill Maya, he wasn't
too keen on spending all of his time on Earth, let
alone with Mags. But after a while, the crisp Kleaton
air became somewhat of a familiar scent to him, a
scent he quite enjoyed. In hell, fire and fury was all
that surrounded Siles; torment, wrath, anguish. There
was nothing new, nothing exciting, nothing... *alive.*

Siles fought with his head and his heart,
thinking of Marina. He cared for her, but something
was... changing. He felt their bond breaking, her

dishonesty and secrets. He saw the way she played with Braum in the cellar, the way she played with Mags...

They were nothing but toys, objects. Marina thought them to be useless, and she wanted to see them suffer. Even though Siles felt a twang of jealousy towards Braum, he knew that Marina didn't care for him. But could he say the same about himself? *Don't hurt her*, Siles wanted to say to Marina. But... why?

Marina's boastful voice plagued his thoughts the entire walk. *We have all of hell! My love, we have it all...*

How naïve of her to think of hell as paradise.

Siles didn't understand her sudden switch, her unquenchable thirst for blood and power. Braum's father came to mind. *How could she take a human life? One that had nothing to do with the mission?* Whether he had been the worst man, the best, or in between, Siles didn't believe that it was her place to take away the gift of living... when he himself never even got the chance.

In 1914, Siles was a soldier in the first world war, fighting alongside the Germans. He grew up in a small town just outside Berlin, and was conscripted into war when he turned twenty. He didn't know any better, just that he was fighting front line for his country. He wanted to see the world, buy his mother a nice country home in Glasgow, marry a beautiful woman – he wanted to live.

Siles witnessed death and destruction with every turn in battle. He watched the older fall, and the young, younger than he, killed violently. Then one day, a fellow comrade, just short of seventeen approached Siles: Karl Ryker.

Amidst all the smoke and ash, Karl and Siles became the best of friends. They fought side by side, they spilt beer and blood, and amidst all of the chaos, they lived. Until... they didn't.

In a morning mission, Karl, Siles and three other soldiers patrolled the trenches at their camp when a suicide bomber ran through. Siles survived, but Karl, wide eyed and spry, no longer spoke; no longer moved, or breathed, or blinked.

In a mass of rage, Siles demanded vengeance, stomping into the commanding officer's tent.

"I have just the job for you." The officer said.

Siles was tasked to infiltrate an enemy camp, alongside Hanz, a nineteen-year-old soldier. It was a suicide mission, one meant for the careless, but he left on a whim.

"Kill the General's son. Take what is most valuable to him and eliminate the threat, *whatever it takes.*" The officer's voice echoed in Siles' mind the entire trip. Day and night, day and night, Siles and his comrade trudged through the muddy terrain.

In the near distance, they spotted a bevy of white tents, awnings and canopies, hidden beneath a hill.

"This is it," Siles pointed to a small, beige tent, isolated from the rest of the enemy camp. "Let us finish this."

The camp was entirely silent, a perfect opportunity for Siles to strike, to take out his vengeance and avenge his dear friend, Karl. If the

General could take away someone he cared for, what was stopping him from doing the same?

Only Siles didn't know then what was at stake for his soul, and when he found out, he didn't know if he could fulfill his mission.

A young boy, doe eyed and spry, lay nestled under a white sheet atop a cot. He wrapped his chubby fingers around a small brown bear, sleeping soundly.

"Is this – Is this *him?*" Siles was unable to move a muscle. "The General's son?"

Hanz nodded, showing no emotion.

"He... he cannot be more than eleven. He will inflict no harm."

Siles didn't expect the General's son to be a child, barely a teenage boy. In his heart, he found it easier to kill a man who endured a list of suffering... a man whose heart was already tainted with sin. But this boy, he had not lived even a sliver of his life yet. He had no true understanding of what was happening, of the darkness in the world.

"Children are forbidden in camps. What is he doing here?" Siles demanded, his voice strained and quiet.

Hanz chewed on a cornflower stem, spitting it out before responding. "Spies say the boy followed the General. Mum's dead, no siblings, no caretakers... No loss." He smirked.

He was following his father. "We cannot –"

His comrade interrupted his concern, nudging him towards the child. "Ay! What are you waiting for? Just, kill the boy." Hanz spoke through hushed breaths.

Siles stood frozen. "He is a child, this is inhumane."

"And he'll turn out like the rest of 'em." Hanz shoved him aside, drawing his blade. "Coward." He spat.

Hanz tiptoed to the child and knelt down, getting ready to strike. A dimly lit lantern sat by the cot, illuminating the young boy's features. A youthful, rounded face, light brown hair. He inhaled a breath, and exhaled contently, pulling his teddy bear closer to his body.

Siles couldn't watch this happen, he couldn't take the life of an innocent boy. No matter the vengeance, he knew he would avenge Karl in another way, somehow, not now. In one quick movement, Siles took out his whistle and blew hard, alerting the enemy camp that there was an intruder. He ran out of the tent and hid behind a distant boulder, watching the enemies pull out his comrade, Hanz.

With flailing arms, Hanz was dragged through the mud, forced to his knees. The enemies tied his wrists together, beating him with wooden bats.

Siles watched his bloodied body, bruised and broken by the enemies... the enemies who killed Karl. Then one of them pulled out a rifle, pressing it against the back of Hanz's head.

A shrill scream.

"*Coward!*"

The booming echo of a gunshot.

Silence.

Siles slugged back to his camp, the burden of his betrayal weighing heavy on his shoulders. He thought he'd made the right decision about sparing the boy's life, until his comrades lifeless corpse, stared back at him with taunting eyes even after his death...
Coward!

The commanding officer found Siles at the camp entrance, hurrying to speak with him. His brute structure stomped to face him, cementing his shoes into the soil.

"Siles." He addressed. "Did you eliminate the threat? Did you kill the boy?" He furrowed his brows. "Where is Hanz?"

Siles collapsed to his knees, defeated, weak and somber. "Dead, sir. I couldn't –" Siles sniffed. "I couldn't do it. I couldn't... I failed, sir."

The commanding officer held no sign of empathy. He signalled for his guard, who handed him a black baton and a pistol. The hot sun beamed down on to Siles, burning his skin. In one quick movement, the officer whipped his face with the baton and aimed the pistol at Siles.

Siles was on the ground, looking up at the hazy silhouette of his commanding officer. For a second, the officer's features blurred to Karl's kind, green eyes. Only his words were different; his words were harsh, cold, *evil.*

The pain was instant, ephemeral.

Death was faster.

The echoed words of the commanding officer lingered, melting together with the cruel cries of Hanz's last breath.

"I have no use for a coward..."

"What's on your mind, baby?" Mags asked, poking Siles' side.

Siles swallowed hard, shaking off the flashbacks of his past and smiled shyly. "Nothing that concerns you."

Mags stopped in her tracks, pulling him to a halt. His eyes met her blue, crystalline stare. Her blonde hair glistened in the moonlight, her cheekbones high and defined. *She is kind of beautiful.*

She put her hands on her hips, smiling kindly. "Don't be afraid to show your heart to me, Siles. I've practically given mine to you."

She pulled him into a warm embrace, burying her face into his chest. He was hesitant, for a moment, then softened at her touch. *I've practically given mine to you*, her words banged against his skull.

Because I've taken it... and you don't even have a clue.

He pushed aside the taunting voices, the thoughts that raised him to be a warrior of hell, his place as an incubus, and he hugged her tightly, savouring the moment of warmth – a warmth immeasurably different from Marina.

Chapter 25

KLEATON'S GATE, PRESENT NIGHT

I sent Tommy off when I was confident that he was mentally capable of driving home. He was frantic for another half an hour, recounting everything that happened between him, Braum and Ky. Though his demeanour drastically changed when he talked about Braum's new girlfriend, Marina, whoever she was. I didn't know what to think or how to feel. His disturbed state sent shivers down my spine; I'd never seen Tommy like that before... *Or anyone for that matter.*

Everything he'd said reminded me of Mags and how she changed within days. All of the parallels lined up in a similar order... uncannily similar.

I shut the door behind me and inhaled a deep breath from the inside of my house. "Finally some fresh air." *Unlike the air I'd been breathing for the past hour.*

I found my dad in his study, nose deep in paperwork. "How'd it go?" he asked.

I leaned against the doorframe. "Manageable." I chuckled. "I'm going to head to bed, night Dad."

"Goodnight kiddo."

I dragged myself up the stairs and slumped down on my mattress, pulling the sheets over my head. A bevy of goosebumps remained on my skin, painting my flesh with unsettling discomfort. I forced myself to close my eyes and drown out the noise nagging in my brain. But it was no use.

I tossed and turned, stretching into every position to make myself comfortable, but I couldn't. Tommy's words ate away at me, and I couldn't prevent my wandering thoughts from thinking about Mags... and Beau.

I blindly pulled open my bedside table and reached for my mother's cross. It always helped calm me down when I had a lot on my mind, and boy did I ever need a sense of relief right about now.

But my fingers only found empty space. *Where is it? I never move it.* I struggled to reach deeper into my drawer, and finally caught hold of the chain. *There you are.* Only, my mother's cross was tangled in something, something... soft.

I used one hand to assist me upwards, checking what the necklace was attached to... and I stopped immediately.

My body fell entirely numb. The tingly sensation of my heightened senses scaled its way to the top of my skin. All I could hear were the turbulent beats of my heart, banging in my ears. *Lub-dub, lub-dub, lub-dub...*

Entangled in the chain of my mother's necklace was the white feather that Beau had given me. *Gabriel's feather.*

A panic frenzy infiltrated my being, controlling my movements. Without thinking, I grabbed hold of the cross, feather and car keys, shutting the door behind me. The cool night surrounded me in still blackness as I leapt into my Honda and pressed on the gas. My mind was manic, my thoughts racing a mile a minute and before I knew it, I was heading in the direction of Glass Hill Condos.

Beau wore a black t-shirt and light grey sweats. Dark scruff lined his jaw and heavy purple bags hung under his eyes. I swallowed hard, feeling a multitude of butterflies dance around in my stomach. I hadn't seen Beau in so long, it almost didn't feel real; his mystifying grey eyes, his midnight hair, those rosy lips... *Get a grip Maya, you're here for a reason.*

As tortuous as it was for me, there was something bigger happening here, something I didn't understand... Something I hoped he could explain.

My gruesome nightmares kept me awake at night, plaguing my dreams. And when I finally had fallen asleep, faint chants of my name whispered through the air. *Maya... Maya...* over and over. I didn't know what it was at the time, I still don't, but all the signs began pointing to the unbelievable... Everything Beau had told me.

I'm not crazy, I'm not crazy. Beau is! I forced my mind to believe this, anything but that implausible fiction tale Beau wanted me to believe. So, I placed the white feather he had given me in an old jewelry box and buried it under a stack of blankets. *It can't be that, it's impossible.* But... it had to be.

Every night that I woke up, the chants sang from the direction of the jewelry box. I just wanted it to end; I felt like I was going insane. I thought about it, holding the feather and praying to Gabriel... as crazy as that sounded. *Why am I thinking about this? This can't be real!*

And then tonight happened.

Tommy came to me, overwrought with fear. *It's like Marina's controlling Braum. He's not himself...* Tommy's words sprayed my mind. Beau had told me that Siles was a demon, an incubus that controlled Mags. Either I was giving in to my insanity, or maybe... Maybe Beau was telling the truth. And then his feather, *Gabriel's* feather... It – It was all impossible. It was locked in the corner of my room, untouched for weeks. Then all of a sudden, it was entangled in my mother's cross. My mother... who Beau protected.

Beau's expression was inscrutable. He looked surprised; whether contented or disappointed, it was hard to tell.

"Can I come in?" I asked, softly. My heart raced.

He pushed the door open and stepped to the side, allowing me to enter before shutting it behind me.

His apartment was cold and reeked of alcohol. Empty bottles lined the top of his kitchen counter and stacks of plates flooded the sink. The shards of glass I had seen weeks ago were still pushed into the corner, a scattered mess.

The hazy memories of my last visit resurfaced in my brain; pulling myself out of the apartment after Beau had told me I was the saviour of a holy war between Heaven and hell, leaving his side for so long but now... now, I was back to square one.

I bit down hard on my bottom lip forcing myself to turn around and look at him. He was sitting on one of the barstools, peering down at the floor. His dark hair swooped down over his forehead, shading his eyes. I couldn't help but stare, stare at the man I thought I knew, but clearly not at all. I wanted to pity him, pity him for being insane and creating a fantasy narrative out of this reality but I couldn't - I couldn't because every part of me felt his honesty.

I cleared my throat, inhaling a heavy breath. "Beau -"

"I'm sorry, Maya." He mumbled, cutting me off. "I'm so fucking sorry."

My feet carried me to his direction. I positioned myself in between his legs, inhaling the scent of pine and whisky radiating off of him. He looked defeated, his shoulders hung low. Glancing around the room, observing the messy chaos he'd been living in since I last saw him seemed to be punishment enough.

I placed a gentle hand on his arm, feeling the electrocuting warmth of his skin. "I needed..." I paused, swallowing hard. "I needed time."

He finally looked up, his grey eyes piercing into mine with intensity. "I know."

I stepped back, digging my nails into the crease of my palm. "I'm ready to talk, if you are," I released.

He nodded and led me to the bedroom, where I had once been a month ago... *when Mags poisoned me.* I took a seat at the edge of the mattress and he sat beside me, twirling his fingers.

I didn't know how to begin. I didn't even know what I wanted to say. I had made an elaborate plan of attack on the drive here, but now he was in front of me, looking so... helpless. *You can do this, Maya. Just talk to him.*

I took a deep breath. "I still think this is nuts."

He chuckled softly, his head aimed downwards. "I would too."

"But... I don't know why I believe it," I whispered.

He darted to me with wide eyes. "You do?"

My hands shook as I pulled out the feather from my sweater pocket. I held it in front of me and examined its opulence. Both sides twinkled like stardust, shining with light. It didn't feel or look like a cheap Halloween prop or a dollar store toy; it looked... *real.* Everything about it was irrefutably mesmerizing, beautiful. The longer I stared, the harder it was to look away.

It's so white... like pearls and snow and... Maya... Maya...

"Maya!" Beau shook me. "Hey, hey." He placed his hand over mine, rubbing my thumb gently.

What the... What... I shut my eyes and shivered, my head feeling woozy. "What was that? What happened?"

"Gabriel's feather. It's fueled with grace." Beau responded, calmly.

I trembled, blocking out my surfacing thoughts of panic. I needed to know the truth, I needed to know everything. If this was all real, and I really was the Puritas, then I was the key to something bigger than all of us. *I need to know.*

I tentatively wrapped my fingers around Beau's, eying him carefully. "Can you do this with me?" I gripped the feather with my other hand. "I don't... I don't know what's going to happen."

Beau gritted his teeth and nodded slowly, taking the feather from my left hand and putting it into my right. He interlocked both of our fingers with the feather in the middle.

"Are you sure?" he asked.

I have to be. "Yes."

"Close your eyes." He paused. "Repeat this, Maya: *To the archangel Gabriel, I pray.*"

I shut my eyes, allowing the encompassing darkness to blanket my vision. Gripping the bedsheet behind me, I concentrated on the soft cotton underneath my fingertips; the normalcy of something so simple... *Something I haven't felt in so long.*

Here goes nothing. "*To the archangel Gabriel... I pray.*"

The blind darkness burst into a kaleidoscope of glass diamonds, warping me into a reality far away from here – a reality of ivory lights, pastel dust and *black* feathers...

I saw it. I saw it all. I was living through Beau's perspective, through his eyes, ever since I was born. I saw my mother raise me as a child, scooping me into her arms, caressing my hair. Beau had watched her for years, then me. I saw the cross that my mother gave Beau before she died... the one he wore around his neck at all times. I watched my mother die. She got shot, by a hooded figure whose identity was never found. I saw Marina and Siles, in the floating crystal orb that Gabriel showed Beau. Blight, he visited Blight the angel in prison the day we first met. And I saw Beau... Beau's scars, Beau's darkness...

Beau... he's... he's an angel. Everything – All of it is true. I am the sole mortal that can walk

through Heaven, purgatory and hell. I have God's grace coursing through my veins. I am the Puritas.

I struggled for a breath, any breath as the light sucked me back into reality. Beau gripped my arm and squeezed my hand tightly, staring at me patiently.

I couldn't contain my quaking being. *It's all true.* "I – I always thought..." I stuttered. "I always thought that my mom was in the wrong place at the wrong time but no." I looked to Beau, shaking my head. Tears welled in my eyes, drowning my vision. "She was meant to be there, wasn't she?"

Beau pressed his lips together and clenched his jaw, nodding his head. "I'm sorry, Maya."

My chin quivered as reality finally sunk in, a reality so far and distant that I didn't know existed... until now. The incomprehensible weighed down on my chest like boulders. I couldn't hold my tears, burying my face in my hands. I sunk to the ground in dismay and felt Beau's soothing warmth cradle my body.

My mother was a sacrifice, so that I could save the afterlife. Me, a nineteen-year-old girl from a small town in the middle of nowhere. Me, a normal girl, who in a month from now would have been attending MU, getting ready to start her adult life. Her *normal* life. *It's... It's all gone.*

Beau held the back of my neck and turned my face up to his. "Do you want to be alone? I can't even imagine what you're –"

"No." The words slipped my mouth. "I need you."

As ridiculous as it sounded, with everything that'd happened since I met Beau Gabriel, needing him was the one thing that finally made sense.

I sunk back into the safety of his arms and wiped my cheeks, laying on his chest. His chin rested on the top of my head perfectly, as if it were meant to be there.

"I'm here Maya," he whispered. "*Always.*"

Chapter 26

HEAVEN

The clear white clouds shimmered with a crystal hue, floating in serenity. A choir of soft, faint voices came and went with the winds. Gabriel found Raphael and Michael in the golden armoury, devising a plan to attack the fallen.

"What are the numbers?" Raphael asked Michael.

Michael was dressed in all white armour with a silver plate covering his chest and arms. His ash blonde hair cascaded down to his shoulders, and his grey eyes beamed with ferocity.

"The mortals love making bad decisions." Michael began, reaching for his helmet. "They're all choosing Lucifer, every single one. Only a fraction of mankind see the golden gate after death; we're losing, brother."

Raphael and Michael heard Gabriel approaching behind the grandeur diamond door.

"Gabriel!" Raphael clapped in joy. "What news do you bring?"

Michael scoffed. "Hopefully something good."

Gabriel flashed a weak smile. He'd just watched Beau tell Maya of her position as the divine mortal, and he was glad, though something was coming and Gabriel knew that... Something much darker. "Beau has made it known to the Puritas."

Raphael and Michael rejoiced in unison.

"Wonderful!" Raphael said.

"Just in time." Michael responded. "Maybe now our numbers will increase." He walked over to Gabriel and placed a stiff hand on his shoulder. "It's getting bad out there, Gabe."

Gabriel didn't speak.

Raphael scrunched his eyebrows warily, pushing back the crimped locks from his face. "Gabriel, what troubles you?"

Gabriel swallowed hard, glancing at his brothers twice over. "Beau is running out of time. He..." Gabriel paused. "He is one sin away from turning into one of *them*... to the dark."

"Mortal or venial?" Raphael questioned.

"Does it matter?" Michael snapped. "I knew that Beau was not suitable for Earth."

An angel never fell to Earth for God's bidding; Beau was the first ever Nuntius. God put his trust in the archangels to select one they found worthy, and to Gabriel, that was Beau. *There is something special about Beau*, Gabriel thought. He was one of the most beautiful angels in all of Heaven, despite his absence of title. When God created Beau, he melded sacred fire and water, a powerful magnitude of opposing elements. Gabriel taught Beau as he aged, educating him on humans and their souls. And within Beau's spirit, Gabriel saw resilience, resolution... hope.

"Send him home and bring forth another angel. Perhaps one with more devotion and less... humanity." Michael commanded.

Gabriel was silent.

Raphael stirred, placing a calm hand on Michael. "Now, now, brother. We mustn't get ahead of ourselves. Gabriel," he turned to face him. "What of the Puritas? Does she believe?"

Gabriel nodded. "Slowly. We must be patient."

Michael ripped away from Raphael's grasp and marched towards the golden chest in the middle of the armoury. The chest was glowing and ardent, brimming with grace. It was divinely sealed by the four healing crystals: clear quartz, rose quartz, jasper and obsidian.

When God bestowed the title of the warrior to Michael, a band of heavenly thrones forged a sword so powerful that only the purest of souls could wield: the Flaming Sword. The celestial weapon lay resting in the golden chest that only the diamond key could unlock. Michael wore it around his neck every passing moment, and ensured that the healing crystals remained intact. Without the crystals, the grace fuelling the Flaming Sword would diminish, weakening its ability to fight against the fallen. Though the crystals remained unbroken and untouched since the beginning of time; the absence of the stones was not a concern.

He placed the diamond key in the chest and unlocked it, pulling out the Flaming Sword. The silver blade glistened against the ivory skies, its power fueled by a thousand thrones and incandescent holy fire.

Michael shoved past Gabriel and Raphael, extending his snow white wings for flight. He turned to look at his brothers one last time, before returning to the battlefield of mist and thorns.

"Patience is our demise."

Whoosh.

Chapter 27

KLEATON'S GATE, PRESENT NIGHT

Ky hadn't left his room in weeks. Clothes scattered the floor, covering his carpet in a heaping mess. He told Tommy and his family that he would be taking an early trip up to his college campus, to learn the ropes and familiarize himself. But in reality, Ky just wanted to be as far away from Kleaton's Gate as possible. He never planned on coming back, not after what happened with Braum.

Ky had spent the past three days writing out anonymous statements to the KG police, explaining everything he had seen. He knew that it was a long shot, but he couldn't harbour his torment any longer. Mike's decrepit body was hanging from the ceiling, covered in blood. The image plagued Ky's thoughts with feral fear; he didn't want to believe Braum could commit such a heinous crime. But Ky didn't know what to think anymore, so he gave up.

Ky didn't give a second thought as to what he was packing in his luggage. He frantically threw clean and dirty clothes in a sack and shoved it in his carry-on. Amidst the clutter, he found a picture of Tommy, him and Braum at the beach two years prior. They wore big smiles and cheered beers. They looked happy.

Tears blurred Ky's eyes as he gently rubbed the photo with his thumb. *What I would do to go back in time...*

"It's a shame." A woman's voice startled him.

Ky jumped and dropped the picture, jolting his body around. Marina sat in the corner chair with her legs overlapping one another. The moonlight twinkled against her red lipstick and pale skin, highlighting her sharp features.

"M... Marina?" Ky stuttered. "Help! Mom!" Ky yelled, bolting for the door.

Within seconds, Marina stood in front of him, guarding the exit with crossed arms. She placed her hand flat on the lock as a red hue radiated from her palm, sizzling.

"Wha – what..." Ky muttered.

Ineffable fear drowned his being. He stumbled back to the wall, shaking incessantly. His eyes darted around the room, trying to find a logical explanation to how Marina got inside without him noticing, but the window was closed and the door was locked. *How... How is she... Help!*

Ky screamed at the top of his lungs. "Help! Please, mom! Dad!"

His hand found the nearest object to his left – an empty peanut tin. He held it out in front of him, trembling, hoping and praying that this was all a dream and she would disappear. But it wasn't a dream, and Marina still remained, smiling before him.

Marina slowly approached, swatting away the tin with force. His room was dimly lit, but the red in her eyes penetrated through the darkness.

"They can't hear you, cretin." With weighted pressure, she pinned Ky against the wall and held him by the neck, curling her fingers around his throat. "Your screams stay in this room."

Ky's legs dangled as she lifted him higher and higher. He gasped for air, digging his nails into Marina's forearm. Trickles of blood dripped from her skin, flowing down her arm. She chuckled, using her other hand to collect a small drop of blood and licked her finger.

"Wh – why... are you doing – this..." Ky let out, losing consciousness.

Marina grimaced as she twisted harder, choking the remaining life out of Ky.

His legs grew numb, weak and frail. The kicking was the first to stop, then his body cooled, and the struggle eased away slowly. His fingers faltered, no longer gripping Marina's arm. The pain became bearable, natural almost. Nothing hurt anymore. A fading light shone in the distance as death slowly forced his eyes closed.

She wanted to be the last thing Ky saw before he took his last breath.

"Because I can." Marina smiled, releasing the corpse of Ky Gerber.

Chapter 28

HELL

$\mathscr{I}$t had been over a month since Siles and Marina had that fight in the garden, since Siles had last seen her. He thought that he'd taken a substantial amount of space from her, enough to reconcile their differences and come back stronger.

Marina wrapped her legs around Siles and bit down hard on his lip. She kissed him passionately, pushing him up against the cave wall.

"I have missed you, Marina..." Siles moaned against her mouth.

Marina chuckled slyly. "I have something to tell you."

Siles continued to kiss her, trailing down her neck then to her collarbone. He pulled her hair and nibbled her ear, gazing at her with contentment.

"Oh... Can't it wait?" he asked, drawing her closer.

She beamed with wide eyes. "I killed Ky Gerber, a friend of Braum's."

The smile Siles wore slowly twisted into a visage of betrayal and disgust. "You *what?*" he yanked away from Marina aggressively.

"Oh you should have seen it, Siles! I held him by the throat and watched the life –"

"Marina," Siles snapped. "Why did you kill him? Did I not express my feelings clearly enough in the garden?"

Marina fixed her tousled hair irately. "Are you... *mad* at me?"

A labyrinth of sentiments strangled his senses. Siles didn't know how to feel anymore. He'd been fighting with his mind for weeks, struggling to decipher where his true nature aligned. Marina meant a lot to him, but ever since Lucifer tasked them to Earth, he felt her slipping, and he didn't know if he could pull her back up.

Siles stepped back. "Why did you kill him, Marina?" he asked, sternly.

Marina fixed her blouse and huffed with aggravation. "Because I wanted to. And what of it?"

"The task was to eradicate Maya. Not kill everyone in sight," Siles spat. "Where is he? Is he in hell, Marina?"

Blood rose to her cheeks. She leaned back on her heels and crossed her arms. "I didn't see him."

Blood rushed to his face. "Another innocent life." Siles buttoned up his shirt and fixed his hair, making his way to the cell exit.

"Where are you going?" Marina demanded.

Siles took a deep breath in, longing for the air on Earth. He wanted to go to Mags. He didn't have a clue why, but the tenderness he'd shared with her was unmistakeable. He had slowly begun to take pity on her. It was never supposed to end like this, in the bloodshed of innocent mortals.

When Siles was tasked to Earth, he had no expectations of this version of humankind. All he could remember was the violence, the destruction of war... *His cowardice.*

He wanted to prove to Lucifer, his commanding officer, Hanz, Karl... that he was not a coward. He could fulfill any mission, and he would get it done right this time around. He'd been training for over a century, and Lucifer selected him to do this – to eradicate Maya. She was a threat to hell, his home. But day by day, Siles began to question where exactly home truly was.

In the beginning, Mags was just an object of strategy, to get closer to Maya. If he were to do this mission, he wanted to know everything. Befriend the enemy, study... analyze... strike. But in turn, a part of him grew fond of Mags. He had kissed her the first night, so no matter what Siles did, Mags would have drifted under his control regardless. Though the more time he spent with her, the less he wanted to use her.

Marina on the other hand, sought out to inflict pain on just about anyone – the taste for blood darkened her heart.

But Siles never relished in these primal acts. In turn, he took interest in observing this obscure version of humankind. Whatever misery Braum had put Mags through in the past, Mags had forgotten in the cellar. Siles remarked the pain in Mags' eyes, the confusion, the fear. Braum was a familiar being to her; they shared history. Whether good or bad, there had been love there, forgiveness and what looked to be... a second chance. In hell, second chances were unheard of – only a burning mortuary of persecuted souls.

But Ky was not among them. His soul most likely found peace in Heaven, or a sentence in purgatory. He was young, he had a life to live... A life no longer. Whoever Ky Gerber was, Mags knew him. And because of Marina, Mags could never see him again.

Siles craned his neck to the side, eyeing Marina in his peripheral vision before exiting the cell. Through gritted teeth, he clenched his fist and seethed, "You can't play God Marina, not even Lucifer can."

Chapter 29

KLEATON'S GATE, PRESENT NIGHT

Mags had just finished a bath when the doorbell rang. Her parents were vacationing at the cottage so she was home alone. *Thank God, my family is so annoying.*

Mags skipped down the stairs and unlocked the door to Siles, his blonde hair sopping wet from the rain.

"Baby!" Mags jumped up and brushed his lips before yanking him inside.

Siles returned the kiss hesitantly, grabbing her hand and leading her to the living room couch.

"Oh, okay. I guess we can do it here." Mags got on top of him, wrapping her legs around his middle.

But Siles pulled her to his side and faced her, taking her hand gently. "Mags, I'm going to do something. But you can't freak out."

Mags laughed and fluffed her hair. "Anything you do is fine by me."

Siles closed his eyes and squeezed her fingers, pressing his lips together before mouthing a foreign word. "*Exsolvo...*"

An acute pain formed in her temples, batting against her skull. "What..." she muttered, wincing. "What are you doing?"

All the light dimmed around Mags, blinking sporadically. She watched the furniture in her living room morph into distorted shapes and colours. A piercing white noise rang through her ears as she fell in and out of consciousness. She peered down to her glowing hands; misty white bubbles drifted away from her skin, weightless and airy. The sharp pain slowly dissipated and the world around her levelled out.

Opening and closing her eyes repeatedly, she looked to the man sitting in front of her, the man from the casino... the man who locked her up in the cellar.

Mags fell down a rabbit hole of terrifying memories as she stared into the emerald eyes of Siles Killian. *Braum...* his battered body in bloody clothes. *Marina...* She was kissing Siles in front of her, attempting to provoke something in Mags she didn't know existed. *Their... their eyes.* Their red eyes sliced into hers, black veins snaking out from underneath their flesh.

"Are you there, Mags?" Siles asked, watching her carefully.

Who... Who are you... What are you...

Mags swallowed hard and fought with her brain, trying to remain calm through her crazed fear. Her thoughts spun out of control trying to decipher the most plausible means for escape. She knew if she ran, Siles would instantly grab her. If she reacted, he'd kill her. *I need to live. I have to live. He can't keep me in a cellar, he can't kill me!*

Mags loved to act in plays. She always got cast as the lead, ever since middle school. She knew that her best bet was to fake an illness, to get him to comfort her, and then when he was out of sight, she'd bolt. *What other choice do I have?*

She placed her hand over her head and coughed with intent. "Ugh, what is happening..." She twitched her jaw. "Siles, can you – can you get me a glass of water. My head hurts."

He nodded with concern and released her hand, making his way for the kitchen.

I need to move. Now! Mags spotted her car keys on the coffee table near the door. The air was still and the tension, immeasurable. Her heart thumped rapidly in her chest, about to explode. As soon as she heard the fridge open, she leapt off the couch and snagged the keys, sprinting out the front door as fast as she could. She heard glass shatter, followed by heavy footsteps trailing shortly behind her.

The rain dribbled down her face, pouring heavily from the sky. She jumped into her car and locked the doors immediately, just as Siles ran out of her house. Mags turned on the ignition and sped out of the driveway before he could catch her. *I need to see Maya. Faster, damnit!* She pushed down hard on the pedal.

Looking back, she saw Siles in the middle of the road, his silhouette drowning in the storm. He collapsed to his knees before the hazy grey atmosphere enclosed, turning him into nothing but a shadow.

Chapter 30

KLEATON'S GATE, PRESENT NIGHT

"So... you're an angel..."

I had finally calmed down after crying for what felt like hours. Beau was patient with me, hovering near just in case I needed him, but gave me enough space to process, well, everything. I could tell that he was searching for a way to comfort me, a way to help me understand better, but there wasn't much he could do. *What could anyone do?*

"I'm a Nuntius, if you want to get technical," Beau chuckled. His smile was gentle. "But yes, I'm an angel."

I swallowed hard, shaking my head. "You know... I've read so many books. So much fiction about things that I never thought existed. I've read about angels, about *you*. I can't believe it's all true."

"Not all of it." Beau leaned back on the mattress. "The devil doesn't have horns."

For the first time in forever, a small laugh escaped my throat.

Beau smiled. "Haven't seen that in a while."

Blood rushed to my cheeks, causing me to blush. I fiddled with my fingers, looking down.

"I checked on you, once." He began, swallowing hard. "To see if you were okay."

I glanced up at him, scrunching my eyebrows in confusion. "When? You... I didn't see you?"

"Gabriel would have given me hell if you had," he laughed.

"Is defying orders not a sin?"

"It is," he flashed a half grin. "But I couldn't find it in me to stay away."

Butterflies fluttered in my stomach. I thought about the countless nights I laid awake in bed, thinking of Beau. *And he thought of me too.*

Amidst all the unbelievable turmoil I endured these past couple of months, I took in this moment. Honestly, it was the only thing that felt *real* to me. Beau was leaning back on his arms, his dark hair messy over his grey eyes. They beamed into mine with intensity, never losing focus.

Beau got under my skin more times than I could count on two hands. He was obnoxious, aggravating and proud. And though it pained me to confess, there was absolutely no denying Beau's undeniable appeal. Everything about him seemed to be carved by angels... *literally.* I faced him, cross-legged with my fingers in my lap.

"What?" Beau chuckled, flashing a grin.

His teeth were white and perfect like polished pearls. His lips... plump and rosy, waiting to be kissed. *Don't kid yourself, you've wanted to for a while.*

His smile softened as he pressed his lips together. He knew what I wanted before I could admit it to myself. *Him.*

In a tentative motion, he slowly rose up from the mattress and slid his hand up my calf, resting it on my knee. My heart exploded in my chest, rattling sporadically. He leaned in closer, gripping my leg tighter. I could almost taste his breath against my mouth, spiced and warm. His lips parted and he shut his eyes, closing the distance between us. *Oh my God... this is happening. Beau Gabriel is going to kiss me. He's right in front of my face... close your eyes damnit!*

"*Your name means handsome in French*!" I blurted, placing my hands firmly on his chest. My cheeks reddened with heightening embarrassment. *Are you – What the hell is wrong with you! Stupid, stupid, stupid.*

Beau squinted his eyes, chortling. He squeezed my thigh, patting it gently before standing up. He scratched his head and glanced quickly around the room before returning his attention back to me. "I'm sorry, I didn't –"

Holy saints, are you serious? "No, no, you didn't. It was me."

"I'm –" he chuckled again, softly. "Are you hungry?" He pointed out the door to the kitchen.

Great, perfect, food! Something has got to save me from my own self-sabotage. "Absolutely."

Beau cooked a steaming pot of bacon carbonara which was surprisingly delicious. I tried to control my thoughts as he kept his back turned to me, wiping the countertop. *I'm human, what can I say.*

"I didn't realize angels could cook." I jested, sitting on the barstool.

Beau stood across from me, cleaning our dishes. "Sometimes I forget that I'm an angel. I've lived on Earth for so long now, Heaven feels like a dream." He paused, turning the water off. "And then Gabriel pays me an unwanted visit, reminding me that I am still in fact, me."

I shyly smiled, still trying to wrap my brain around the fact that Beau was an angel from Heaven, standing before me... cooking. Is this what all angels looked like? Did they all have perfect, sandy skin? Grey eyes? A ridiculous body... *tattoos.*

"Can I ask you a question?"

Beau stopped cleaning and crossed his arms, leaning against the counter. "Shoot."

My eyes trailed the length of his arm. "What does your tattoo mean? I've always wanted to ask, but –"

He flashed a small grin. "I wasn't lying when I said it's a cover up." He stretched out his arm, flexing it subtly. "When I fell, Gabriel transferred his grace to me, enough of it at least. Hurt like hell, Jesus."

We laughed together.

"His grace left some pretty nasty scars and I hated it. So, a few decades later, I walked my ass into the first tattoo shop I saw and got all the white covered." He glanced up at me, his eyes poking with affection. "Stupid, or smart?"

I narrowed my gaze, tapping my cheek with a sarcastic finger. "Stupid *and* smart."

He smiled, pushing his body off the counter. "I like the sound of that."

I pressed my lips together, glancing around the room. My eyes caught sight of the broken shards of glass in the corner. "You know, you may know how to cook, but you're not the best housekeeper are you?" I teased.

Beau fell silent.

When I held Gabriel's feather, I caught a quick glimpse of Beau punching the mirror, scratching at his scars. I knew he had them, but I didn't understand why it angered him so much. *Did they hurt? Did someone do that to him?*

"Can I see them?" I asked, warily.

Beau clenched his jaw and gripped the countertop. He didn't say anything, only stared past me to the shards of glass on the ground.

"You don't need to show me, I was just –"

"I'll show you." He said, cutting me off.

With noticeable hesitation, he turned around, carefully pulling his shirt over his head. His back muscles flexed underneath the two dark slivers trailing down his back. Black veins coiled underneath his skin, pulsing in beats. Some veins spiked out like thorns, darker than others. Almost his entire spine was bruised and violet.

What the... I was stupefied, unable to contain my shock. *What is... What are those...* My jaw dropped as I stared, unconsciously reaching out to touch his skin.

"That," Beau turned around quickly, grabbing my wrist. "I can't allow you to do."

I slowly eased back into reality, swallowing hard. "I'm sorry." I shook my head, completely lost for words. "What... happened?"

He sighed, his jaw twitching. "Let's just say, an angel doesn't always act like an angel."

A thousand questions plagued my brain, all of which I didn't know how to ask. I sensed the visible discomfort he was feeling, hell, I wouldn't even know how to live with that burden on my back... *literally.* But as much as I wanted to know why, pushing Beau's limits was the last thing I wanted to do. And after everything I just found out, I think pushing myself would be even worse.

My phone startled me, vibrating in my pocket. The caller ID read: **DAD.**

Oh shit. I completely lost track of time. I glanced at the oven clock which read: **1:02am.**

I cleared my throat quickly, praying I wouldn't hear a yell on the other line. "Dad, I'm sorry. I'll explain later, I'll be home –"

"Maya, it's Mags! I left my phone at my place, I need – I need you, now! I'm at your place, please get here!"

I stared at the empty nothingness that hid behind my eyelids. My stomach dropped entirely. The familiar tone of Mags' sweet voice rendered me with an influx of conflicting emotions.

"M – Mags?" I trembled, my brain trying to comprehend the possibility that my best friend could really be at my house. *Is that really you?*

An eruption of sobbing bled through the other line, and without a conscious thought, I knew this was Mags. *This is her. She needs me... My Mags is back.*

I put her on speaker and gathered my things in a hurry, scrambling for the door. "Mags, Mags! I'm coming. You're at my place?"

"Let me drive you." Beau suggested.

I shook my head, grabbing my keys. "Come with me."

I hadn't been paying much attention to the speed limit on my drive home.

"So this is why you didn't want to take my car." Beau gasped, holding on to the dashboard.

I kept a straight face as I pushed harder on the pedal. I glanced at him once and shrugged. "You drive like an angel."

We made it to my place in under twenty minutes. I barely pulled into the house when Mags ran out frantically, flailing her arms. Her hair was wet and she was wearing striped pyjama shorts and a pink tank top.

"Maya!" Mags jumped into my arms and squeezed tightly. "Maya, Maya, get inside! Who are..." she looked to Beau, then back to me. "Fuck, I don't have time for this." She yanked Beau and me by our hands and locked the door behind us.

Mags huffed, ducking from my hallway window. Her hug was the same as I remember; the comforting hugs she always used to give me. Even through her feral panic, I embraced the familiarity. The good kind.

"Mags, what's going on?" I asked, pulling the blinds shut.

She looked Beau up and down and crossed her arms. "Is this who I think it is?"

I nodded with a smile, observing Mags' twitching brow, her overprotective stature and frayed blonde locks. *My best friend is here.*

"Beau... *Garbally?*" Mags questioned with intent to annoy.

Beau laughed. "Close enough."

She narrowed her eyes. "You know, I may be running away from a potential serial killer but if you ever hurt Maya, Beau I swear to you –"

Beau's eyes grew wide. "Siles?"

Mags interlocked our fingers and hugged my arm, pulling me away from Beau. "How do you know him?" She began to spaz. "Oh my God, you're not going to lock me in a cellar too? Maya, get away from him!"

"*Cellar?*" I wrinkled my face in confusion.

Beau whipped away from Mags and I, marching towards the door. "I'm going to fucking kill him. Is he with you? Where is he?"

I grabbed his arm and pulled him to my side. "You're not going anywhere right now."

He stared at me for a few moments, his tense shoulders slowly easing at my touch. The corner of his lip upturned slightly and he took his place by my side without further protest.

After double checking my locks, I led Mags to the couch, wrapping a throw blanket around her shoulders. "Here, Mags. I'll make you some tea."

I poured some water into a pot and turned the stove to high, returning back to the living room. "Okay, what the hell happened?"

Mags was eyeing Beau with discontent.

"He's fine, Mags. Seriously." I reassured her.

She rolled her eyes. "Fine." She huffed. "I don't remember anything, Maya. I'm serious. It's like the past two months of my life were just erased from my brain. But – " she stuttered. "I do remember... I was locked in this cellar. And... and... Braum was there covered in blood..."

My stomach twisted. "*Braum?*" I asked, swallowing hard. *Tommy.*

"Yes, oh my God. Siles and Marina tied us to these fucking chairs and went all crazy! I don't even know what happened... they're on drugs I think." Her small hands shook ceaselessly. "I saw these black veins under their eyes and then... they said some word. They said a word and I couldn't talk anymore. Braum and I, we couldn't speak." She was silent for a few moments, then slapped her thighs with frustration. "And what the hell happened to my hair!"

Ha, I was waiting for that.

Heavy footsteps came stomping down the stairs, and my dad appeared in his navy housecoat and slippers.

"A party of four," he yawned. "I let Mags in, she said she needed to see you." He looked to Beau in confusion, raising his eyebrows. "Hi there."

Beau ran his fingers through his messy hair and extended a hand out to my dad. "Beau Gabriel." He smiled.

My dad leaned back on his heel and shook his hand sternly. "You the boy my daughter's been crying about?"

This is my worst nightmare.

Beau glanced at me quickly and scratched his temple, chuckling. *Shit, I forgot he could hear my thoughts.*

"No sir, I hope not." Beau responded.

My dad tapped his shoulder and sluggishly walked towards the kitchen. "Good man." He then called out to me. "Maya, water's done boiling."

I jogged over and plopped a teabag into a white mug, waiting for my dad to go upstairs.

"Night kiddo. Don't make too much noise." He smiled, kissing the top of my head.

When he finally left, I sat down next to Mags and handed her the cup.

"Your dad's nice." Beau smirked.

I waved him off and turned my attention to Mags. "You said you couldn't speak... why? What did you do?"

Mags stared at me suspiciously. "How are you so calm right now? I got abducted!"

I swallowed hard, looking to Beau. He was leaning on the doorframe with arms crossed, avoiding eye contact. *You're on your own*, is what his demeanour read.

I wasn't calm, nor was I downplaying anything that happened to her. I wanted to know, I wanted to hear it all. But my brain was still registering everything that'd happened to me, and the initial shock definitely hadn't settled in yet. More than anything, all that I cared about was having the real Mags back.

"Mags," I took in a breath. "I'm going to sound completely crazy right now and I know you're already freaked out as is, but I need you safe. Okay?" I held her hand tightly.

She nodded her head slowly, staring at me with wide blue eyes.

God, now I understand how Beau felt when he was trying to tell me everything.

"Wasn't easy." Beau shrugged, looking in my direction.

"Stop that." I said, flatly.

Mags threw her hands in the air in exasperation "Stop what? What are you two doing? What is fucking happening!"

Beau walked over to us, pulling out Gabriel's feather from his pocket and handed it to me. It felt like silk in my fingers, glimmering with light.

Mags eyed it intently and set aside her tea. "What is that?"

"A feather." Beau answered drily.

She shot him a look. "I know what it is, moron. What are you doing with it?"

I had to be careful with my words. I knew that if I told Mags everything, she wouldn't believe me. I had to show her. That was the only way that I believed. *Here goes nothing.*

"Do you trust me?" I asked, wrapping her fingers around the feather.

She opened her mouth to protest but I interrupted her.

"Mags, do you trust me?" I demanded once more.

She pressed her lips together and nodded.

"Repeat with me... *To the archangel Gabriel, I pray.*"

Mags raised her eyebrows and shook her head. "Maya, what –"

I pleaded, desperate. "Please, just do it Mags."

She swallowed and released a breath, shutting her eyes. "*To the archangel Gabriel, I pray...*"

Within seconds, Mags' head flew up and her sitting posture was pulled erect. Her pupils melted into a milky white orb as she stared blankly at the wall across the room. An ivory hue radiated from the feather, coiling itself around Mags' entire arm. *Holy saints... Did I look like that too?*

I glanced to Beau with concern, squeezing her fingers tightly. "Is she okay? Is it working?"

He nodded once, observing her with cautiousness.

After a few minutes of anxious waiting, Mags shook her head and opened her beaming ocean eyes. She took one look at me and Beau, stumbling onto my carpet in panic.

"What the – what the fuck! *What the fuck!*" Mags yelled, scurrying for the front door. She bolted outside and tripped on her feet, plummeting onto my lawn.

Beau rolled his eyes. "Well this got dramatic fast."

I shoved past Beau and chased after her, pinning her to the grass. She flailed her arms in a crazed frenzy, sobbing uncontrollably.

"This isn't real, you *drugged* me! This isn't real! What the fuck kind of hallucinogens are you on, Maya!" she screamed. "*Help!*"

"Mags, calm down!"

Her eyes grew wide, bloodshot and feral.. "You expect me – to be fucking calm? What... Beau... He's – He had wings and you! You're some kind of... All because I touched a feather! I touched..." her speech began to slur. "I touched a..." Her limp body fell light, and she passed out.

I sat on my lawn, huffing with breath. Mags lay in the grass, her body plastered in sweat. I honestly didn't know what reaction to expect, so I thought her response was quite fair. The way I dealt with Beau's news was hibernating for weeks, and I hadn't even seen everything at that point. Once again, her reaction was completely justified. All I could hope for was a calmer Mags when she woke up. *That's a long shot.*

"Beau, help me carry her inside." I waved him over.

I dimmed the lights and placed a blanket over Mags, letting her rest on the living room couch.

"We have to find Siles and Marina." I shook my head, grabbing a red bull out of the fridge. "Tommy told me Marina killed Braum's dad, or made him do it, I don't know. Regardless, he was an innocent person." *Not the best person, but he didn't deserve death.*

"They're impossible to track. Not even Gabriel could and he's watching from Heaven. Lucifer must've cloaked them." Beau responded.

I still couldn't wrap my head around this life... *My* life. Lucifer sent two demons to Earth to try and kill me, Lucifer, Satan himself... *This is going to take some time to get used to.*

✛

"So what do we do now?" I asked, leaning against my countertop.

Beau trudged towards me, taking the can out of my grip. He placed both his hands on my cheeks and lifted my chin. His grey eyes intensified the longer he stared, leaving little to no space between us.

When Beau and I first met, I could sense the hesitation of his touch. He never got too close, and if he had, he made sure to retreat almost instantly. But now, there was no hesitation at all. With confidence, he handled me like I was his. *He wanted to be near me.*

Surges of heat rose to my face, causing me to blush.

"Do you trust me?" he asked, circling my skin with his thumb.

I nodded, goosebumps covered my arms.

"Do you really believe all of this? You know, that you're the Puritas?"

My thoughts bounced in my brain. *Did I? I* bit the inside of my cheeks and ripped my eyes away from his. "I have no other choice but to believe. I saw my mother die... for this, for me." Tears welled up in my eyes. *Don't cry. You've cried enough.*

Beau backed up, dropping his hands to his side. He clenched his jaw and glanced at Mags, knocked out on the couch. "Looks like you and I are going on a road trip."

I scrunched my eyebrows in confusion. "Where?"

He pulled out Gabriel's feather from his pocket and squeezed tightly. "Port Hope."

Chapter 31

KLEATON'S GATE, PRESENT NIGHT

Siles followed Mags to Maya's home and crouched underneath the outdoor windowsill, completely out of sight. The blinds were drawn but he made out a small crack in the corner, where he spotted Mags sleeping on the couch.

At first, Siles regretted releasing her from his control. *I'm doing her a favour, how dare she!* His initial instinct was to kill her coldly for running away, like he was trained to do in hell. But he saw the fear in her eyes, the fear that *he* caused. There was no denying the truth any longer; somewhere along the way, he had begun to care for Mags.

When she sped down the road, Siles contemplated using his power to stop her car... But he didn't. *What's the point?* He thought. *Just kill Maya. Get this menial task over with and forget about Earth.*

When he reached Maya's, Siles felt Beau's strong, palpable grace penetrating through the brick premises. *Cursed angel.* He paced around the house, searching for open entries. Through the blanket of darkness, Siles made out a faint yellow light radiating from one of the bedroom windows. The illumination allowed him to see that the latch was unlocked, making it easy for entry. *Perfect, I'll wait until Maya's alone.*

That's when he took his place underneath the windowsill and saw Mags through the sliver of glass, lying peacefully with her eyes closed on the couch. He stared at her, pressing his lips together. All of the memories they had made came flooding back, stamping his brain with guilt. Lucifer's taunting voice boomed in his head, banging against his skull with threat. But for the first time, Siles ignored it. He was about to kill her best friend, the one person Mags trusted with her life... the person who made her feel *alive*, and she wouldn't even know. *I'm sorry, Maggie.*

Another figure approached, flickering in the corner of Siles' peripheral vision. Her brown hair was bunched into a bun, her petite frame wabbling into view. She looked tired, holding a cup and a bowl of towels. She too, stared at Mags, standing over her for a few moments.

Siles recounted the sole encounter he had with Maya, the night at the casino. At first glance, he thought she was quite beautiful. In Lucifer's orbionyx, Siles couldn't really tell by the blurry display. But up close, Maya held a hard shield – strong, assertive and tough. *So... This is the Puritas.* At first, Siles wanted to draw her in, play on her vices like any demon would. He had the opportunity to show forth his abilities, everything he'd been training for since he fell... Though oddly enough, a part of him accepted that he couldn't. A part of him knew he didn't deserve to.

Maya sat down and crossed her legs in front of sleeping Mags. She placed a small folded towel on her forehead and brushed away strands of her hair with gentle fingers. Siles closed his eyes, thinking back to all the moments he did exactly that with Mags... Memories that only existed under his control.

Burning embers began to sizzle from Siles' hands, a snake of fire trailing up his arm. *I... I can't.* He watched Maya lean her head on Mags' arm, closing her eyes. *I won't.*

Lucifer trained his fallen to be strong, to avoid vulnerability, that love was an incurable venom and hatred was the true salvation of humanity. Though the more Siles thought of Lucifer's words, the more distant they became. Maybe Lucifer had it all wrong... Siles thought, staring at the unbreakable bond between two humans who found peace in each other... who found love. Water burned his eyes, as he forced himself up off the ground. *Hatred is an incurable venom. Love is the true salvation of humanity.*

And he walked away.

HELL

"What the fuck have you done!" Marina screamed, clawing Siles with anger.

Lucifer dragged Marina and Siles back to hell after watching him walk away from the Puritas, a failed mission. After revealing to Marina that Siles released Mags from his control, the darkness inside of her amplified.

Lucifer's black suit sparkled with hell dust, twinkling with the remnants of condemned souls. "It's a shame, Siles. Pity." Lucifer pouted, sardonically. "You intentionally defied my orders."

"Worthy of eternal punishment, you snake! Traitor!" Marina spat, emphasizing her final word. "*Coward!*"

Siles killed the fire that burned in his core, standing with a straight face. *Coward, coward...* The words from his commanding officer repeated in his brain. *Coward...* Hanz's dying breath. *Coward!* Marina's disdain.

He knew that he'd disobeyed the mission that Lucifer assigned him, but he fought with his fire and fear to remain strong. He saw what condemning lives did to Marina, preying on the innocent... playing

God. Siles believed to the worst of people, eternal punishment was imperative. But to the rest, the ones who had a life yet to live, taking that away was dishonorable, *evil*. He trained in Lucifer's army, working his way to the top. But what good was that to waste on dishonest drudgery?

"You're a demon. You are no angel." Marina scowled. "*Burn*, you pathetic bastard!" She stomped past Siles, shoving him with her shoulder.

Lucifer turned on his heel, raising a giddy arm. "Now, where are you going, my sweet?"

Marina's red hair flamed through the bloody hue lights of hell. She clenched her jaw, burning her eyes into Siles' before walking into the red portal of Earth. "To finish the job."

And she was gone.

Lucifer's sinister laugh echoed through the cave walls, encompassing Siles with disconcerting fear. His courage diminished, fleeing away to the shadows of the darkness.

"Siles, Siles, Siles." Lucifer clicked his tongue, stepping off his throne. "What do we do, what do we do?"

In calm motions, Lucifer stretched his fingers, using his power to chain Siles' arms in burning cuffs that exploded with hellfire.

"*Ah!*" he wailed in agony, sinking to the ground.

Lucifer stomped up to him, lifting him firmly by the neck. With his free hand, he tore off Siles' shirt and disintegrated it to ash. His grey eyes flashed into blobs of red, burning into Siles as black veins slowly emerged from beneath his skin.

Lucifer threw him to the ground and kicked him to his stomach, calling for the guards to hold his limp body erect.

"Let me paint you a picture," Lucifer spoke fast, gelling back his hair rampantly. "I prefer them to be animated, don't you, *pet.*"

A vein in Lucifer's forehead twitched as he extended a hand out behind him, keeping his stare on Siles. A black mist sprouted from the granite floor, twirling into three silhouettes. Through glossy vision, Siles made out the familiar profiles of his past: the brute structure of his commanding officer, the dark stare of Hanz, and Karl... his innocent green eyes turned black, dripping with tar.

"No! *No!*" Siles screamed, locked in the grasp of Lucifer's demons. Their bodies were painted with bullet holes, oozing with bloody pus. They strode towards him, pulling out sharp blades from the ashy mist.

Hanz was the first to strike, driving his blade through Siles' stomach.

"*Argh!*" Siles wailed, digging his nails into his palm. Hanz wore a twisted smile, smirking as he carved a letter into his skin.

Next to approach was the commanding officer, wasting no time to stab Siles violently in the side. Siles cried in pain as the he, too, carved letters into his flesh.

Hanz and the commanding officer busted into dust, leaving only Siles and Karl, facing each other in the throne room.

"P... Please." Siles begged, his limbs giving out to excruciating torment. "You know me..."

Karl's dark expression held no signs of empathy as he dragged out a burning dagger, and drove it straight through his heart. He twisted the knife, carving the final letter onto Siles' chest.

Karl stepped back and eyed Siles. His red eyes were vacant and hallow, observing the withering demon, painted by gore and sweat. "*I only hear the screams of a sheep.*"

And he vanished.

Lucifer clapped, jumping up and down. "What a show! What a – guards, don't you agree?" He snapped his fingers and a square mirror appeared in the center of the throne room. There were no words to explain the fatigue that Siles felt, the suffering and the torment. He wanted to die... but he was already dead.

With what little energy Siles had left, he slowly lifted his head to look at his reflection in the mirror. Blood dribbled down his arm, starting from where Siles had buried his nails in his palm. Gore leaked from several different holes on his body, pooling around his feet. And in the center of his chest, black and blue lettering was carved downwards, sealed by Lucifer's eternal fire.

$$COWARD$$

Tears waterfalled down Siles' cheeks, painting his face with guilt and anguish. He felt no courage, no resilience, only weakness. *I'm nothing, I'm nothing... I'm a coward.*

"What a lovely marking, isn't it?" Lucifer snapped his fingers once more and the mirror shattered. "Now, what do we say in hell?"

Siles was unresponsive.

Lucifer's eyes bulged as he curled his fingers around Siles' neck, squeezing with fury. "*What...*" Lucifer began through chattering teeth. "*Do... We... Say...*"

Siles could barely open his eyes. Lucifer's voice was a harsh whisper in the distant corner of his mind, but the pain increased. Lucifer's burning fingertips scorched Siles' throat, forcing the words to come out.

"*Love is...*" Siles choked, his lips crusted with blood. "*Love is an incurable... an incurable venom and hatred... salvation.*"

Lucifer released him, brushing off his veiny hands. "Take him to the cages." He grimaced, commanding the guards.

Coward... Siles wept in agonizing pain. As the guards pulled him by the arms, his limp feet dragged against the cold grounds of hell. *Coward...* He faded in and out of consciousness, seeing sharp flashes of red. A trail of blood followed Siles, his chest swelling with charred contamination.

"*Coward...*" Siles whispered. "*Cowa...*"

Silence.

Chapter 32

KLEATON'S GATE, PRESENT NIGHT

Get up... Maya...

My tired eyes adjusted to the dim light of the living room. I scratched at my scalp, peering down at the giant red circle on my arm from the pressure of my head. *Shit, I fell asleep!* My phone read: **3:18am.**

Mags was still passed out from earlier and Beau sat on the loveseat across from the couch. He smiled when he noticed me stir.

"I didn't know you talked in your sleep." He chuckled, fiddling with his fingers.

My cheeks flushed with embarrassment. "No I don't!" I denied, hiding my blush. "What did I say?"

He got up from his slump and plopped his elbows on his knees. "Somethin' like... *God, Beau, why don't you just shut up and kiss me?*"

I scoffed with annoyance, throwing a cushion at his face. "Why didn't you wake me up?"

"I didn't want you grumpy," he shrugged, playfully.

I rubbed my eyes and looked at Mags. Her mouth was wide open and drool dripped down her chin. *Well, at least she's not yelling anymore.*

I motioned for Beau to come to the kitchen so we wouldn't wake her.

"When do you want to leave?" I asked, finishing off my red bull from earlier. *Ew, it's warm.*

He scratched the nape of his neck and tilted his head to the side. "Want the truth?"

"Nothing but." I replied, choking back the remaining contents of my drink.

Beau crossed his arms, looking to the stove clock. "Now."

I coughed instantly, checking the time again. "Now? Right now? Beau it's the middle of the night. You just – *we* just sprung the fact that you're, you know and I'm, well..." I trailed off.

"Yeah, I know, Maya. But Siles and Marina are going to come after you, and I can't..." he paused, taking in a heavy breath. "I *won't* let that happen."

Fatigue strangled my senses, though drifted off to a gruesome image of Siles standing over me, my beating heart in his hands. I shuddered at the thought, wondering if it was Siles haunting my nightmares all this time. *No, it can't be. Those were just stupid dreams.*

Nonetheless, the thought of being killed by a demon didn't seem all that pleasant. But what would I even say to my dad? *Hey dad, so I'm actually the key to stopping a holy war and I'm running off with a boy who is also an angel but I'll be fine. And mom, well mom was actually* – Wait.

"Did my dad know what my mom was?" I questioned, furrowing my brows. "That she was a sacrifice, so that I could –"

"No." A simple response.

I pressed my lips together and scratched at my elbow, glancing at the time once again. "And when we get to Port Hope, what then? What happens when I drink from the chalice?"

God, that really sunk in. Just saying that out loud made it very real. I knew that I'd been avoiding referring to myself as something greater than I was, because I just didn't feel like anything other than ordinary. I sometimes waited for something to happen that would pull me back out of this dream and suck me back into reality... But this was reality.

I had seen all of it, I believed Beau... but what would happen to me? Would I grow wings? What am I drinking? *What exactly do I need to do...*

"I wish I could tell you, Maya, but I don't even know." Beau said, reading my thoughts. "What I do know, is staying in Kleaton's Gate is going to do more harm than good. Those demons are out there and..." Beau swallowed, faltering.

He grew fidgety, unable to look me in the eyes. His hesitation to speak was unnervingly off-putting. A blade of tension sliced our space in two, the air heavy and cold. His fingers curled around the corner of my countertop as he stared downwards.

"Beau?" I asked, approaching him slowly. "I know they're demons but you have the grace of an archangel... That – that's stronger... Right?"

Beau clenched his jaw. "The night I visited you, when we weren't speaking," he began, "I crossed paths with Marina."

My eyes grew wide. "You... You what? And you didn't think to tell me?"

"I didn't want to scare you." His expression was inscrutable, vacant. "I'm strong," he shook his head, "But so is she."

I didn't speak. I didn't know what to say. Beau was quiet, careful. He stood proud and tall in every situation, but not this one. He looked almost... *afraid.*

After a few moments of silence he finally looked up at me, his grey eyes hallow and dark. He remained silent, taking slow steps towards me. I swallowed hard as he cupped my face, his unreadable stare bleeding into mine. All of his apparent indiscretion slowly dissolved, the vacant darkness of his eyes fading into a familiar grey. He leaned down, brushing his soft lips against mine gently, then pulled back before I could return his kiss.

"I don't want them near you," he whispered.

Chapter 33

LONDON, ENGLAND, 1924

*B*eau walked the streets of England alone. Rain pattered gently against his black umbrella while a misty fog swept the streets. A crow circled the buildings above, the wind carrying its caws.

The bar chatter echoed through the night as intoxicated folk made their way home.

Beau wore a grey peacoat and black boots. His dark hair was slicked back messily underneath his hat. He enjoyed walking in the night, when the noise dwindled and his surroundings were empty.

Earth was nothing like he expected. He had seen the wars, the sins and the people like no other. At first, Beau had a hard time adjusting. *How are mortals so vile?* He used to say. But the beauty of Earth was unmatched. The scenery, the personalities, the women...

Beau turned around quickly, sensing a presence.

A lady dressed in red held a blue umbrella. Beau was astonished by her beauty. She was tall and lean with flowing black hair. Her long dress was covered by a red shawl paired with matching cherry lipstick.

"Two people can walk in the same direction, can they not?" she smiled. Her pearly white teeth illuminated the darkness. She had the most crisp English accent.

Beau snapped out of his trance and shook his head. "Of course, m'lady." Beau extended a hand out in front of him.

Her heels clicked against the cobblestone walkway as she passed Beau with a smirk.

"What is a fine woman like you doing out so late at night?" Beau asked, matching her pace.

"I could ask the same about you." She joked, slyly.

Beau beamed from ear. "Deary, I can assure you I am no woman."

"I would have never guessed." She responded. A dimple indented her cheek.

A dark cork tree stood shaded in the distance; small mushrooms lined the path they walked along. Beau had never seen so many mushrooms of a peculiar size before, and with his lack of coins, plucking a few for a free stew wouldn't hurt...

"Unless you wish for death, I wouldn't dare touch those." The woman giggled, facing ahead.

"Oh? And why not?"

She stopped and turned around, lifting the corner of her lips to a smile. "A death cap mushroom rarely shows mercy."

Death cap... That was enough for Beau to shelve his intrigue and move away from the fungi.

He watched the mysterious woman, trudging forward slowly. *What a vision...* Beau thought. *Educated and alluring.* The lady walked with grace, her head held high. Beau was astonished. *I have never seen anyone more beautiful.*

"Well?" she turned back to him. "Are you not going to walk me home?"

Beau grinned excitedly, following after her like a stray puppy. They talked and laughed the whole way. Even though the night was gloomy, Beau radiated with happiness.

They stopped at a small stone building beside a brewery, plastered with ivy vines. "This is me." The lady said.

Beau's smile fell into a pout. He only talked to her for under half an hour, but he felt like he'd known her for eternity. "The night is still young." Beau added, blushing.

The lady scrunched her face and chuckled. "I have an early morning, but I had a very nice time with you…"

"Beau."

She smiled, folding her umbrella. Her brown eyes twinkled even in the night. "Beau."

Beau felt giddy inside. Butterflies danced and twirled in his stomach and he couldn't hold back his growing infatuation. "May I see you again? I must."

The lady turned around, placing a hand on her hip. "You really want to?"

Beau nodded several times. "I will wait all night in the rain just to hear you say yes, my lady."

She tilted her head back and laughed, placing her hand over her mouth. "Yes, yes."

"I'll be here at seven tomorrow night. Wear something pretty." Beau turned to walk away, but quickly ran back up the stairs before she shut the door. "I didn't catch your name."

The lady leaned her head against the doorframe and shook her head with a smile. "Rosanna Hiver."

VENICE, ITALY, 1925

Beau and Rosanna spent a year together travelling all of Europe. Halfway through their endeavours, Rosanna dropped a bomb on Beau that was difficult to process.

"You're a... a *demon*." Beau stuttered. He couldn't believe the woman he fell for sprouted from an evil seed on Lucifer's behest.

Rosanna placed her hands on Beau's cheeks. "I *was* a roam. I was Beau, before I met you."

Beau drew away quickly with disgust. "How could you never tell me this? Why now, Rosy? When I've fallen for you?"

Tears welled in her eyes. "I was ashamed. When you told me you were an angel I thought, how could I ever tell the purest of hearts that I am the opposite. How could I have done that to you?"

"You've just done that to me, Rosy!" Beau yelled. His chest huffed up and down as he stared into her eyes. "Was this all planned, then? The crow I heard that night, that was you was it not?"

Before Beau met Rosanna, Lucifer granted her the ability to turn into a crow and circle above the taverns of bustling crowds. These demons were called roams. He tasked her to seduce married mortals, in which she'd spend the night and steal their rings as a token of infidelity. Lucifer then waited for those humans to die and fall to hell, where he'd hand them back their ring to wear for all eternity. *Guilt is a new form of punishment,* Lucifer would say.

Rosanna began to sob. "You were never an option of prey, my love... you stole my heart."

Beau's eyes grew wide. He hadn't realized Rosanna reciprocated the feelings that he had felt... the love.

He walked up to her and cupped her face, wiping the tears away from her cheeks. "You love me?" he asked.

She gently nodded, placing her hand against his. "More than I ever thought I was capable of."

He lowered his lips to hers, kissing slowly then passionately. He pushed her up against the small bungalow wall they had been staying at. She let out a soft moan as he made his way down her neck, exploring various parts of her skin. He showered her with adoration, using only his fingers.

Moonlight poured through the window as they made love, reflecting the colour of Beau's white scars fading one shade darker...

"You'd look absolutely dashing in that one, Beau." Rosanna pointed to a mannequin dressed in a grey-maroon ensemble.

They walked the streets of Italy at noon, hunting for outfits to wear for the Summer's Eve masquerade ball.

Beau squeezed her hand with a smile, flipping down his hat to passerby. "If you like it, I like it."

Rosanna spotted an old antique jewellers with a sign reading:

FREE CUSTOMIZATIONS

She pepped up and pushed him towards the men's tailors they had passed earlier. "You go and get your suit. I'll meet you there."

Beau smiled and kissed her forehead. "What has gotten you so chipper?"

She smirked and pushed him again. "Go on, go on!"

Beau obeyed and turned around to look at her every chance he got until he reached the tailors. The suit he had his eyes on held a hefty price tag which worried Beau. He wanted to look good for her and it was evident that she fancied that specific ensemble.

"Are there any discounts, good sir?" Beau asked the shop owner.

"Sure." He smiled, smoking a cigar. "One lira off."

Beau winced at his sarcasm, checking the price tag again. He paced around for a few minutes but always returned to the first mannequin.

The shop manager walked towards him with a hand over his protruding stomach. "Lad, I would try the shop down the road. It's called the dumpster, great assortment of fine rags." He spat.

A dark urge came over Beau that he never felt before. He tugged the man by the collar and lifted him up. The veins in his arms bulged as he stared into the man's eyes, using his grace to compel him.

The shop owner walked over to the mannequin and ripped off the tag of the suit. In a trance, he handed over the ensemble to Beau. "Free, sir."

Without realizing what he'd done, Beau panicked and stumbled backwards, taking the suit in hand and running out the door.

Rosanna was just approaching the shop when Beau bumped into her. "Oh, I'm so sorry my love."

Her eyes twinkled. "You got the suit!"

Beau nervously fixed his shirt, clearing his throat. "Oh, yes – yes, I did. For you." He eyed the shop owner who still looked to be in a state of reverie, staring into nothing. "Let's get you a dress, shall we?"

"Well, all right." Rosanna smiled, hooking her arm around Beau's.

As they walked off, Beau took one last glance at the tailors and scratched at the discomfort in his back. *What pains me...*

Rosanna and Beau walked hand in hand into a mansion fit for royalty. Crystal chandeliers hung from the ceilings while the diamond imperial staircases twinkled in the light. The Summer's Eve masquerade ball was always hosted by various different princes and lords who passed through Venice.

Everywhere they turned, a beautiful man or woman was dressed in exquisite attire sewn by elite seamstresses. Rosanna wore a silk silver gown paired with a black feathered mask. Her hair was curled into an updo and Beau was taken by her beauty once again.

"You're the most beautiful woman in the room." Beau smiled, leading her to a waltz.

She smirked. "Because every woman in here is disguised."

Beau pulled her closer. He wore a burgundy vest with matching suspenders, covered by a grey suit. His dark hair was combed backwards neatly.

"Even without a mask, no woman will ever compare to you."

They danced and danced all night, relishing in the love they found with each other. Beau thought to have finally discovered happiness. While he fell from Heaven for the mission of Sophie Brixton, she was decades away from being born. Along his journey, he found his soulmate. *I care not that she is a demon, she has my heart. She loves me back. She is my home.*

Ten minutes before midnight, Rosanna pulled Beau away from the horde of people. She grinned and kissed him gently. "I have a present for you."

Beau smiled, leaning in. "Rosy..."

She fumbled with her glittered clutch, pulling out two rings, one silver and one gold. Rosanna slid the silver one onto his finger and squealed. "It fits!" she exclaimed.

"What is this for, Rosy?" Beau questioned, chuckling at her excitement.

Rosanna placed the silver ring in his hand and wrapped his fingers closed. "Meet me at the east-wing balcony at midnight." And ran off.

The Gates of Gabriel | 268

Beau's smile lines sank deeply into his cheeks. He took out the ring from his palm and examined it closely. It was a crude metal with a cursive engravement on the inside: R. *R... for Rosanna.*

He shook his head and looked down, slipping the ring onto his fourth finger. *This is it. A promise ring, to solidify our love.* He was eager to see what she had in store for him at midnight, so he made his way to the balcony early.

Beau pushed through crowds of people, mapping his way to the east-wing. The mansion was immense, a maze of beauty. There were plenty of open drawing rooms, several refreshment carts, and a stretch of people for as far as the eye could see. After climbing two staircases, he found the double door exit to the balcony.

The air was still, crisp and cool. Stars sparkled in the night sky, waving at Beau with ivory light. The midnight bell chimed, echoing through the estate. Beau searched the perimeter of the balcony, expecting Rosanna to be there. Though, there was not a soul in sight. He glanced around curiously, wondering if he had gone the right way. *Hm, my mistake.*

As he was leaving, a shiny fabric twinkled in his peripheral vision. As he came closer, an unpleasant, apprehensive feeling engulfed his senses. But what Beau discovered was far from what he expected.

What Beau found left his heart shattered in pieces.

A piece of silver cloth from Rosanna's dress sat perfectly on the ledge of the balcony, caught on a rusted nail. Written in black ink, it said:

Dearest Beau,

> *A roam roams and settles not. Demons know no love but pain. As men I've seen have feared me not, an angel grieves the loss in vain. I know no love, for you no less, a trick is what I see. As easy as the sun will set, you are no love to me.*

> *Rosanna*

Beau trembled, sinking to his knees in agony. The distant tick of a clock was all he allowed himself to hear, while time slowed down around him. Soon after he read the words, the chatter of crowds below grew distant, drowning into the wind. His ears rang loudly, imagining the sweet sound of her voice as she crumbled his heart. He re-read the words over and over again, pleading to the skies above to leave Earth behind. He tore the cloth in half and threw it over the balcony, enraged at the vulnerability he'd shown Rosanna. Uncontrollable tears streamed down his face as he slid the ring off his finger and buried it into the depths of his pocket. A burning wrath deluged his senses, taking full control of his core. His back burned like fire as he sank to his knees.

If only you had stayed, so I could write you a letter of my own. If only you had remained, so I could kiss your treacherous lips one last time. If only you were not a demon, maybe you would have loved me righteously. If only you hadn't broken my heart... I would believe that love exists. I vow to the angels and thrones that once my mission is fulfilled, I will return home. I will flee as far away from our memories as my grace can take me. I swear to you Rosanna... No piece of this world, the next, or the afterlife will ever break me again.

Chapter 34

PINESTONE, PRESENT NIGHT

"*T*ommy's on his way." I said to Beau, biting anxiously at my fingernail.

After gathering a few of my things in a backpack, Beau brought us to one of his 'escape cabins' a half hour out from Kleaton's Gate. I chose not to talk about the moment we'd shared in my kitchen, when Beau *kissed* me. The moment came and went, and no words were exchanged after it happened. Did I want to talk about it? Absolutely. Did he? *Doubt it.* So instead, I buried my trifling thoughts and posed another question.

"What exactly is an escape cabin?" I'd asked him before we left.

"A place I go when I want to be alone." He had responded.

My features shrunk in bewilderment. "But... aren't you always alone?"

"Huh, you're right. Weird how I can't get enough of myself, isn't it?" He jested.

After our conversation, we got to work on ensuring the security of everyone involved. I told him I wasn't going anywhere until I knew all of my friends and family were safe, and I meant that. Beau used his grace to compel my dad into staying at a hotel for a few days while I was gone, and sealed the door shut with holy fire. As much as it pained me to see my dad helpless and unaware, I couldn't risk his safety. If Marina went after Braum and his father, I didn't want to find out who'd be next. Not only that, Siles was still out there just waiting to pounce.

"Is Mags still asleep?" I asked, pacing around the living room.

The cabin was all brick and mahogany wood. A fireplace sat in the corner, accompanied by a vintage green sofa and a coffee table. A small kitchen was positioned towards the back, beside the sole bedroom.

The bed squeaked loudly from behind the bedroom door, followed by a shrill scream.

"Don't think so," Beau responded.

"Stay here, I got this."

He put his hands up and chuckled. "I'm glad, because I don't."

I made my way to the bedroom and turned the doorknob, locking it behind me.

Mags was on the bed with her knees up. She rocked back and forth, fixing her tousled hair.

"Maya, what - where am I? Is Beau here? Am I still drugged?" she freaked, flailing her arms in the air. "Let me out, this is crazy!"

Oh, how I missed sleeping Mags.

I took in a deep breath. "You were never drugged Mags." *But you tried to poison me, funny. Remember that? Okay Maya, don't start.*

She sunk to the edge of the bed, sobbing. "It can't be real... angels, demons. You, you're some kind of - some kind of..."

She trailed off, burying her face in her hands. It was hard to watch my best friend so disoriented, so confused. But if anyone knew what she was going through, it was me. Beau was an angel, he'd always been an angel. My whole life I've been, well, Maya Brixton. An ordinary girl who lived in small town Kleaton's Gate... until I met Beau. Now, I'm something sacred, something *divine*. And worst of all, I had to believe that. *It just doesn't seem real.*

I leaned back on the wall, looking down. "It's hard for me too, Mags."

She kept silent, rubbing her snotty nose.

"Whether you believe me or not, something bigger than both of us is happening and I need you safe."

A knock on the door startled me. Beau spoke from the other side. "Tommy's here."

I swallowed hard and approached Mags, grabbing hold of her hand. "Do you trust me?"

A long exhale. "As long as you don't put another magical feather in my face." Mags chuckled through congested tears.

There she is.

"I won't, if you promise that you won't try and poison me again." I knew she had no idea what I was talking about, and it made me giggle.

She paled. "I... *What?*"

Ha-ha, oh Mags. She almost killed me and had no idea. This will be quite the story to tell over a few glasses of wine.

"I'll explain later." I smiled and let her go. "Stay put for a minute, I'll be back."

Tommy stood in the doorway dressed in all black, his hair untidy and greased with sweat, shaking incessantly. He had a blank face, mumbling a cast of words to himself.

All of the calmness I'd felt talking to Mags was long gone. My heart beat an octave higher, rattling in my chest. I approached him tentatively, eyeing his erratic movements. "Tommy?"

"*Ky's dead. Ky is dead... Ky's dead.*" He repeated, over and over.

A sharp pain lodged itself in my chest.

No. No... No.

I didn't want to believe it, I *couldn't* believe it. Ky... Ky Gerber. I've – I've known him for years. We made memories together, we went camping, we shared the same love for cream puffs and blueberry

waffles , we – we... *He can't be. He can't be gone.*
He's not gone.

I froze, swallowing down the barbed wire
strangling my esophagus. My heartbeat was turbulent,
I couldn't hold a breath.

Beau rushed to pull him inside, locking the
front door of the cabin.

"What... did you say?" I asked in an
overwhelming state of shock, hoping it was a joke.
But every part of me told me it wasn't. Every part of
me knew.

"I – I was almost here, I was driving... Ky's
mom called me and said she found him dead in his
room. Suicide... *suicide.*" He shook his head,
trembling. "Suicide! *A fucking suicide!*" He sobbed,
slamming the floor underneath him. "What
happened to my fucking life!"

Beau's eyes found mine, dark and dim. He
looked to me with worry, empathy. But I looked
through him, envisioning Ky. *Whoever did this, Siles,*
Marina, I swear to –

A creek interrupted my thoughts. Mags
walked out of the bedroom slowly, creeping up
behind me.

I couldn't say the words.

"What's going on? *Tommy?*" she questioned,
moving towards him. "What about Ky?"

Tommy buried his face in his hands. "He's
fucking dead! Mike's dead, Ky is dead, fuck for all I
know Braum's dead too!"

A piercing whine escaped Mags' throat as she
fell against the wall, running her fingers through her

hair. She crawled over to Tommy and hugged him, sobbing into his arms.

The world around me was no longer mine. I didn't know how to react. Time was measured, slow and deliberate. Every second that ticked by was worse than the last. *Tick-tock, tick-tock.*

My throat was hoarse, scratchy. I wanted to speak, I wanted to say something to make it all go away. But what was left to say? Ky... Ky was gone. *How the hell did it come to this? What do I have to do? What the hell do I do! How do I stop this?*

Beau shot me a look of urgency and quickly pulled my arm. "Maya... Maya, look at me." He cupped my face in his hands, rubbing my cheekbones with his thumbs.

I didn't look at him, I couldn't. I stared at Tommy and Mags sulking on the ground, tempted to join them.

I was encapsulated by guilt, like somehow everything was my fault. I was the Puritas, my mother died for me to win a holy war. Beau was an angel, demons killed people I cared about. They wanted me, not them. I was the problem. *I am the problem.*

"You are not the problem, stop that!" Beau held me in place, pleading for my attention.

When my eyes found his, he leaned his forehead against mine. "We have to go, okay? I'll seal this door; no one, not even a demon can penetrate it. Maya," he wiped the tears from my cheek. "You drink from that chalice, you absorb the grace God gave you when you were born. You're untouchable and Lucifer has no choice but to call back his demons."

Everything in me wanted to give up, to give in to the demons and let them take me. Anything to save my friends, my family. It was clear now they would hurt anyone in their path just to get to me.

"Ky didn't commit suicide." I muttered. My lips were dry.

Beau clenched his jaw. "Considering recent events, I'd think that highly unlikely."

I shut my eyes, forcing all the water out. *Be brave Maya. Your mother didn't die for nothing. You are who you are, you've seen it with your own two eyes. You can't escape this life, you have to embrace it. For your sake and for everyone else's, you are more powerful than you know.*

I moved away from Beau's touch and knelt down to Mags and Tommy. "No one else is going to die." I embraced both of them. "Stay here and wait for me to come back. I have to make things right."

I didn't give them time to respond. I signalled for Beau and exited the cabin, making my way for the car. Beau shortly followed, placing his hand against the entrance. A vibrant white hue radiated from beneath his palm, outlining the doorframe in ivory stardust. He knelt on the ground, mumbling a few words to himself. In a flash, the entire perimeter of the house lit up in crystalline beams and receded into the ground beneath it.

He jogged to the car and shut the door, starting the ignition. I took one last glance at the cabin before we pulled out of the driveway, releasing my final tear. *I'm going to make things right.*

"Let's go to Port Hope." I said.

Chapter 35

HELL

Siles awoke in a caged, dark room. In the distance, he could make out blue-fire torches lining the cave walls. His weak muscles ached with intense pain and his stomach, an empty pit. The whole of his chest was crusted with dried blood from Lucifer's carving.

"*Auxilium!*" Siles yelled for aid, coughing out blood clots. When his swollen eyes finally came to, he quickly realized that he wasn't on Earth... but hell.

The faint echo of snickering demons loomed over Siles, followed by loud cries of lost souls, trapped in the stone.

Siles slumped back down, leaning against the cold bars with stinging discomfort. "*I am... a coward.*"

His mind wandered to Mags, and if Marina got to her. *She would kill Mags before Maya, just because of me...* Siles thought. It blew his mind how he ended up in the exact position he'd spent the last century running away from. Just a few months ago, he had been a warrior in Lucifer's army, training for the fight against the enemy. But now, Siles was uncertain of who the true enemy really was.

"*Are you afraid of pain?*" An indistinct voice asked in the darkness.

Siles scampered away from the cage bars, startled. "Who's there?" He saw no one.

"Cowards are afraid of pain." The voice spoke again. "From what I see, you are no coward."

Across from him, a glint of metal gleamed in the darkness. The soft, clanging sound of rusty bars echoed through the cave. Siles narrowed his eyes, making out a shaded face in the dim light of the torches. She was a woman, he gathered that from her long hair. But that's all he could see.

"Lucifer will never pity you, and the ones that will are locked up, like you and I." Her voice was clearer now. She had a distinct accent.

A small orange light beamed from within her cell, radiating a glowing yellow hue.

The ones that will are locked up, like you and I. "There... there are *more?*" Siles questioned.

"Many. I have seen the guards drag down demons like dogs, because they rebelled against Lucifer's tactics." Her tone was raspy and strained, as if she hadn't used her voice in decades.

Siles had never seen this part of hell before. He was used to the glamour, the enriching vices that Lucifer allowed him to see. He spent his days in comforted rooms, surrounded by luscious embers and glittering shadows. The depths of hell – these parts were foreign, unknown... *frightening.*

"How long have you been down here?" Siles asked, concerned.

No response.

He leaned against the cold bars once again, extending his legs. His back ached with twisting pain in any way he tried to sit. "Well, since we're partners in this prison, why don't you tell me how you ended up here?"

For a few moments, only the soft sound of crackling fire was heard.

Then, her faint voice. "*Love.*"

Siles clenched his jaw, squeezing his fingers into a fist. *Love is an incurable venom... hatred is the salvation of humanity.* Lucifer trained the fallen to dismiss the thought of humanness, kindness, love or light. He said that knowing tenderness would release the dragons of hell, the worst eternal punishment and the gravest violation of any kind. And yet, Earth dismissed all of Lucifer's teachings. Siles found life again, a life untouched by fire and flame – a life he wanted to live. Mags made him feel something; the importance of humanity. Right and wrong, a conscience that Lucifer forbade.

Siles cleared his throat, pushing away the past he could never return to. "Lucifer tasked me to Earth, to eradicate a mortal." He mocked Lucifer. "*My father is making a fool out of me... Her and her angel companion must be stopped.*" He laughed, shaking his head. "You know, I –"

"Her what?" The woman's voice interrupted, sharply. "Who is this angel?"

Siles scrunched his eyebrows. "Why?"

"The name!" she yelled, desperate.

"B – Beau." He responded, aghast.

Silence.

Siles hadn't heard anything for a while. He tried calling out, over and over again, but she never responded. It was as if she was never there, a hallucination of Siles' diminishing psyche. The sound of crackling fire filled the air for hours, until suddenly, the yellow hue from across his cell rolled under his bars.

Siles picked up the orange crystal and held it in his hands. He examined it thoroughly, gazing at the dancing black lines encased inside of it.

"What is this?" Siles asked, twirling it in his fingers.

The woman held her face against the bars, shaded by the dark atmosphere. "When Lucifer caged me, I bottled my remaining power into this crystal from Earth. Consume it, and you will turn into a crow. Fly to the portal and fulfill what needs to be done."

Siles' heart pounded against his chest. *Could this be? Could I really return to Earth?* Siles fought with his head and his heart. He didn't know this demon, and she knew nothing of him. *This could be a trick.* But for some reason, he didn't feel like this was the case. He felt like he could trust her. *What do I have to lose? I'm spending eternity in here anyways.*

"If this is true, why haven't you consumed it?" Siles asked, doubtfully.

A stressed breath. "I have no reason to return to Earth," the woman whispered, a tinge of sadness in her voice.

Siles squeezed his eyes shut and prepared for the worst possible outcome. *A crow*, he thought. *Roams are ancient demons. Who are you...*

With tentative movements, he held the crystal to his mouth and swallowed hard. A sizzling bubble formed in his stomach, burning his chest. Siles screamed in anguish as his fingers popped out of his sockets, morphing into black claws. *This isn't a trick! I'm going to Earth!*

In between sore breaths, Siles huffed, "I promise to get you out of here once I get back." He shouted in pain, attempting to level his breathing. "What is... your name, demon – What is it?"

The woman snickered softly, fading back into the shadows of her cage. "*Rosanna.*"

Chapter 36

BEECH COUNTY, 24 HOURS

*P*ort Hope was under a day's drive down a plain, yet scenic highway. There was nothing but distant mountains and fog, though every so often a glimmer of sun peaked through the clouds. Beau and I had been on the road for almost eight hours, taking turns at the wheel. Given the circumstances, I couldn't think of someone better to have shared a car with. *Not that I had much of a choice.*

"Isn't this fun?" Beau bantered, nudging my arm playfully. "You've got me all to yourself."

I rolled my eyes, holding in a laugh. "Huh, you think I would've gotten used to it by now." I kept my gaze forward, but I knew he was smiling.

"Come on, ask me questions." Beau gave me a genial shove.

"Questions?" I laughed, thinking about the vast list of things I've wanted to know since I met Beau. "Do you have all of eternity?"

A small smirk. "Technically, yes."

Funny. "What does Heaven look like?"

"Boring, next question."

My eyebrows raised in surprise, my mouth twitching to a jested grin. "You can't do that! Heaven must be a beautiful place."

For a moment, Beau was silent, contemplating quietly. Then he licked his lips, and turned his gaze to me. "Heaven is home," he began. "And sometimes home isn't always a place."

I caught my breath. My cheeks were on fire. He turned his attention back to the road, one hand on the wheel and the other on the gear shift. *Sometimes home isn't always a place...*

Before I could respond, he poked my thigh and released, "Next question."

After a while, my tongue was dry and my lips crusted with dried saliva. It was half past noon and my stomach yearned for a meal.

"We have to pull over, I might die of starvation." I groaned, wrapping my arms around my middle.

Beau laughed, laying his palm flat against the steering wheel. "I was waiting for you to say that."

He took the next exit off to Beech County, pulling into the first diner we saw. There were two people sitting at the bar drinking coffee and four tables occupied by small families and couples. The air carried the scent of bacon and eggs which my stomach growled at.

"Anywhere you'd like." The kind waitress said upon entry.

We sat down next to an old jukebox that's sole purpose looked to be collecting dust. Beau chuckled, scanning the menu. "Haven't seen that in ages."

I never took into account how old Beau really was. He'd been on Earth for so long, it puzzled me how he still enjoyed it. "When did you fall?" I asked.

"What?"

"From Heaven."

Beau smiled without taking his eyes off the menu, clicking his tongue. "Never ask a man's age."

Flashbacks to one of our very first conversations came to mind. "So you aren't twenty-two?" I smirked.

He held his hand to his heart, jokingly offended. "I believe that I look twenty-two, therefore, I am."

I chuckled, staring at the pixelated image of a clubhouse sandwich. *That would be so good right now.* My mouth could have practically devoured the picture right then and there. My stomach rumbled loudly as I finalized my decision, rubbing my middle. *I think we're in agreement.*

"No really," I pried. "How many lifetimes have you lived? Three thousand?"

"Fuck, feels like it." He laced his fingers together, planting them on the table. "I fell in 1842, so if you do the math then I'm –"

"Old." I responded quickly, smirking.

He looked up at me, flashing his pearly smile. His grey eyes twinkled against the radiating sunlight. "Very old."

A young blonde woman wearing a high ponytail and a white checkered ensemble approached us, flipping open a notepad. *Finally.* "Hi there, my name's Layla, what can I get you both?" she asked, peppy.

No need to ask me twice. "Chicken clubhouse on rye please." I pushed the menu towards her and smiled.

She wrote it down quickly and turned to Beau, blushing. "Oh and um, for you, sir?" She batted her eyelashes.

Of course. I internally rolled my eyes. Every instance I've had with Beau had been like this. All women viewed him as some Greek god, insatiably desirable. I've counted at least five different occasions where I'd seen drool practically fall out of girls' mouths – and those were only the times I'd *noticed.*

It never bothered me... not really anyway. I never thought about what Beau and I were, never had time to. I thought about our kiss, how he barely brushed his lips against mine but the feeling lingered for days.

I felt stupid thinking about something so minor in comparison to everything else. It wasn't really a priority in my mind, it couldn't be, considering he and I never had a sense of normalcy since being together. And a kiss? Well, people kiss all the time...

I wanted to ask him about it, why he did it or how it made him feel but I guess it wasn't a priority on his mind either. Though now, for some reason, I wanted to bring it up. Maybe it was because our waitress was getting cheeky with him, or maybe, just maybe, I felt a twang of jealousy. But I wasn't about to give Beau the satisfaction of another girl fawning over him, when one was practically on her knees begging for a second of his attention.

The corner of Beau's lips upturned as he pointed to the Belgian waffles.

"Extra syrup on the side?" Layla asked, puckering her lips. "Tell you what, I'll give it to you for free."

She gathered our menus and walked away, looking back once before fleeing into the kitchen.

"*Extra syrup on the side...*" I mocked.

Beau's eyes lit up as he shrugged, laughing. "Oh shut up."

We walked out of the diner with full stomachs. Layla ended up writing her number down on the receipt, unaware that he was paying for both of us.

"I'm sorry," she gasped. "I didn't realize yous' were an item."

"We aren't."

"We are." Beau countered.

I blushed, pressing my lips into a small smile.

The sun was at its peak, hitting mid-afternoon. I'd heard of Beech County as being one of the nicest spots for hiking trails, but it appeared to be much more than that. Trees encompassed the town, blossoming with different coloured leaves. The atmosphere smelt of lake water and evergreen. Shops were connected in a line downtown, and there were not many cars. In a town where everything seemed close-knit, there would be no reason to own a vehicle if everything was within walking distance.

"Do you remember what day you fell?" I asked, getting in the driver's seat.

Beau clicked his seatbelt and leaned forward. "Hard to forget."

"Okay, so... spill." I said curiously, taking a sip of my iced tea.

A huff. "Today, a hundred and seventy-eight years ago."

The tea caught my esophagus, burning as I forced it down my throat. I almost died. "Are you serious? And you never thought to tell me?"

He leaned back and stretched his arms. "Didn't think I needed to."

I stared into his grey eyes, searching for something. I didn't know what in that moment, but I couldn't look away. An idea buzzed in my brain, one that I could very well end up regretting later on, but *screw it*. I've always been quite impulsive, and having Mags around fuelled my fire. For whatever reason, though, amidst all the craziness that was going on, I felt like I could be.

We were hours away from Kleaton's Gate, all my friends and family were off the grid and there were no signs of Marina and Siles tracking us. I wanted one night, to not worry, to not feel *responsible...* to forget. Since Beau and I had met, we'd never done anything together but worry. There were so many secrets, so much pain, everything but happiness. I stared at him with wide eyes, this man, *angel*, that despite all the tribulations we endured, made me happy.

My body took control of my senses and without thinking, I started the ignition and made my way for the town square.

"Where – Maya, where are we going? The exit's that way?" He pointed out the window.

I stopped at the traffic light and turned to face him. "You fell from Heaven on this day well over a century ago. Technically, it's your birthday."

Beau laughed hesitantly. "I guess?"
He must have read my mind because the sheepish smile that he wore now faded into a downturned frown. "No, Maya, we don't have time for this."

I waved him off. "Beau I know it seems –"

"Reckless? Unnecessary? Idiotic?" he contested.

I let out a sigh of exasperation, determined to get my way. "You're confident your grace can hold its protection?"

One thing I came to learn about Beau was his undeniable weakness to flattery. If his abilities ever came into question, he would stroke it with pride.

"Of course." He clapped back. *Right where I want him.*

"The first place Siles and Marina would think to look for us is with Mags, especially since she just got out of his control. If your grace is impenetrable, they won't be able to get in. Mags can make them believe we're inside the cabin, meanwhile we're here. Hours away from them." I proposed, fidgeting with my fingers.

Silence. I took it as my permission to continue.

"They would never suspect I would leave my best friend, my dad, anyone I cared about just out in the open. Beau, I'm saying we have time."

I decide against speaking anything further, allowing him to process my suggestion.

I understood how it sounded, and truthfully, it was more concerning to myself than anyone else. I was afraid, I was terrified. When the time comes to drink from that chalice, who would I become? Would I die and reincarnate into a spirit, able to walk the afterlife? Would I see my mom again? *I can't handle this anymore. I want to be normal, I want to be Maya Brixton again. The ordinary, nineteen-year-old girl who no one really knows. The girl who drinks pear smoothies and reads books all day. I'm still so young*

– I want to dance, and travel and move far away with Mags to the school of my dreams. I want a good job, a safe job. And I want to live a long, happy, healthy life and die in my sleep, only to meet my mom again when the time comes.

But no.

My life, as it turns out, was nothing short of a disaster. I've entered the gates of Beau Gabriel, and I am locked in for eternity.

Beau cleared his throat, breaking the silence. "What is this really about, Maya?"

I exhaled. "I just think we should take some time to relax. We've been driving for hours and –"

"Don't lie to me," he released, his stare undefiable.

Tears welled in my waterline. I knew Beau could read my thoughts, but he wanted me to say it out loud. He wanted me to be honest with him. He wanted my vulnerability.

"I'm so tired of everything, Beau." My chin quivered, attempting to keep the sadness at bay. "Braum's dad is dead, Ky is dead, everything – all of it, my life, everyone's lives... Everything is just so messed up now."

Tears glossed my vision, blurring my sight. *I can't drive like this.* I pulled over to the side of the road, parking on the gravel pavement.

I turned to Beau, his expression unreadable.

"I was so normal before I met you." I chewed on my lip, looking down at my fingers. "I had a good plan, a *normal* plan. School, work... Maybe one day, I would have owned a dog." I shook my head, chuckling flatly. "And now, people are dying, demons are tormenting everyone in my life... because of me."

Beau opened his mouth to protest but I couldn't bear any more words of comfort. All I heard were the soft sobs escaping my throat.

"My mom's life got taken, because of me."

Beau unbuckled his seatbelt, drawing me into his arms. We sat for a while, his warmth protecting me from the intrusive thoughts and grim feelings.

I was never much of a crier, up until now. I felt like crying was the only thing I knew how to do. The last thing I wanted was a pity party. There were people who had it much worse, I knew that. Hell, Beau lived on Earth for so long – no wonder his skin was impenetrable.

But me, I – I was unprepared, for all of it. I got thrown into this mess of a life, and I wanted to hate Beau for it. Everything went wrong when he came into the picture. *Stop this, Maya. This wasn't his doing.*

I knew that. I knew it wasn't Beau's fault, none of it was. He didn't ask this of me, a higher power did. For whatever reason, my mom had to die so I could live. For whatever reason, I was the key to something bigger than any of us could've imagined. *But I don't want to imagine it. Not right now, not tonight.*

Beau released me gently, wiping the tears from my cheeks. "What did you have in mind?"

I sniffled. "What?"

"My birthday," he smiled softly. "Cake? Balloons?"

I laughed, rubbing my puffy eyes. "Seriously? You're okay with it?"

"You're the party planner." He reached over the gear shift and turned the car keys, starting the ignition. "I can wear a blindfold if you don't want me to see your surprises."

I swatted his arm and bit my lip, beaming from ear to ear. Beau nudged his head forward and I pulled onto the street.

Nerves of excitement took over my entire being, dissipating all feelings of pain and strife. I pushed my foot on the gas and continued to the destination of normalcy. I knew what tomorrow would bring – I would be in Port Hope, accepting my destiny as the key to stopping a holy war. But if something were to go wrong tomorrow, I would deal with it tomorrow, as the *Puritas*. What I did have was this moment, alone with Beau, on what could be my last day of being *Maya Brixton*.

I glanced once more at Beau and smiled ahead, throwing any sign of painful irrationality out of my mind. "Happy birthday, Beau."

Chapter 37

PINESTONE, 22 HOURS

Mags paced around the room, twirling her hair nervously. She didn't know if she believed everything she'd seen over the last few hours, but the only choice she really had was to accept the unbelievable.

"Why the fuck won't you open!" Tommy yelled, violently fiddling with the doorknob. He eventually gave up and paced around the room, holding his hands above his head. "What the fuck are we doing here, Mags?"

Yet another question Mags didn't have the answer to. Despite the confusion, the haziness and the secrets, Mags was confident in one thing: she trusted Maya. For the last little while of her life, Mags couldn't recount a single thing that happened, other than the cellar. Though, one thing she was positively certain about was that panicking was going to get them killed.

"Just leave it, Tommy." Mags said, slumping down against the wall.

"How are you so calm right now?" Tommy raged. "Ky is dead, Mike is dead, Maya and... whoever the *fuck* kidnapped us and –"

"Just shut up, Tommy! Jesus!" Mags snapped.

Every single thought in Mags' head pounced in her brain, banging against her skull. Within the past twenty-four hours, she discovered that her supposed hookup was a demon, Beau was an angel and Maya was some saviour of the holy war. *My best friend... has power. Beau... is an angel, with wings and Siles... he's a – he's a demon from hell. Siles... Parts of me cared for Siles... but all this time, he wanted me dead. He wants me –*

In the corner of her eye, Mags noticed a red hue illuminating the crack underneath the door. She scrunched her eyebrows and quickly placed a finger over her lip, directing Tommy to stay quiet. Tommy moved back slowly as Mags approached the front entrance, tiptoeing carefully.

Bang! Bang! Bang! The door vibrated loudly, causing her to leap off the ground.

"I know you're in there!" a woman spat. A pit of nails scratched against Mags' insides. She recognized that voice, clear as day. "I can *smell* you."

Tommy began to shake. "Marina..." he uttered.

Marina... the girl from the cellar... with Siles.

Cold shivers constricted every fibre of Mags' being. She remembered how Marina took complete control over Braum, and the slow burn of her own free-will fleeing her body.

The wooden door began to melt into nothing, disintegrating to ash. There, Marina stood with fire blazing at her fingertips. "Finally." She smirked.

Mags grabbed hold of Tommy's hand, closing her eyes. She didn't know what was going to happen, what ways Marina would torture her. She thought about her family and if they would find her out here one day. Her dead body, rotting in the unknown. When it would come time to her funeral, her cause of death would read: Murdered by Demon. *I hope it doesn't hurt...*

But Marina couldn't enter.

She slammed at the opening repeatedly, while a white hue bubbled through the transparency of the door.

"What is this!" Marina snapped. She screamed throwing a ball of fire, but the white hue deflected her power.

Tommy gasped in shock. "Did she just..." Tommy choked. "Mags, was that –"

Only then did Mags accept the truth of everything. Beau had sealed the door with his grace, which is why Marina couldn't get in. *Beau really is an angel... She can't get in. Siles isn't here anymore. He can't control me. Everything is real, this is real. I am living in a world where demons walk the Earth, and one is standing right in front of me.*

A surge of power came over Mags, adrenaline filling her veins. She dusted off her knees and marched to the door, facing Marina through the impenetrable barrier.

Mags smiled, knowing there was nothing Marina could do. Marina's eyes turned blood red as black veins coiled around the perimeter of her face. She growled infuriatingly, banging her hand against the invisible shield.

"Careful Marina, your *demon* is showing." Mags taunted.

Marina huffed with anger. "You will lose. I will kill everyone you love! Starting with that useless Puritas!"

Mags wasn't very religious, even though her mom raised her to believe in a higher power. She was aware of the stories people told – Lucifer fell from Paradise, dragging down thrones of angels on his influence. There was always a separation in the world, the great divide of good and evil. Standing before her, a real demon, a monster that despite her power, could not control it.

Mags had faith in Maya and surprisingly... in Beau. Though she didn't really know Beau, Mags was always good at reading people. Now, did angels count as people? That was a mystery. But Mags saw how calculated Beau was. She didn't believe he would use his abilities for the wrong reasons. She saw his patience, his will to do good. There was something about Beau... A troubled past with redemption? And who grants redemption? Never the fallen. She knew that the good always triumphed the bad, even when it didn't seem that way.

I have faith...

Without hesitation, Mags reached through the door and grabbed Marina's shirt by the collar. She gripped the fabric and yanked her closer to the barrier. The grace scorched Marina's cheek, burning a black slab of lava into her skin.

She released the yelping Marina who stumbled back, holding her face with two hands.

Mags crossed her arms and scowled at the cowering demon who now seemed so helpless. "I'd like to see you try."

Chapter 38

BEECH COUNTY, 18 HOURS

I spent the late afternoon picking out an outfit for Beau along the strip of downtown Beech County. There were only a few vintage clothing shops, but I managed to make do with what I had. The sun had just set and I couldn't be bothered to spend all night plucking shirts from shelves when I had birthday plans for us. Beau dressed decently well, but rather plain. Mind you, it worked for him, but I would be lying if I said I didn't fantasize about him in a nice button up and some slacks that hugged the curve of his –

"Maya, room key please." Beau smirked, interrupting my thoughts.

Ah, yuck. I shook my head and blushed, rummaging through my purse for the stupid card.

Beau moved in front of me, leaning against our room door. His natural musk of pine and mint drowned my senses as he grabbed hold of my chin and lifted it to face him. "If you want, I can show you those curves right now."

Oh my God... I keep forgetting he can read my thoughts. I shoved past him, concealing the small smile that crept on my face.

I checked us in to the first hotel that was within walking distance of the two pubs in the area. We had made a quick pit stop to the liquor store before entering the building – God knows how expensive purchasing drinks was at the bar. I hadn't ever seen Beau drunk, but from what I remember of his impressive Whisky collection, he was no stranger to alcohol.

"You know Maya, I watched you run in front of a car when you were eight because you wanted to see if the driver would stop," he began, closing the door behind us. "I've seen you jump over a firepit to prove that you wouldn't burn to death, and yet, this still may be the dumbest idea you've ever had." He laughed, plopping down onto the double bed.

I always forgot that Beau had known me for so long, watching me from afar ever since I was born. I remember when he first told me that, it kept me up at night – realizing how old Beau really was and how well he truly knew me. And yet here I was, knowing only the parts he allowed himself to show me.

Beau had been around for almost two centuries... Who did he meet? What sins has he committed that turned his scars black? What places has he visited? What girls has he... *Never mind.*

I cleared my throat, shrugging my shoulders. "A dumb idea is better than no idea at all." I heard my dad's lackluster advice prod its way into my brain. *I'm too young to be that old.*

I set my backpack down, examining my surroundings. The room was quite small, but cozy. There was a standard bathroom, a wall mounted TV, a floor length mirror and a closet all encased by periwinkle walls.

I walked over to the window which overlooked a lake, encompassed by willow trees and boat docks. When my mom was still alive, my dad would drive us to our family cottage in Springs County, about two hours out of Kleaton's Gate. I would sit by the window, much like this one, with my mom at my side and watch the loons swim by. She used to tell me about her childhood then, how much she loved the water. *How much she loved me.*

"You know," Beau approached, positioning himself next to me. "I would capture the moon if I could."

I glanced up at him in bewilderment. "What?" I chuckled softly. "What do you mean?"

He kept his eyes forward, staring at the moonlight illuminating the calm waters. "Before the fall, Lucifer fought with God, arguing about power and control – just completely senseless. But God didn't give up on him, didn't *want* to. So, He gave Lucifer the opportunity to prove himself, to prove that he could control such a great deal of power and grace without fault."

I watched him without saying a word. This was the first time I'd seen Beau talk about his home, his history... about *Heaven.*

"God granted Lucifer the power of the moon. It signified that even through the darkness, there would always be light."

I shook my head, lost for words. "Wait... So, Lucifer controls the moon?"

"In theory."

"But – he fell? Why didn't God take that away from him? He's horrible."

Beau turned to me, his eyes glossed with a silver sheen. "God can't take away anything that He's given. That's why you're important."

My mouth dried, thinking about me, the *Puritas*, and whatever power I held that God bestowed upon me. I didn't understand it; the grace I possessed that could give me the ability to fulfill such a task – whatever this task entailed. *But I have to do it, for my mom, for everyone.*

"Because... Because I can lift condemned souls, *somehow.*"

He nodded, turning to face the window again. "Somehow."

Beau was silent for a few moments, half of his face shaded by the shadows of the cornered darkness. Then, he took in a tired breath and relaxed.

"We can't see the moon from Heaven, only the sun. God is the sun, the light – Lucifer is the moon." He faced me, tension slicing the space between our breaths. "A shining star among a sea of devils."

I kept my jaw tight, staring at the evident torment in his eyes. I'd never seen Beau so vulnerable before, so bare and exposed. He'd never shown this side of himself to me, *ever*.

He glanced one last time at the moon and leaned his back against the window. "I'd capture the moon just to see it shine in Heaven. I don't understand how something so bright can be in possession of something so dark."

I tempered my breaths as best as I could, my heart hammering in my chest. "This is the first time you talked about your past."

"You never really asked." His stature was still and composed.

"Is it weird that I'm afraid to?"

He lifted an eyebrow and chuckled softly. "It'd be weird if you *weren't* afraid."

I faced him with intent, and he mirrored my movements. "Do you ever get lonely? You've lived on Earth for so long and you're always... alone." I questioned, regretting it almost instantly. "I – I don't mean that in a bad way, I think it's good to be alone sometimes. I just... You went from being surrounded by angels all the time, to being the sole angel to walk the Earth."

"You're right."

"Do you have any friends?"

A light laugh. "I've made a few." He turned his gaze back to the view outside our window. "I never did well with attachments."

I figured that much. Beau had always been stand-offish, since the day I met him. He had a personality that welcomed you in, but at a distance. Everything he did, every move, every word was precise. He controlled his surroundings, never straying off the stream. But... what made him this way?

"Not everyone is going to hurt you, you know?" I contested. I don't know why I assumed that someone hurt him. I guess, to me, coldness sprouted from pain... and Beau had told me nothing of his.

He remained silent, his eyes fixated on mine.

"I mean," I spoke carefully. "At the end of the day, we all need someone. I'm sure not everyone will love you, but if you close yourself off, you're limiting your chances of finding something good."

"Maybe that's the point." His answer was abrupt and distant, even though he stood right next to me.

I had never seen Beau so stoic and unmoved, yet riling with emotion all at the same time. It was... *odd.* Sad? I didn't know what to make of it.

"Or maybe..." I swallowed, "You're just waiting for someone to fix the things someone broke in you."

His jaw twitched, his eyes zeroing into mine with painful intent. A flicker of sadness blanketed his vision – that, was evident.

"You're very wise." He wore a dark expression as he chuckled, brushing a loose strand of hair from my face. "*Observant.*"

My heart thumped in my chest. "Then why? Why don't you do attachments?"

He inhaled a deep breath, biting down on his bottom teeth. His eyes diverted to the window for a moment, then met mine with precision. "Because once you let someone in, you give them the power to break your heart."

I couldn't even find the words to respond before he moved back into the room and rummaged through the bags of clothing I purchased at the strip.

"I prefer to keep my heart intact," he spoke flatly, analyzing the new black button up. He snagged the slacks and dress shirt, making his way for the bathroom.

Before he shut the door, his eyes met mine, shimmering with grey sparkle. "At least for now."

I pushed away my heavy conversation with Beau earlier, and patted down my grey bodycon dress. I wanted to talk to him about everything, about his past, about whatever hurt him. But I was determined to make this night lighthearted, *fun. It's technically his birthday... and he made mine quite eventful. I'd like to return the favour.*

I strapped on some nude heels that I saw at the boutique, and made my way to the floor length mirror. *Not too bad, Maya.* My dress was relatively short, with slight ruffles at the bottom and thin spaghetti straps. It hugged my frame perfectly, the scoop neckline giving my breasts a little lift. Honestly, Mags would have been proud of me.

Mags.

Is she safe? Is Tommy?

I couldn't help but worry. What if Beau's grace didn't hold up, and Marina or Siles got to both of them? *Snap out of it Maya, just call her.* So I did.

Three rings. "Hello?"

A sigh of relief flooded over me. "Mags, you're okay."

"Barely, Marina decided to pay a vis... – Give me the phone! – Leave it, Tom – Sorry Maya, Tommy's been frantic ever since it happened." Mags said.

My heart raced. Marina tracked down Mags instantly, could she have found my dad? Did she get in?

"Mags, what happened? Where is she?" I paced around the room, biting my nails.

"You would have been so proud of me Maya. I showed the bitch!" I heard Mags clap and Tommy grunt in the background. "She tried to get in, but whatever mojo Beau did to protect us really kicked her ass. She couldn't make it through the door!"

Every muscle in my body relaxed. *Phew, so his grace really did work.* At least they were safe. *That means my dad is okay.* "Where is she now?"

Silence.

"Mags?" I questioned. "Mags."

Mags cleared her throat, speaking lowly. "Erhm... I - think she's dead? She might be dead. She's just laying in the door entrance limp, like a dead fish."

I couldn't help but chuckle at the thought. *Am I really laughing at the fact a demon is dead in front of my best friend?* My humour must be broken. Though, a surge of relief inundated my body. If Marina really was dead, then that eliminated one extra threat. But Mags never mentioned Siles, only Marina. *Crap.*

"Was Siles with her?" I demanded, drawing my hair up into a ponytail.

A sharp response. "No."

It never fully sunk into me that Mags, throughout whatever torture Siles put her through, developed a relationship with him. I thought it was absolutely absurd that she even cared in the first place - he manipulated her, used her. Though, I guess being attached to someone, even if you aren't consciously aware holds a greater emotion than I will ever be able to understand. *But... you do understand.*

"Where are you?" Mags interrupted my thoughts.

Various different noises sounded from the bathroom, followed by the faint squeak of the tap turning on.

I cleared my throat, knowing Mags would lose her mind over Beau and I staying at a hotel alone together. Even though our lives were far from normal, some mundane romantic angst was enough to make her forget an earthquake.

"I'm uh – Beau and I are going to hit the road again tomorrow. We're just at a hotel right now." I left it at that.

The line was silent for a few moments and then a shrill shriek pierced my eardrum.

"Ah! You and Beau are at a hotel, right now? Maya, Maya this is huge. Did you pack lingerie? Did you shave? Oh – what about that lotion we bought from –"

I heard the tap shut off from the bathroom and the fumbling of the doorknob.

"Mags, I'll call you later, glad you're safe. I love you."

Protest. "Wait –"

But I hung up as soon as Beau stepped out.

A tingly sensation ran down the back of my arms, finding its way to the tips of my fingers. Beau leaned against the doorframe, rolling up the sleeves of his black dress shirt. I dug my nail into the crease of my palm, attempting to focus on anything but him... yeah, it was impossible. The black slacks I got him reached just above his ankle, shaping his quads perfectly. His dark button down was undone, revealing the golden cross my mother gave him against his tan skin. A speckle of grey twinkled in his eyes as he ran his fingers through his midnight hair, roughing it up.

I've fallen in love with so many fictional characters in stories, described in such a way like him, but to see it with my own eyes was ethereal. He was an angel... dressed like a devil.

Through my trance, I almost didn't realize him come towards me, picking up my hand and twirling me into a spin. He pulled me against his body, lacing us together. His fingers trailed down my spine, halting just above my tailbone. He let them linger a while longer before lightly pulling the elastic out of my ponytail.

His grey eyes seared into mine like fire, burning with intensity. "I like your hair down," he released.

My brown waves cascaded down the sides of my face, camouflaging my blushed cheeks. I opened my mouth to say something, anything to show my feigned disgust, but I didn't have any. Beau Gabriel quite literally took my breath away.

He twirled me again, halting me halfway so that my back was against his chest. He kept one arm locked around my middle, and the other tracing the curve of my hip.

His lips found the crook my neck, brushing lightly over thin skin. "I should've finished what I started in your kitchen."

I swallowed hard, blood rushing to my cheeks. *Our kiss.*

He released me and stepped back with a smirk, giving my body a look down. "Can I make you a drink?" he asked innocently, holding up a bottle of tequila.

I gasped. He knew exactly what he was doing. *No, no, no. You can not have this effect on me any longer. Two can play that game.*

I marched towards the sole table in our room and grabbed the liquor out of his hands. My eyes never left his as I took a swig of tequila, and pushed the bottle hard against his chest.

He bit the inside of his cheek, wearing a half grin.

With all the confidence I had in me, I fluffed my hair and stepped forward. "Your move." I winked.

Chapter 39

PINESTONE, 14 HOURS

"So we just wait here until Maya gets back?" Tommy asked through panic breaths.

Since hours had passed, Mags thought that Tommy would've calmed down by now, but even she couldn't comprehend her own tranquility. *Shock, it has to be shock.*

Mags nodded, sitting at the edge of the bed. She watched Tommy cross his legs, picking a scab on his knee. She'd never seen him in such a disoriented state before. His hair was disheveled and it looked like he hadn't showered for days... *Smelt like it too.*

Mags didn't blame him though, she couldn't. Even though Braum's dad was a horrible father, seeing his mutilated corpse would have sent anyone over the deep end. Not only that, Ky was dead... Tommy's best friend in the entire world, besides Braum who was completely off the grid.

"Are Maya and Beau..." Tommy began but quickly cut himself off. "Never mind."

Mags stared blankly at the wall, zoning out before registering what Tommy had asked. She immediately darted her eyes to him in discontent.

"Never mind is right." She combatted. End of discussion. Mags pulled out her phone and made her way for the door. "I'm going to call Maya, but please, for the love of God Tommy, take a shower. You *have* time."

Tommy grunted. "I don't even have clean clothes."

One thing Mags believed in was 'self-care on sadness Saturdays." *Saturdays are the end of a week, so cry it out to prepare for sunny Sundays.* She understood Tommy's zombie-like state, hell if she let herself feel it she would probably be worse, but it disgusted her that he wanted to live in his own filth for a second longer.

She walked to the closet and pulled out one of Beau's t-shirts and a pair of sweatpants, throwing it at Tommy's face. "Maybe Beau's closet can give you some insight on how to dress."

Mags' phone vibrated violently in her pocket. She nudged her head forward to Tommy then quickly shut the door behind her.

Maya. *Good God what a relief.* "Hello?"

"Mags, you're okay." Her tone was shaky and panicked, but Mags reassured her that everything was fine.

She explained to Maya what had happened with Marina, boasting her accomplishment. "You would have been so proud of me Maya!" Mags added.

When Maya asked about Siles, Mags' smile drooped low. Even though she didn't remember much of their time together, the feeling lingered – the feeling of being in love. In the cellar, Siles called her 'Maggie,' a name practically extinct to everyone around her. *Did he care?* He couldn't.

Mags didn't let him get her down. He was dangerous, he wanted to end her life. *He's a demon.* That is what she told herself and that is what got her by... even if she didn't believe it.

Then Maya told Mags she was alone in a hotel with Beau, which sent her somber state into an opposing bliss. *Beau the angel is about to commit one hell of a sin,* Mags snickered to herself.

After Maya hung up, Mags leaned sluggishly against the wall, listening to the faint hum of the shower. She slumped down and drew her knees up, burying her face in her hands. A small tear escaped her eye, finding its way to her lips. She didn't feel anything, she didn't let herself, but her body couldn't handle it anymore.

She sobbed until she felt lightheaded, and her consciousness pushed her into a deep sleep.

Mags hadn't realized that she dozed off. It was only when she heard her name being called that she woke up. *How long has it been?*

She rubbed her eyes, scanning the familiar surroundings of the wood cabin walls. She pulled out her phone and saw that four hours had passed. *How the hell did I manage to sleep on the ground? I definitely needed the rest.*

With one light shove, she twisted her body around and opened the bedroom door behind her. Tommy was sound asleep, curled up against the wall in a wool blanket. *If Tommy isn't calling my name, then who...*

"Mags!" A familiar voice yelled. A male voice, one that echoed in her mind every second.

With weary steps, she tiptoed her way to the open entrance, swallowing back the frog that tried to pry its way out of her throat.

Marina was gone.

And in her place, *he* stood.

His ashy blonde hair swooped over his forehead, tangled. He wore black trousers that were ripped up the sides and his chest was oozing with pus, bruised and beaten. Down his torso, an infected, scabbed word was carved in his flesh: *COWARD*.

Mags shuddered, staring at the dark plum circle encasing his left eye and below it, a gaping cut from his ear to his chin.

Tears waterfalled down Mags' cheeks, she couldn't help it. Whatever happened to him, whoever hurt him, had the intent to make him suffer. An empathetic pain filled her limbic system. She slowly walked up to the open entrance, placing her hand flat against the grace-fueled barrier.

"S - *Siles?*" Mags asked, stuttering. She couldn't believe that he was standing before her. "What... what happened to you?"

She analyzed his features, whatever features she could make out clearly. There were barely any.

He swallowed hard, searching for something within Mags' eyes. He bit down hard on his bottom teeth and crouched to the ground, running his fingers through the soil.

"She was here, wasn't she?" he began, crumbling dirt in his palm. "Did she hurt you?"

Mags pulled her hand away from the entrance and crossed her arms over her chest. "Marina? No, no. She - she couldn't get inside."

Siles stood up and looked to Mags with weak eyes. "Good."

Mags swallowed hard. She didn't know what Siles wanted or how he found her, but she assumed it wasn't anything good. She wanted to channel that same adrenaline, that indestructible power she had facing off to Marina, but Siles was different. She felt weak, small... *vulnerable.*

"Are you here to kill me?" Mags asked, her voice cracking. "You can't. You can't get through. Beau - he sealed the door, you can't -"

"I'm not going to hurt you," Siles interrupted softly. "*Maggie*."

Heat rose to her face. *Maggie*. "Then why... Why are you here?"

Silence.

"She's – she's going to kill Maya, isn't she?" Mags asked through chattering teeth. She knew the answer to that question.

Marina was alive. She told Maya hours ago that she wasn't, but she was, and she was out for blood. That much, Mags knew. But what she didn't understand was why Siles came to her.

He nodded his head slowly. Silence followed for a few moments before he turned to face Mags. "I'm going to stop her."

Mags didn't know how to feel. He only recently tried to kill her, controlled her for months but now he was trying to stop Marina? Was this a trap? Could she even trust him? Why would she?

But a part of her did. He released her from his control, and Mags couldn't decipher why. There were so many questions, but if Marina wasn't dead, she would make sure Maya was. That was the priority.

Mags knew she couldn't leave, even if she wanted to. She had to trust Siles; it was her only option.

"Why are you doing this?" Mags asked, tears glossing her vision. "Why do you want to help?"

Siles' expression was inscrutable. He turned away from Mags, looking off into the distance. When he turned back to her, his eyes were crimson, fading slowly to the shade of a spring clover. He clenched his fist, as sparks began to fizzle beneath his palm, burning the soil beneath him to ash.

"I no longer side with Lucifer."

Chapter 40

BEECH COUNTY, 14 HOURS

Beau and I stopped at the first pub closest to our hotel, the *Jack Rabbit*. It was decently busy, and we were definitely way too overdressed to blend in with the crowd of mid-thirties wearing jean jackets and flannels.

Upon entry, several people looked in our direction which skyrocketed my anxiety. If it weren't for the few shots of tequila I had, I would have run for the hills by now.

Beau wrapped his arm around my waist, digging his fingers into my hip as we passed by a table full of bikers catcalling me. He darted his eyes in their direction, holding his stare until we made it to the actual bar.

"What gives?" I giggled, innocently. *I would be lying if I said I didn't enjoy it, but I had to ask all the same.*

He released me from his grasp, watching the biker table like a hawk. In a tense motion, he bumped the side of his fist against the bar twice then turned his attention to me.

He chuckled, but didn't say anything. Instead, he spoke to the bartender who was an older brunette covered in tattoos.

"Two shots of gin," Beau smirked. "And can I send a couple of mixed drinks to the table in the corner?" *The bikers. What is he doing?*

The brunette pursed her lips, flipping two shot glasses upside down. "You know Barny and Suds? Boy, I really wouldn't dare try them kid."

She slid us the two shots of gin and shook her head with a smile. Behind me, I could hear the bikers whistling and slamming down their beers. Even through the blaring classic rock, I made out the sound of shattering glass coming from their direction.

"Reece!" An overweight biker with a southern accent called. He was looking at the bartender. "Get your ass over here, will ya darlin'? Suds broke a mug." Roaring laughter rose from the group.

Beau slapped a twenty on the bar. "Don't forget to put that little umbrella in their cocktails." He winked.

The bartender half-smiled and pointed a finger at Beau, snagging the twenty and shoving it in her pocket. "You're good kid," she laughed.

She stirred two fizzy orange drinks, plopping two paper umbrellas inside and made her way to the table of six bikers.

I immediately turned to Beau with wide eyes, my palms sweating. "What was the point of that?"

He threw back his gin shot and dragged his pointer across his top lip, clearing the alcohol that glossed the corner of his mouth. I blushed.

"Drink," he nudged the shot glass to my hand. "It's good for you."

He laughed out loud, playful and innocent, watching me intently. I could tell the alcohol was starting to hit him. His cheeks were flushed rosy and his grey eyes twinkled a shade brighter.

I shook my head with a smile and took the shot back, before turning around to two of the bikers standing right behind Beau and I.

They smelled of cigars and gasoline, sending the gin almost straight up my esophagus. The one on the left had curly black hair covered by a red bandana. On his neck was a tattoo of an eagle spread across his throat. He wore a leather vest and a brown buckle with a hammered, metal symbol. The biker standing next to Beau was the one who called for the bartender earlier. Up close, he looked even more repulsive. A pearl scar sliced his eye and his teeth were yellow and crooked.

"This some kind of joke, punk?" The one with the scar asked, holding up the cocktail Beau ordered to their table.

Beau stood up as if he had a death wish, leaving little to no space between him and the biker. He gave him a look down with disdain, before flashing a saccharine smile.

"Barny and Suds, I take it?" Beau laughed. "I don't even get a thank you?"

I wanted to yell at him right then and there. The room started to spin and the flashing lights blurred together in a spiral of random colours.

I placed my hand on his shoulder and stood up, attempting to control my buzz. "Beau, let's just go."

The biker with the neck tattoo stepped forward, biting down on his knuckles. "Well would you look at that pretty thing," he clicked his tongue, inspecting me with beady eyes. "Be lyin' if I said I didn't notice those legs when you opened the door. Think you can open somethin' else –"

Before I could process the moment, Beau grabbed the cocktail out of the bikers hand and threw it in his eyes. The biker with the neck tattoo lunged for him but Beau ducked out of the way, kicking behind his knee. He fell to the ground in wailing pain, struggling to get up.

The other bikers got up from their seats, pulling out pocket knives. I felt vomit rising up from my throat as drool escaped the side of my mouth. My heart rattled in my chest; beads of sweat dripped down my forehead like a waterfall.

In a flash, Beau grabbed me by the hand and ran me out of the bar. The night's wind slapped me in the face, settling my senses. Beau led me behind the pub, encasing me in his grasp. He pressed me tightly against the brick wall, covering my mouth with one hand.

"What –" I muttered.

He buried his face in my neck, mumbling a few words. Instantly, my whole body went numb, as if I was paralyzed. Flashes of heat and ice ran through my veins, pulsating under my skin. I watched as the group of bikers ran out of the pub and stared directly in our direction, only for them to curse and stomp back into the bar. *They... they can't see us.*

Beau held me against him for another minute before releasing me when there was no sign of the bikers anymore.

He burst into a feral laughter, but I was too shocked to comprehend what had just happened.

"Did you just... did you make us..." I managed to say through staccato breaths.

Beau wiped his teary eyes. "Make us invisible? Yeah, that was precious."

Fury boiled through my veins. The buzz I had was long gone and I wanted to slap him across the face. I watched his smug expression with crossed arms. *They pulled pocket knives out of their jackets... he could have gotten me killed. And for what? For what! Wasn't Beau my protector?*

I couldn't control my anger. I walked up to him and shoved his shoulders with every ounce of might I had left. "Are you fucking insane, Beau?"

His laughter disappeared into the winds. "What's wrong? Can't handle a little trouble?"

"Not when it can get me killed!" I fumed.

I shoved past him, struggling to walk through the grass with high heels. I had just about enough of this night, the night that I planned for Beau and I to have fun. But he had to go and be reckless, for whatever reason. I saw it now; why he got the scars. He was careless, he did whatever he wanted to do and he didn't care about who he endangered. Yes Beau was sent to watch over me, but he just put me in a situation that could've ended everything... and he laughed about it. *This was a mistake.*

Before I could take another wobbly step, Beau was in front of me, pushing my body against the craggy brick wall. The moonlight gleamed down, illuminating the golden cross around his neck. He caged me in his arms, securing them on either side of my face. His grey eyes burned into mine, twinkling with lust. I felt his warm breath linger against my skin, hovering above my lips. He stared at me for a few moments, then moved one hand to my shoulder, tracing my collarbone slowly with his fingertips.

I swallowed hard, frozen in place. I couldn't move. *I didn't want to move.*

"If you knew what they were thinking," he whispered, trailing his fingers up the side of my neck. "You would've done the same thing."

"B... Beau..." I stuttered through erratic breaths. "What are you doing?"

His grey eyes, dark like coal, stared at me with hunger, longing... *want.* "Taking out my anger."

Before I could blink, he smashed his lips against mine, violent and thirsty. It took me a second to register that Beau was kissing me, but when I did, I fully gave in. I fantasized about this moment more times than I could count; it almost didn't feel real.

This was nothing like when he first kissed me. Back then, he was gentle, soft. But now... his lips were cemented on mine, and nothing was gentle about it.

He gnawed at my bottom lip until his tongue found mine, slashing against it with purpose. Butterflies danced in my stomach, banging against each other. His kiss was sinful, fuelled by lust. My hair was entangled in his fingers as he yanked it back, planting kisses down my neck all the way to my collarbone. He wanted this for a while, I tasted it. All the built up tension over the past few months ended in this moment. The events of tonight were a distant memory in my brain. All that I craved was Beau Gabriel.

I wrapped my legs around him as he picked me up, kissing me harder, *hungrier.* He pressed his groin against me, sewing our bodies together. A soft moan escaped his lips. "Maya..." he released.

I cupped the sides of his face and brushed his lips softly before pulling away. He wasn't done with me, I saw it, but he couldn't contest. *The cards are in my hands now.*

"Let's go back to our room," I smirked.

Chapter 41

BEECH COUNTY, 13 HOURS

*B*eau kept his lips against mine as he fumbled with the room key, unable to take his hands off of me. *Or maybe I can't take my hands off him.*

We stumbled in and Beau kicked the door shut, swooping me up with one arm and held the back of my neck with his free hand. My senses amplified, craving every inch of him more and more as he pushed me gently on the bed, ripping his black dress shirt off. Buttons soared through the air and clattered against the floor.

"Oops," he smirked against my lips, caressing every part of my body.

Every kiss, every touch felt ethereal. He satiated every part of me without effort. I had been in a relationship with Tommy, and of course we had our fair share of intimate moments, but none like this... this was incomparable.

He pulled back, knees on either side of my body and scanned me up and down. My cheeks flushed. I had never seen someone look at me with such desire, such *want*.

I ran my fingers up and down his abdomen, giggling playfully. "That shirt was twenty dollars, you know?"

He chuckled, brushing my brown locks away from my face. He gently pushed the spaghetti strap off my shoulder in one careful movement, then the other. A tingly sensation began to form between my legs, so I pushed them tighter together.

"And how much..." he began, outlining my silhouette with his finger. "Was this dress?"

He tugged at the fabric, ripping the ruffles off the bottom hem like tape. "I hope it wasn't expensive."

I swallowed hard, pulling him down on top of me, but he pulled away once more. He searched my eyes for approval, I could tell. He *wanted* me, that much I saw, but he didn't want to do anything without my consent. I shut my eyes and smiled, thinking loud thoughts, fully aware that he could read my mind. *I want you, Beau Gabriel.*

A small smile crept over his lips as he melted into me, bunching the bulk of my dress in one hand and pulling it down my legs. His fingers danced all over my skin, running over my lace bra and in between my thighs.

"*Beau...*"I moaned softly against his lips. *I want you... I need you.*

In an instant, Beau tensed up and drew back, balling his fist against the side of the bed. He looked down at me and clenched his jaw before leaping off the mattress.

Embarrassment, guilt, worry, panic, all the emotions bubbled inside of me as I covered myself with the white sheets. What – what happened? *What did I do?*

"Nothing." He said through gritted teeth, finding his black t-shirt. His chest heaved up and down.

I kept my eyes on him as I searched for my clothes, throwing on my wool sweater from earlier. I walked over to him with tentative movements, reaching out to touch his shoulder but he moved away.

"Beau..." I whispered, fighting back tears.

I was so open with him, vulnerable. I let him touch me, kiss me, hell, I almost gave *myself* to him. How could he treat me so coldly? What did I do? *What the hell did I do!*

He sat on the edge of the bed with his hand between his legs, huffing with frustration. When he looked up at me, I could see the pain in his eyes.

"It's not that I –" he started, but cut himself off. After a few moments, he stood up and walked up to me, cupping my face in his hands. "Fuck, Maya, I want you more than anything," he breathed. "I've wanted this, *us*, for longer than you know."

I shook my head in confusion, placing one hand over his. "Then why..."

He swallowed hard and slowly turned his back to face me. I gasped in shock. My hands shook as I reached out to touch the cornucopia of black veins pulsating underneath Beau's skin. His scars were off-black, connecting in various different directions like a gigantic spiderweb.

He quickly turned around and grabbed my hand, staring into my eyes.

"Does it..." I stuttered, unable to form a proper sentence. "Does it hurt?"

He nodded. "If I give in to one more vice, Maya..." he bit down hard on his bottom teeth, flexing his jaw. "I'm going to become one of Lucifer's fallen. I can't, I won't –"

My innocence. Beau refused to take my innocence. I folded him into my arms, running my fingers through his hair. I wanted to stay like this, embraced forever. He wrapped one arm around my waist and held one hand on the back of my head.

"You won't," I promised him. "I can't lose you."

We stood still in time, holding each other like that was all we had left.

In the distance, I heard my phone vibrate in my purse. If it were any other circumstance I would have tossed my phone out the window, but a gut feeling told me to pick up.

When I clicked open my cell, I saw that I had twenty-three missed calls from Mags. *No, no, no, no. Shit!*

I dialed her number immediately and heard her panicked voice. "Maya, you need to leave, you need to get to Port Hope now! Do you hear me?"

I furrowed my brows in confusion, checking the time. **12:08am.** "Mags, what's wrong? We have time?"

"No!" she snapped. A muffled male voice sounded in the distance, only it didn't sound like Tommy's. I swallowed hard, glancing to Beau. I put the phone on speaker.

A static noise followed and then I heard a man clear his throat. "Maya?"

"Yes?"

"It's Siles."

Before I could speak, Beau darted for the phone, pulling it out of my hands. "I'm going to fucking kill you. If you touch Mags you rodent piece of –"

"I didn't hurt her. I'm not going to hurt her." Siles was calm. In the distance I could hear Mags say, "He's not going to hurt me."

Siles continued. "We don't have time for this, Marina's gone. Mags thought she was dead, she isn't. If Marina hasn't found you yet, she will. Lucifer gave us an orbionyx to track your whereabouts."

Beau's eyes went lifeless. He spoke slowly underneath his breath, shaking his head. "That's how they found us."

I bit my fingernail anxiously. "*Orbionyx?*" I asked.

"In Heaven, we use orbiopal. It's a crystal orb that can show you specific points in time, but only for a few moments." He turned to me, his eyes darkening by the second. "Why didn't you tell me about Marina?"

Before I could protest, he hung up the phone and grabbed his keys off the table, pulling me towards the door. "We're leaving."

I struggled out of his grip. "I don't even have pants on!"

The veins in his neck protruded as he flung back around in anger. "Then put your fucking pants on, Maya, she will kill you! She will kill you in cold blood and she won't think twice! Fuck!" He seethed. In panting breaths, he spoke, "If Lucifer wants you, he will claim you."

He stared down to the ground and stretched out his hand, white sparks fizzled at his fingertips. I had never seen Beau so angry before, so enraged. I paced back and quickly threw my jeans on, leaving the rest of the room in a heaping disaster.

I shoved past him, holding the door open for him to walk out. When he did, he planted one swift kiss across my lips. "You're the only hope I have left." He whispered.

Chapter 42

PORT HOPE, 2 HOURS

The entire drive to Port Hope was in silence. It took us eleven hours to get there, and Beau insisted on driving the entire way. I didn't know what to say, so I slept for most of the trip.

Beau was angry, angry that I didn't tell him about Marina. But I knew if I had, he would have wanted to leave immediately and I thought she was truly dead... *Never trusting Mags again.* But it wasn't her fault, if anything it was mine. How could I think one normal night with Beau would actually be *normal.*

"Where is this place?" I asked Beau, fiddling with my fingers.

He didn't answer, only pressed on the gas harder. I didn't contest.

After a half an hour, Beau pulled off the highway and took a sharp turn down a narrow road. Drooping trees lined the sides of the route, shading the sunlight from coming in. Even though it was almost noon, it looked like nighttime.

He slowed down when we reached an abandoned liquor store, and parked his car next to a decrepit shed. I swallowed hard, goosebumps breaking the barrier of my skin.

I opened my mouth to end the silence, but he cut me off.

"I'm not angry." His grey eyes burned into mine like ice, softening the longer he stared. "I just don't want anything to happen to you."

I wanted to say a million things, but I thought it best to keep silent. Instead, I flashed him a genuine smile and nodded my head.

He unlatched his seatbelt and reached over my legs, popping open the glove compartment. Inside, he pulled out Gabriel's feathers, a piece of white cloth, and a silver blade before getting out of the car.

The knife shone like mirrored glass in every way he turned it. A pit fell hard in my stomach... *I hope to God he doesn't have to use that.*

I sat still, analyzing the dark forest encircling me. No light penetrated through the cracks of the leaves; it was just a conglomeration of phthalo green and black wood. *Where are we?*

Beau knocked on the glass and opened up the passenger door, leaning over my body and clicking the seatbelt. "Come on, Marina could be anywhere."

I obeyed. I didn't have a choice. I had no idea what I was walking into. *This is really happening right now. I'm supposed to drink from a chalice, and become... become what? The Puritas? What do I do then? Where will I go? What is going to happen to me?*

As we passed the desolate liquor store, I caught a glimpse of the graffiti stained windows. Lined symbols and letters covered the brick. An odd sense of familiarity loomed over me. *Have I been here before?* Beads of sweat dripped down my face and I shivered against Beau.

He kept me close, lacing our fingers together. It calmed me down... sort of. I felt like I was being watched, I couldn't shake the feeling. Like every single one of my nightmares, I had seen this before. I was walking in a shaded wood, someone was chasing me in a... in a... *No.* In *this* forest.

Shivers ran down my spine and pricked my skin like barbwire. *Were my nightmares warning me? Did I really predict this? No, this can't be happening.*

A rustling sound behind me caused me to jump. A squirrel ran out from the fern, disappearing into a log.

I cleared my throat, shuddering next to Beau. We walked for a few more minutes before he stopped at a large willow tree, pushing aside the leaves. Engraved in the bark was a dark handprint, blinking in beats. My eyes grew wide.

"We're here." He released, placing his hand over the handprint. It was Beau's.

He signaled for me to stick with him and stepped through hanging vines. I heard the distant sound of slashing waves, light peaking through the hanging leaves. *This is it.* With one heavy breath, I shut my eyes and left my entire life behind.

I faced a rocky precipice, planting my feet on the stone. Mist swept the ground like dancing spirits, trapped beneath the rocks. All I could see in the horizon was the dark sea, splashing violently over smaller peaks. The cloudy skies hid the sun.

Beau was ahead of me, walking right to the edge of the cliff. He took in a deep breath and crouched down, running his hands along the cold stone beneath him.

I approached him slowly, the wind slapped my skin with light force.

"It has to be here." He muttered under his breath. He closed his eyes and placed his palm flat against the ground. A white hue radiated from underneath his fingertips, penetrating every crack and crevasse like a silver snake.

I couldn't process what was happening. The waves roared as if they were speaking, trying to communicate with me. A grim feeling resurfaced, the feeling of being watched.

Beau finally got up and moved to a small dent in the stone, concaved like a bowl. I watched as he mumbled a few words and shot a beaming white light out of his palm, cracking open the rock.

My head felt heavy, witnessing the impossible. In moments like this, I found it very difficult to differentiate reality from fiction. None of it seemed real, it couldn't be. *What if I never met Beau and all of this, the past few months of my life was just a twisted dream... a fragment of my imagination? It has to be. This can't be my life.* But somehow, it was.

He buried his arm into the stone, struggling to grab something. After a few moments, he pulled *it* out.

I dropped to my knees beside him, staring at the crystalized opulence that was *the* chalice, the Holy Grail. I had read about this in books before, how beautiful it was, but to see it... the original cup forged by the angels themselves was indescribable. Four gems encompassed the golden bowl, glimmering with glowing radiance. *I have never seen anything more beautiful.*

Beau wrapped his fingers around mine, facing me with weak eyes. "Maya..."

"What do I have to do?" I asked, unable to keep my eyes off the chalice.

"Maya," he repeated. "Look at me."

His grey eyes pierced into mine with purpose. The wind began to pick up and the clouds concealed the sun completely. I didn't want to look at him, I couldn't. It took everything in me to rip my gaze away from the chalice.

He cupped my face, unravelling the piece of white cloth from his pocket. With shaky hands, he placed it in my palm and closed my fingers.

I watched him pull out Gabriel's beaming white feathers, holding them over the cup. He mumbled a few words to himself, stretching his neck to the sky. I could hear the shakiness, see the trembling of his hands. Then just like that, Gabriel's feathers crumbled into dust. I peered over to look into the cup, and gasped. Inside was a vortex of shimmering white liquid, glistening like snow.

Beau pulled me in close, leaning his forehead against mine. I felt the warmth of his breath against my lips.

"I don't..." he began, shaking his head. His grip on the nape of my neck was tense. "I don't know what's going to happen next. I don't – I'm sorry for everything that's happened to you."

In that moment, my life flashed before my eyes. Everything from the past few months came flooding back like a tidal wave. *Why did it have to be me? Why was I destined for this life? Why did my mom have to die... for something unknown. What awaited me? Death, maybe? And when I do drink from this cup, how do I possess such a great deal of power without hurting myself? I'm human... I'm a mortal... I'm... I'm nothing.*

I pulled away from Beau, allowing the wind to slice the heavy space between our faces. The waves crashed harder against the rocks, calling out to the sea. The only light that surrounded me beamed from inside the chalice.

I looked into Beau's twinkling grey eyes, finding nothing but pain. Only it wasn't his... it was a mirror of mine.

With tentative movements, I smoothed out the cloth Beau had given me. On it was a scribble of dark words in a language I couldn't comprehend.

I wrinkled my face in confusion, swallowing hard. "I don't understand." *Was I supposed to?*

"It's Latin." Beau said through pursed lips, looking down to the chalice. "Gabriel told me that before you drink from the Holy Grail, you have to say these words. It will allow the grace to be consumable. You have to believe you are divine, that you are willing to do whatever it takes to fight on our side of this war."

Divine... What a laughable thought. *Me.*

"I know, Maya. I know." Beau read my thoughts. "It's impossible to believe the impossible. But you were chosen," he pushed the chalice towards me. "I don't know what comes next, but I will be by your side. That, I swear on my grace and the Heaven's above. I promise that I –"

"*Maya!*" A shrill scream called out behind me, carried by the winds.

When I had those nightmares that kept me lying awake for weeks, I only equated them to fragments of past trauma, maybe even movies I'd seen... Never a warning. I would have been a fool to believe something was actually following me, something or *someone* wanted me dead. No, it couldn't be. *I have way too active of an imagination*, I thought.

But they were real.

They were warnings.

I recognized that scream, the desperation of his voice. I hadn't heard it in a while, but every memory I had of it unlocked in an instant. His wail exploded in my brain like a ticking time bomb, ready to erupt. It was only a matter of time until I turned around to face who was standing from a distance.

The wind blew the red locks from her visage, exposing a sharp nose and scarlet lips. A vacant hole indented her cheek, black and charred. The clicking sound of her tall boots blended with the crashing waves. Beside her, Braum's sluggish body struggled to keep her pace. His knees were dusted with bruises and his legs were plastered in bloody cuts. Every step he took appeared to hurt more than the last, his face twisted with agony. His torso was bare with an inverted crossed carved in the centre of his chest, infected with oozing yellow pus.

I almost gagged at the sight.

Braum was a walking corpse.

I threw my hand over my mouth as she approached Beau and I, stopping close enough that I could see all the damage she evidently inflicted on Braum.

I read his eyes. He didn't say anything, but tears waterfalled down his cheeks as he held his frail arm in one hand.

Then *she* blocked my view of him.

"I don't think we've officially met." She flashed the most daunting smile, a smile of snakes.

Though the wind howled and the waves screeched, I could still hear her name clearer than anything else around me.

"I'm Marina."

Chapter 43

PORT HOPE, 30 MINUTES

"Braum..." I couldn't manage to say anything else. I was encompassed by the gruesome scene that was *Braum*.

His chest heaved up and down. A croak escaped his mouth, loud enough for me to hear but not loud enough for me to understand.

Beau stepped in front of me, shielding me with one arm. A beaming white hue radiated underneath his palm, fizzling at his fingertips.

"Leave, Marina." He demanded.

A crisp laugh rose from her throat. "No, I think I'll stay."

She tugged on Braum, pulling him directly in front of her. In a swift movement, she wrapped her arms around his chest and ignited a flame, slowly carving a symbol over his heart. His deafening screams ruptured my eardrum, echoing through the air.

Without thinking, my feet began to run in his direction. *I need to help him, I can't let him die!* But Beau grabbed my waist, pulling me behind him roughly.

"*Look at him!*" I screamed at Beau, spitting through chattering teeth. My eyes watered, my body shook.

No matter what Braum did in the past, he didn't deserve to die like this. This couldn't be his fate, it couldn't be. No one deserved the wounds he wore, the wounds she gave him.

Braum's exhausted body fell to the stone. Marina laughed, grabbing him by the hair and pulling his limp stature erect.

"Give me the girl, *angel*." She seethed. Her eyes flashed red as she stepped forward. "Let me end your agony."

Beau clenched his fist in fury. "I let you slip once. That won't happen again."

Marina dropped Braum from her grasp, allowing him to fall to his knees. She dusted off her hands, licking the blood off her fingers.

Her eyes met mine, intensifying the longer she held my gaze. The red hue radiating from her pupils bled into my psyche like fire, burning all of my thoughts away. My head thumped in pain following a synchronized pattern, rattling against my skull. A heat waved surged through my body, tangling itself into all my emotions. Tears began to flow down my cheeks, painting my face, though anger filled my veins. Sadness overwhelmed me as I looked to Braum, pleading through silence. And yet, when I glanced at Beau, a pulsating feeling surged below, sending goosebumps to my skin. *What is happening to me...*

Marina smirked in the distance. "My, my. The angel hasn't been honest with you, has he *Puritas?*" She spat.

I darted my gaze to Beau, trying to control the tsunami of emotions I felt, but he wouldn't look at me.

"What is she talking about, Beau?" I asked. No response.

"*Beau!*" I demanded in a heated rage. "What is she talking about?" My thoughts wouldn't silence.

"Tragic, really." Marina chimed in. "Girl meets boy, girl falls in love, boy uses her to get over a heartbreak and flaps his merry wings home." Her laugh echoed in my brain.

I didn't know how to feel, how to process anything. My heart thumped in my chest, an overwhelming sensation of jealousy flooded my core. *Heartbreak? Home? Beau was in love?*

"A long time ago," Beau whispered, reading my thoughts. He turned to look at me, his eyes dark as ink. He reached out to touch me but I moved away from him.

A raindrop hit my forehead, then another, and another. The grey clouds enveloped the sky, sealing away any trace of sunlight.

"Maya, it's time." Beau said, grabbing hold of the Holy Grail.

"You know I met her, Beau, Rosanna... *Rosy*, I believe you called her?" Marina's words coiled around my brain, asphyxiating my sense of rationality.

Rosanna... Rosy. Rosanna... *Ros... R.* R. The engravement in that ring he kept in his car. The one I asked him about that made him stiff. The reason why he didn't do attachments. *She* was the reason. There was a girl. *A girl that wasn't me.*

My eyes narrowed as I looked to Beau, but he stood frozen, looking down to the stone.

"Oh, she just broke your little heart to pieces didn't she, Beau? And you couldn't recover, you still can't. And Maya's your only way home, away from her for good." Marina's gaze slithered to me, her red eyes darkening like crimson. "The only woman you have ever loved... is a *demon*."

The urge to hurl myself over the cliff grew stronger. I imagined myself, my fresh blood splattered against the sharp peaks, plastering the stone like paint. My remains would float into the sea, baiting the creatures of the trench. That would be easier, easier than the life God recklessly bestowed on me. *I don't care about this, I don't care about anything or anyone. The world can burn.*

Beau jumped in front of me, blocking my view of Marina. I struggled to get away from his grip, but he was too strong. He held me in place, cupping my face.

"She's getting in your head, Maya. Please, look at me." He spoke desperately.

I couldn't. My eyes swelled. Wrath engulfed my being.

"She's a demon, these are their tricks. They play with your head, your emotions, fears, everything! Maya," he breathed, rubbing my tears with his thumb. "Maya, listen to me."

Fury. "You loved a demon, don't give me that shit Beau!" I spat. Blades of red fire flashed in beats all around me. I didn't want to drink from the Holy Grail, I didn't want to become the Puritas... *I don't want to avenge my mother.*

I glanced at Marina who kept her gaze fixated on me, twirling her fingers in a circular motion. A growing orb began to form, spanning into a dark silhouette... a silhouette covered by a dark hood. *My... my nightmares.*

I tumbled backwards, placing a shaky hand in front of my face as the figure approached, faceless and slender.

"B... Beau," I choked, unable to rip my eyes away from the shadow. "Beau!"

My surroundings spun into a spiral of green fern and thick branches. *I was back in the forest.*

"Get back!" I yelled, searching for a blade-tipped rock, anything sharp, anything that could protect me.

But there was nothing.

A tar-like mud softened over my core, enveloping my middle like thick ribbons. I began to submerge, deeper and deeper into the ground as the figure stopped right in front of me, pulling out a silver blade.

"No!" I screamed, flailing my arms.

The figure crouched down, eye level with me now. The crooked trees whispered to me, preparing me for the pain.

"Who..." I stuttered, my eyes burning with liquid. "Who are you?"

The figure watched me behind a shaded mask, then carefully lifted its hands to remove its hood. I gasped, recoiling as far as I possibly could go, but the mud trapped me in place.

"*Hello, Maya...*" The figure slithered, her familiar brown hair burnt and scraggly. Her complexion was the same, her bone structure was sunken, her eyes... were not hazel. They were black.

She laughed, placing the blade to my throat. It was the same laugh I heard in my nightmare, the same laugh that escaped my throat instead of a scream.

The dark figure was me.

My throat was a caged inferno, my screams straining my vocal chords. I shut my eyes, preparing for death, *inviting it.* But then, the world around me spun into the familiar precipice. I was no longer a prisoner of heavy tar, but of the cold stone cliff. A surging burn erupted in my arm, engulfing all sense of reality. I felt the weight of Beau's hand wrapped around my wrist, pricking my skin like pins and needles. Through blurry vision, beams of white light penetrated each viewpoint of my eyes, blinding the atmosphere once again. *Has the rain stopped? Is the sun out?*

Ringing erupted in my ear, tuning out my surroundings. Time slowed; all my instincts were heavily sedated. Through squinted vision, I made out the hazy silhouette of Beau, marching away from me towards a glob of red. A dance of black and scarlet twisted in the air as distant screams echoed through the winds.

Maya! Maya... A male called.

Maya... Grail... Drink...

"Beau..." I mumbled, reaching out.

My emotions slowly settled as I regained my vision. Through the violent rain, I saw Beau kneeling over Marina's body with a hand around her throat. Braum was lying further off in the distance... unmoving.

I covered my mouth with my hands.

"Maya, the Grail!" Beau yelled.

I used whatever strength I had to push myself off the cold stone, scrambling to my feet. The white hue radiating from the Holy Grail was shining in a concaved crevice.

Growls and shouts of pain sounded from Beau's end. I turned to see Marina straddling him, choking him with a chain of red fire.

I didn't give it a second thought. "*Beau!*" I yelled, sprinting towards him.

Through the hazy grey and pattering rain, I caught a glimpse of his eyes. They were hollow, the darkest shade of ebony. Black veins crawled up his arms, making their way to his neck.

Beau mouthed something to me, a word he'd said to me before. It barely escaped his lips, but I heard it in my mind, loud and clear.

"*Always...*"

And with that, he let out a single, puncturing cry, and slammed his hand against the stone beneath him.

An energy so powerful pushed me into the air, sending my body flying back. I landed on my side, scraping the length of my arm on a pointed rock. A piercing pain cracked the back of my skull, sending sharp zaps down my spin. The ringing in my ears grew louder than ever, chanting a stinging white noise.

The metallic taste of blood filled my mouth. My eyes fought to stay open, but it was no use. Everything was spinning, everything was falling, I couldn't breathe... *I can't –*

Beau...

A raindrop slipped into my mouth, then another, and another. I had no telling of how much time had passed since my body shut down. The skies were still painted with grey clouds. I pushed myself off the ground and scratched my eyes, peering down at the blood dripping from my forearm. A wet grime coated the back of my neck, trickling down my back. I placed my shaky fingers to the back of my head, feeling an open sore underneath my hair.

What happened...

Flashes of my memory resurfaced. A brute power flung me through the sky, a rippling energy that Beau caused when he slammed his hand onto the stone.

Beau.

Through the heavy rain I caught a glimpse of him in the distance, his body lying still on his back.

I scrambled to my feet but crashed down when my legs gave out. A sharp rock lodged itself into my thigh. Tears filled my waterline, spilling down my face as I scrunched the fabric of my sweater and took a deep breath. In one quick movement, I pulled out the rock and yelped in gruelling pain. Blood flowed out of my exposed skin, staining the stone with goopy crimson. I used the sharp edge of the rock to cut a piece of my sweater, and tied it with pressure around my thigh.

With whatever strength I had left, I slowly crawled towards Beau.

Marina's motionless body was further away, face down.

"Beau," I let out through dry lips.

I reached out to touch him but was shocked backwards. A white ring circled the perimeter of where their bodies lay. With that, an invisible barrier encompassed them, trapping them inside.

What... What is this? No... No!

"Beau!" I yelled, slamming my hand violently against the barrier. A wave of transparent glimmer rippled in front of me but never broke.

"Beau!" I cried. *Beau wake up, wake up, I know you can hear me, I know you fucking hear me! Wake up, I need you, I... I need you.*

Moments passed and his inert body began to stir. Through weak eyes, his head turned to me. He flashed a small smile, reaching out a feeble finger.

You aren't dead. You aren't dead, you're still with me.

"Beau..." I released, shaking.

Then *it* happened.

All I could do was watch.

A black vine emerged from beneath the stone, coiling itself around his mouth, slamming his head down forcefully against the rock.

His eyes, dark as a raven's wing, shuddered rapidly with pain.

Hundreds of black veins stemmed from beneath him, encasing his body like a cocoon. They wrapped around his legs, his arms, his neck, piercing his sides with their thorned edges.

The scream wouldn't escape my throat. Maybe it was tired of yelling. Maybe my breath couldn't handle one more second of air.

I watched blood pool beneath him, pouring out of his skin like magma as the vines twirled beneath his flesh.

The ringing continued.

The rain continued.

The clouds were grey.

But his eyes were not.

An erratic rumbling broke the stone in front of me, opening a black hole underneath Beau's twisted body. Red hues radiated from inside the pit, violent flames cascading upwards.

Beau... No... Beau!

A combination of rain and tears glossed my vision, coating my eyelashes. I choked on my breath, banging against the transparent barrier. Everything around me spun in nauseating motion as I begged... and I begged.

With whatever strength Beau still had left, he managed to turn his head slightly to me, struggling to reach out.

The last thing I saw of Beau Gabriel was the flash of crimson in his eyes, before the black hole swallowed him into an abyss of nothing.

Chapter 44

PORT HOPE

I couldn't move.

I couldn't breathe.

I didn't want to.

I stared into the empty space of nothing. Just a concave dent of black ash, floating in the space that once held Beau's body. Not a trace of him was left...

There was nothing.

Nothing to hold on to, nothing I cared to hold on to.

Beau was gone.

After what felt like eternity, I managed to conjure the strength to stand up. Dried blood stained my clothes and hands, nestling underneath my fingernails. My body ached in discomfort, painful sores covered me like second skin.

I chewed on my cracked lips, dragging one foot in front of the other. They weighed down like anchors as I finally stepped into the concave of where Beau *was*.

The invisible barrier that separated Beau and I broke when Beau got taken. *Taken. Taken...*

I ran my fingers though the ashy soil, crumbling it and letting it slip through my fingers. *Like Beau did.*

In the corner of my eye, the twinkle of an object caught my peripheral vision. I crawled over to it, dusting the dark soil off the knife. It was the silver blade Beau carried.

I swallowed hard, clasping it tightly in my palm until a string of blood dribbled down my forearm. I felt something. *That is all I want.*

All of our memories came flooding back into my mind like a tidal wave, drowning out my surroundings. And with his absence, a piece of my past and present slipped away, as if nothing existed before and after him. What future we still held existed only in my mind, poisoning me.

I remember when I first saw you... I couldn't look at anything else. I remember when you found

me at the cemetery; I was naïve then, I wanted to hate
you. You drove around with me all night, to find my
best friend who you knew nothing about... but you
knew everything about me – you've known me my
entire life. I remember our kiss... the way you felt
pressed up against me... I will never feel that again.
You're... you're gone, Beau.

      In the distance, I saw Marina's lifeless corpse
sprawled on the stone. I bit my lip, shaking
incessantly. An earthquake of rage cracked every
realm of consciousness and I yelled, running ferally in
the direction of her corpse.

      I drove the blade through her un-beating
heart. Then again, and again. Splashes of blood
splattered against my face. The tearing of flesh against
my knife filled me with sickishly sweet fury. *You took*
everything from me! You took everything from me!
You took...

      "*Maya!*" A voice called out. "Maya, stop!"

      Arms enveloped me tightly, pulling my
shaking hands away from Marina.

      "She's dead." He said.

      I looked up to the sight of Siles, his bruised
face inches away from mine.

      I nimbly moved away, holding Beau's silver
blade in front of me. I gripped the handle tightly,
shoving it further in his direction.

      "What are you doing here?" I demanded. "I
won't hesitate... I'll kill you Siles, I'll fucking kill
you!" I spat, grimacing. Tears waterfalled down my
face, staining my skin like lighting. *I don't want to cry*

anymore. I can't. He's gone. There's nothing I can do.

"Maya..." Siles released, stepping away from me.

I scanned his broken appearance. His pants were tattered and ripped, and the wounds on his body looked comparable to Braum's. The word *COWARD* was carved into his flesh, seeping with boils. His eyes read no signs of threat, and even if they did... there was nothing left in me that cared.

I dropped to my knees, burying my fingers into the soil. "Just kill me." I whispered under my breath, allowing my limbs to fall weak.

When he didn't respond, I darted my eyes to his. "*Kill me!*" I shouted.

I failed. I let Marina control my emotions. I let her play me like a puppet, while she hurt Beau... While she hurt Braum... While she –

"Where did he go..." I sobbed, punching the soil with my fist. "*Where did you go, Beau...*"

Siles was still for a moment, then walked over to Marina's corpse. I watched him crouch down, running his hand over her chest. He shut his eyes, taking a minute to himself. Then he got up, and moved further along the stone, until he reached another body... one I only assumed was Braum's.

Just like he did Marina, he crouched down and let his hand hover. He ran his finger over Braum's skin and flinched.

"He's alive." Siles uttered.

My eyes grew wide as I hurried to Siles' side. "Braum? Braum's alive?"

"No, Beau," he released sternly.

I couldn't believe him, *I can't believe him.* "I..." I started, shaking my head. "No. I watched him die."

I glanced to Siles who had his eye on the symbol Marina carved into Braum's skin.

Siles met my gaze, his green eyes flashing emerald. "He's in hell, Maya."

Beau's in hell. But... I couldn't process what I was hearing. "How? He didn't do anything? I know his scars were fading but he wasn't... he wasn't close. He had time, he had –"

"He took the life of a mortal." Siles interrupted, peering down to Braum. "Do you see this symbol?" He pointed at Braum's heart. "That's a binding mark. Marina bound her life to Braum's."

I shook my head in disbelief. "What? Why would she do that?"

He pressed his lips together, clenching his jaw. "Marina's smart. She knew Beau would kill her, but she also knew that one more mortal sin would cost him eternal punishment. So she bound the two. Her life, to a mortal." His eyes burned into mine like fire. "Beau's a part of the fallen now."

Beau's blast. It... It killed Braum and Marina. But – "How could he have killed Marina? She's a demon, *you're* a demon. You're already dead."

Siles shifted. "On Earth, it's possible to kill a demon in human form. Marina is somewhere in hell, though I don't know what Lucifer plans to do with her. More than likely, she is just a pile of ash or dust, maybe food for the serpents. She can no longer harm you."

I closed my eyes and focused on my breathing, embracing the sound of howling winds. *Beau is alive.*

After a few moments, I moved away from Braum's corpse, and stabilized myself upwards. I craned my neck to where Beau got sucked into hell, pushing away the memory. *The black vines pierced his skin, slithering inside of him like vipers. They tore at him, tied him, constricted him. Even though his mouth was covered, I could feel his screams. Everything in him tried to reach out to me, desperate and defeated... But his eyes... His eyes were alive. They were frantic, eager. They told me everything. They told me... They told me I could save him.*

With careful steps, I walked towards the crevasse of ashy soil. The rain subsided and the clouds parted to an opening sun, beaming down on a small, golden object beneath the rubble.

I knew what it was before I bent down to retrieve it. I knew the direction it pointed towards. I knew the sign my *mother* was trying to give me.

In my hands was her cross, the one Beau wore around his neck. A joke it would be to bring such a symbol of purity into the place of eternal damnation, pain and darkness. I could have laughed at the thought.

I waved for Siles. He was at my side in seconds, leaving space. I pulled out the white cloth Beau had given me and handed it to him.

"Can you translate this for me?" I asked, hastily.

He gnawed at his bottom lip, squinting his eyes. He was silent for a few moments, then cleared his throat.

"From the chalice I drink holds the power of the trinity. By His name, I accept its grace."

I took in the words, repeating it in my brain with each step I took.

From the chalice I drink... the power of the trinity. From the chalice I drink... I accept its grace.

The waves were calm, settling around the sharp peaks. The sunlight illuminated the edge of the precipice, spotlighting the Holy Grail, buried in the stone.

Siles trailed behind me as I walked towards it. Every stride carried a new wave of power, a new sense of urgency. I clasped my mother's cross in my hand and marched to the edge of the cliff.

The wind fluttered against my skin, the sun beaming down on me with purpose. *I have hope.*

When I reached the chalice, I turned to Siles who kept a substantial distance behind me.

"Can we save him?" I demanded, digging my nails into my palm.

With one swift nod he knelt down. "You can do more than save him, *Puritas.*"

In what felt like forever, I managed a small smile. I crouched down and grabbed the Holy Grail, wrapping my slender fingers around the stem. Its golden opulence glimmered in the light, radiating with a crystalizing white hue. The still liquid began to move, swirling in the cup like a vortex of diamonds.

The waves crashed behind me.

The sun rays absorbed into my skin like fire.

I took in one last breath of being Maya Brixton. One last look of the world around me, the world I *used* to know. The world before I entered the gates of Beau *Gabriel.*

I closed my eyes and put the rim of the chalice to my lips.

"From the chalice I drink holds the power of the trinity. By His name, I accept its grace..." *I am the Puritas.*

And I drank.

THE GATES OF

GABRIEL

MARIE-FRANCE LEGER

† Author's Note †

I was asked once, *"Why do you like to read?"*

I was asked why I preferred to bury my nose beneath a book rather than paperwork, or taxes – real life things, *I suppose.*

I didn't have a quick response. Much like novels, I nod my head to a slow burn. So instead, I let the questioner sit with their question for a while.

When no response was given, I turned my head and smiled. *"Books saved my life."*

I'm sure many people have different reasons why they enjoy reading. I'm sure books have quite literally, saved someone's life. Though in my case, books showed me who I was – and who I am meant to be.

I quite enjoy reading because it's timeless. We live in an ever-moving age, where nothing old is new. This disgusts certain people, because adaptation to the current is *everything.* So, we frown upon old habits, old buildings, vacant sceneries and hollow escapes – we frown on these things, because they've lost their sparkle [to some, maybe].

Not to me.

I dreamt of the characters I read, the places they lived, the love that they lost [and found]. I spoke in accents I could not understand, and laughed alone in the quaint corners of my bedroom to the quick wit of the noblemen and princes. I raced a wild horse alongside a mage, traversing the open plain of purple flowers and rocky hills. There was a moment in time where I led my people in an army against a wicked kingdom who took everything from me... and I won.

I did all of this – because of reading.

You see, there is more to life than what people tell you. We glorify the mundane because that is all we know – all we *care* to know. But when you find yourself alone, what do you think about? Are you truly happy with the metal table you sit behind or the cold coffee you consume?

Ponder this for a moment.

"I cannot."

"You cannot, or you will not?"

I was asked a few months later, *"Why do you write?"*

I was asked why I prefer to scribble down fiction over doing my homework, or responding to emails – important things, *I suppose.*

Though this, I responded faster than the questioner could blink. *"Because there are worlds in my head who seek occupants."*

Dear readers,

Allow my writing to seek you.

Allow my writing to place you in one of these worlds... One of *my* worlds.

Allow me to show you, who you are meant to be.

From one main character to another,

Embrace your magic,

Just as I have.

✝

Hi reader, you've made it to the end!

Thank you so much for reading my book. I hope that you enjoyed the first epic journey of Beau and Maya.

This is my first debut of a YA fantasy novel, and I'm eager to continue writing more in this genre.

As a young writer, I realize that I may not have as much experience as a veteran author that has been writing for over thirty years, but I enjoy the process of writing all the same.

I encourage anyone who loves to read, loves to write, or loves to strengthen their imagination to push their limits and create a world of magic, passion, and hope – hope for a world less mundane, filled with colour.

I have been writing ever since I could walk, scribbling together words that didn't make sense to anyone other than me. Nonetheless, I loved to do it, so I continued.

Diving into the imagination of another human is a gift, and I can only hope that you liked mine.

I'm looking forward to our next talk at the end of *The Gates of Raphael*, the sequel to *The Gates of Gabriel*! Good day fellow reader, and may your creative light shine through.

Marie-France Leger

† Author's Playlist †

I can only assume that my readers love to create little scenarios in their head accompanied by music (if you don't, that's totally fine too)… So, I've come up with a playlist that in my opinion, encapsulates many of the emotions I felt while writing TGOG. I would absolutely love to hear your playlists as well! My DM's are open on Instagram (@mariefranceleger) for anyone who would like to talk!

- ❖ **Can You Feel My Heart** – Bring Me The Horizon
- ❖ **Babylon** – Normandie
- ❖ **Angel** – Theory of a Deadman
- ❖ **Alibi (3 A.M.)** – Empara Mi (Beau and Maya after the bar... Am I right?)
- ❖ **Anthem of the Angels** – Breaking Benjamin
- ❖ **My Understandings** – Of Mice & Men
- ❖ **Your Guardian Angel** – The Red Jumpsuit Apparatus
- ❖ **Play with Fire** – Sam Tinnesz (Oh, Marina...)
- ❖ **Fallen Angel** – Three Days Grace
- ❖ **Who Will Pray**? – We Came As Romans
- ❖ **Porn Star Dancing** – My Darkest Days (... This song is definitely meant for Braum, haha!)
- ❖ **Do it for Me** – Rosenfeld
- ❖ **Ashes** – Stellar
- ❖ **Paralyzed** – NF
- ❖ **Paint It, Black** – Ciara
- ❖ **Lights Out** – Royal Blood
- ❖ **Riptide** – Grandson

THE GATES OF

RAPHAEL

MARIE-FRANCE LEGER

THRONE ROOM, HELL

The torch flames swayed against the ember-fueled walls of hell. Lucifer sat against his red-velvet throne, playing with his orbionyx. The black orb previewed a familiar angel strapped to a marble table, struggling with his restraints. Lucifer couldn't hear his screams, but he smiled all the same.

"Master," one of Lucifer's guards marched into the room, curtseying. He stopped before the throne and trembled as Lucifer pierced his orbionyx with his pointed nail, bursting the orb.

Lucifer stared at the guard in disdain, grimacing at his inferior stance.

"You cower like a *saint*," Lucifer spat, leaning back on his chair. "Speak."

The guard bowed once more and rose to face him, unsure if he should look at him directly. "M – Master... there is – there is someone here to see you."

Lucifer rolled his eyes, igniting a flame on his fingertips. "Not in the mood."

"B – but... Master, it is of urgency."

A loud growl escaped Lucifer's throat. Carrying the flame on his fingertips, Lucifer twirled his hand in the air, sprouting a scarlet snake. Its body coiled around Lucifer's forearm then made its way down the side of his throne. The guard shuddered in fear as the snake slithered towards him, stopping just before his feet. In one quick motion, the snake lurched for his ankle, sinking its sharp fangs into the guards skin.

Within seconds, the guard began to convulse and fell to the ground, foaming at the mouth. The snake burst into embers, disappearing into the air.

Lucifer clapped and laughed out loud, waving his hands forward to open the throne room doors.

Waiting behind them were two guards holding a youthful looking man with golden hair, dressed in white linen.

Lucifer allowed them to enter, crossing his legs impatiently.

The guards led the man to Lucifer's throne, pushing him to the ground before Lucifer's feet.

"Master, he has an offering for you." The tall guard said, and backed away.

The man with the golden hair shook as his *grey* eyes met Lucifer's beaming red pupils.

"How delightful," Lucifer smirked. He diverted his attention to the tall guard and used his power to fling him against the wall.

"You bring an angel into my home, unchained?" Lucifer growled, choking the guard with invisible force.

"I – I... I brought a gift, Lucifer." The man with the golden hair muttered, lowering his posture to the ground like a dog.

Lucifer released the tall guard and stared viscously at the angel before him. "What did you just call me?" He snapped.

The angel trembled, unable to look at him. "Luc – Master... Master, I'm sorry, Mast –"

"Tell me why I shouldn't send you to the cage of the damned right now, *angel.*" Lucifer interrupted curtly.

With shaky hands, the angel lifted up his white linen drapes, ripping a small taupe pouch off the seam of his cloth. The pouch jingled as the angel pulled out four stones, radiating a white hue of Heaven's grace.

Lucifer's eyes grew wide. He knew exactly what these stones were and where they came from. Only they weren't just any stones. They were opulent crystals. He knew what great power these crystals contained, what they meant for the army in Heaven.

In a state of implausibility, Lucifer trudged carefully towards the angel, staring at the glowing richness of the crystals in his hands.

Each step Lucifer took down his throne, he recited the name of the crystals. "*Rose quartz... clear quartz... jasper*, and," he stopped directly in front of the angel. "*Obsidian*."

"The crystals that contain the flaming sword, Master. Michael's sword." The angel smiled, lifting his hands open.

The innards of each crystal swayed with delicate movements, swirling with an eddy of grace.

Lucifer picked each crystal up, analyzing with temperance before placing them back in the angel's hand and stepping back.

"How did you..." For the first time in his existence, Lucifer was lost for words. "Is this a trick?"

A crisp laugh rose from the angel's throat. "Coming from the father of lies, I find this quite amusing."

Lucifer lost all sense of patience, burning his stare into the grey eyes of the frail angel. Black veins surfaced to Lucifer's skin, pulsating as he hoisted him upwards by the neck. "Who are you?" he demanded.

Through staggered breaths, the angel managed a smile through the struggle. Muttering slowly, the angel released, "Blight."

Printed in Great Britain
by Amazon